# Dedication

For the legitimate entertainers in the industry.

# Acknowledgements

With special thanks to the magnificent rock legend, Joe Lynn Turner, for his brilliant and invaluable contributions to my previous rocker novels, One Take Jake, and One Take Jake: Last Call.

Also, I owe huge gratitude to Arlo Guthrie, who generously provided an informative and interesting perspective on New York's social structures.

Additionally, I'd like to thank the following celebs and rock icons for agreeing to be in this novel:

unrivaled vocalist, Graham Bonnet;

famed astronaut and musician, Chris Hadfield;

honored author and SNL alumni, comedian Victoria Jackson;

eminent rocker, Howard Leese;

celebrated bassist, Dave Fowler;

the beautiful and talented songstress, Astrid Young;

N.Y. Times Best Selling author, David Baldacci;

U.K. acclaimed celebrity impressionist, Stevie Riks;

distinguished rocker and MTV personality, Dez Bailey;

electronic music pioneer and vocalist, Gary Numan;

Canadian drum idol, Paul Delong;

the epic Swedish Metal band, Freak Kitchen;

"Dibby" and Southern rock icons The Marshall Tucker Band.

***Thank you all for your correspondence, support, and encouragement. Jay***

# Little Blue

## *Jay Lang*

### *Print ISBNs*
Amazon print 9780228633747
Barnes & Noble 9780228633754
Ingram Spark 9780228633761
BWL Print 9780228633778

Copyright 2025 by Jay Lang
Editor Victoria Chatham
Cover artist Michelle Lee

# Table of Contents

# Chapter 1

My gaze locks on the hospital bed where, under the tangled mess of tubes, wires, and electrodes, my child lies motionless. I step toward her, my feet moving on their own. "Daddy's here, Little Blue. You can wake up now," I whisper.

Kim, my daughter's mother, sniffs. "The doctors found Fentanyl in her system."

"That's impossible." I gently stroke Little Blue's hair. "She would never take drugs."

Tears stream down my cheeks as I stare at my child, willing her to wake up. I reach down to touch her cold hand, and a loud, continuous beep erupts from the equipment.

Kim panics. "What's going on?"

Footsteps echo down the hallway, and two nurses enter the room. One rushes to a gray machine positioned beside Little Blue's bed. The nurse's hands move swiftly as she presses a series of buttons on the screen.

She motions for me to step aside as a doctor bursts into the room. He heads directly to Little Blue's bed, his movements precise and urgent as he takes her vitals. I stand paralyzed, helplessly watching as the doctor barks out, "Code blue," and one of the nurses darts out of the room. The doctor turns and motions towards the door, "she's gone into cardiac arrest," he says, "I need you to wait in the hallway."

Kim screams. "Oh my God! Please help my baby!"

Her father wraps his arms around her and ushers her out of the room. His wife, sobbing uncontrollably, follows close behind.

"You too, sir." The doctor points to the door.

I shake my head. "I need to be with my child. I can't leave her alone."

Two nurses enter, pushing a cart loaded with medical equipment. One of them locks eyes with me. "You have to leave."

Reluctantly, I step backwards, keeping my eyes fixed on my daughter—my only child—lying vulnerable amidst a flurry of frantic medical staff. This can't be real. I'm in a nightmare I can't escape.

Kim's anguished cries reverberate down the hallway, mingling with the sounds of urgent activity. I'm helpless as I witness the chaos unfolding around me.

And then, just as swiftly as the medical team had rushed in to save my child, all activity stops, and the team files out of the room. No one meets my gaze. The last to exit is the doctor. He stops before me, takes a deep breath, and shakes his head. "I'm sorry," he says. "We did everything we could. But between her brain injury and the drugs in her system, her heart just wasn't strong enough."

He touches my shoulder before walking down the hall to deliver the news to Kim and her parents. Moments later, Kim's primal scream pierces the air, followed by the sounds of her collapsing to the floor.

Enveloped in a fog of shock and disbelief, I turn away from the room where my child lies and move towards her mother, each step heavier as the weight of the doctor's words settles in. Amidst the agony and confusion, a grim certainty emerges from deep in my guts: the bright light that was my daughter has been extinguished, not by a tragic accident but by some nameless evil.

* * *

Two years later
*I am not alive, and I am not dead. I am somewhere in between.*


* * *


Blood and filth swirl around the old bucket as I rinse the ragged strands of the mop.

My boss, Skully, approaches from behind and presses an envelope against my chest. "It's your check. Take it."

What the old man lacks in subtleness, he makes up for in heart. Because of him, I have a job, a rare opportunity in the struggling community of Hell's Kitchen. After what happened to my daughter two years ago and the depression that followed, Skully lets me work alone, relieving me of the burden of social interaction.

Keeping my eyes fixed on the mop, I nod slightly and slip the envelope into my back pocket. As Skully begins to walk away, I hear the squeak from his sneakers when he stops and turns on the freshly washed floor.

"And Jude, before you go home tonight, make sure to count the towels," he growls. "I swear, someone is walking away with all our stock." He resumes walking.

Skully is well into his eighties, riddled with arthritis and hunched over in pain, yet he still puts in a full day at the boxing gym he founded some fifty years ago. Black-and-white pictures tacked across the paint-chipped walls tell the story of a once popular gym frequented by high-profile fighters who came to Skully's to warm up before a big event.

Boxing never held any appeal to me before. As a musician, I always found fulfilment in writing songs that resonated with people. The idea of sliding on gloves and beating the shit out of someone never occurred to me until that fateful night two years ago. Now, I find myself transformed into a short-tempered pessimist, with a cold disposition. It's incredible how the potency of pain can alter who we are.

* * *

After flipping the switch that silences the incessant buzz of the fluorescent lights, I set the alarm and secure the reinforced door to the gym.

I walk down West 35th Street, where the blare of sirens from passing emergency vehicles barely fazes me. The sirens are a routine occurrence here in Hell's Kitchen; the locals don't notice them anymore. Approaching 9th Ave, I notice flashing lights and a crowd gathering in front of Tucky's, a bar where I used to perform in my music days.

Drawing closer to the scene, I overhear the crowd discussing what happened. It seems a man was leaving the bar when a vehicle pulled up, and someone inside opened fire, shooting him in the head.

Making my way through the crowd, I hear a commanding voice ring out, "Alright, clear the area. Return to your homes and allow us to do our jobs."

The crowd moves on, and I'm left with feelings of regret about selling my car for much-needed cash. Even though I loathed sitting in city traffic, at least I wasn't battling my way through these chaotic streets on foot.

* * *

The subway car reeks from a mixture of perfume, cologne, and sweat. I make my way down the aisle in search of an empty seat. Once at the back, I notice a man stand up, preparing to exit at the next stop. Seizing the opportunity, I swoop past him and settle into the warm seat. Beside me, a woman around thirty is engrossed in a noisy game on her phone.

I turn away, and my gaze briefly catches my reflection in the window. I scarcely recognize the person staring back at me. It's staggering how much I've aged in two short years.

Before Little Blue's passing, I was fit and healthy. I practiced yoga three times a week and frequented the rec center for swims whenever time allowed. Standing at five foot ten, I wasn't particularly tall, falling squarely within the realm of average height. But my face had vitality back then, and although I'd never been muscular, I had maintained a toned physique. I was, in fact, the quintessential rocker—dark hair, tattoos, and an endless bounty of energy. Now, my face is gaunt, my once thick, black hair is thin and wispy, and my body resembles the eerie caretaker who haunts the graveyards in horror films.

When the automated voice announces an upcoming stop over the loudspeaker, the woman beside me rises from her seat and gestures for me to let her out.

I shift uncomfortably on the hard plastic seat, feeling the discomfort of my wallet pressing against my back pocket.

The subway comes to a stop, and half a dozen people exit while double that number climb on board. Among them is a robust old woman clad in a smock dress, long mismatched socks, and plastic slip-on sandals. Her red, fuzzy hair spills out from under a misshapen straw hat, and streaks of dirt adorn her aged, round face. In her hand is a large plastic tote with a broken strap.

She heads down the aisle toward the vacant seat next to mine. Sighing, I shift to the window seat and divert my gaze to discourage any interaction. I can't help but catch a whiff of her breath—a dense mixture of sour puke and alcohol that hangs in the air around us.

"Hey, thanks for saving me this seat. You knew I was coming, didn'tcha?" She nudges me with her elbow, letting out a cackle. I force a grin in response, and she returns the sentiment, revealing four rotten teeth.

It figures—I go to great lengths to avoid interaction with people, and here I am, pinned to the wall, inches away from a booze-soaked nut bar."You know what? You're kinda cute." She snorts, then raises her voice so everyone sitting in the next five rows can hear. "But you ain't tappin' this until I see a ring on my finger." She holds up a grubby hand and wiggles her digits.

Embarrassed, I try to reason with my eccentric seatmate. "If it's all the same to you, I'd rather not talk." I keep facing forward in an attempt to avoid her putrid breath.

Ignoring my remarks, she leans forward, her face far too close to mine. "You're a sad, sad man, aren't you? What's the matter? Did someone break your heart? Or maybe someone died. Is that what happened?" She bursts into maniacal laughter. "Boo hoo. Poor baby. You're not going to cry, are you? Maybe I should get you a tissue."

She turns her attention to the crowded room and yells at the top of her lungs, "Hey, does anyone have an extra tissue? We've got a crier back here."

I stand. "Move, I'm getting out."

"Hey, calm down. I was just trying to get a rise out of you. I'll behave now, I promise." She mimes zipping her lips shut.

"I'm serious. Move so I can get out."

"Geez. Someone has their panties in a knot. Fine, fine. Have it your way." She struggles to get her huge bulk out of the way, grunting as she stands and moves into the aisle, finally letting me free from my unbearable confinement.

I speed up the aisle, getting away as fast as I can, but she hollers out behind me, "You owe me twenty bucks for that little grope session."

I close my eyes and grab onto a pole, praying for my stop to come quickly.

I hear something fall to the floor, and in front of me, a man wearing headphones leans over and picks up his wallet. He grins and shrugs. I return the grin, but a fleeting reminder has me checking my back pocket. To my horror, my wallet is missing. I glance back at the crazy woman, who is now staring out the window. *Son of a bitch. How did she manage to rob me without me noticing?*

I stomp back down the aisle and stop in front of the looney bird. "Give me my damn wallet, now." I stick out my hand.

She avoids my gaze. "I don't know what you're talking about, mister. I don't have your—"

"Now! Or I'm calling the cops."

After a moment, she sighs loudly and reaches into her tote. "You really can't take a joke, can you?" She retrieves my wallet and pushes it in my direction.

I slide it back into my pocket. "If you needed a couple bucks, you should've just asked."

Her eyes widen, making her look even crazier. "I don't need no handouts. I work for a living!"

I laugh. "You're a thief. How is that working for a living? You are certifiably nuts."

The subway comes to a stop, and along with a dozen others, I jump off and onto the platform. I'm out of the station and heading towards 52$^{nd}$ Street when I hear a gravelly voice behind me. "Jude. Wait!"

My name isn't uncommon, so I don't turn around. Again, the voice rings out: "Jude Edward Rossi."

I stop and turn at the sound of my full name, and much to my horror, the crazy old bag lady is approaching, waving her arm in the air.

"How do you know my name?"

She snorts. "Duh! Think about it."

I remember that she had my wallet. "What in the hell do you want?"

"Nothin'. I just happen to be goin' the same way as you."

A nagging suspicion creeps over me. I stand far enough away to make sure my pockets remain out of her reach.

"I don't have far to go," she insists. "Can I walk with you? A woman like me isn't safe alone at night."

*A woman like her? Who does she think she is, a Victoria's Secret model?*

Being within a ten-mile radius of the crazy old woman makes me nervous, but my late mother's words force themselves to the forefront of my mind: "There is never a reason not to be kind to the elderly." I wonder if her intention included this cunning old woman.

I shrug. "Just keep your hands away from my wallet."

She cackles. "You're still mad about that? I don't see why. You got it back with nothing taken. You should feel grateful. Maybe next time you'll keep your wallet in a safer place."

I resume walking but slow my pace. I wouldn't want to give her a heart attack, even if the crazy klepto did steal my wallet and humiliate me on the subway.

"So, you never asked my name," she pants as she walks. "Aren't you curious?"

"No. Not really."

"My name is Madge," she says proudly.

*That's fitting. Mad Madge.* "So, tell me, Madge, where are you heading?"

Ignoring my question, she points to an old brick building across the road. "You see that place? I was born there."

Disinterested, I remain quiet.

"Yep. During the five years we lived there, my father worked at a wool factory, and my mother was a janitor at the Clinton Liberal Institute—Clara Barton was a student at the time."

I stop in my tracks, staring at Madge in disbelief. "Clara Barton, the nurse who founded The Red Cross?"

"I don't know of any other Clara Bartons."

I shake my head and scoff. "You must think I'm a bloody idiot."

"How so?"

"Clara Barton was a student at The Clinton Liberal Institute in 1850. Nice try, Madge. I took History in school."

"Are you insinuating that I'm lying?"

I shake my head and continue walking.

"It's cold tonight." Madge pants as she struggles to keep up.

Disgusted with her lies, I keep my head down, silently watching the pavement pass under my feet.

"I said, it's cold out tonight. Don't you think?"

I don't answer. The truth is, over the past two years, I've been devoid of the sensations of heat or cold. On windy days, my hair blows around wildly, occasionally striking my face, yet I remain oblivious to the temperature.

Similarly, my clothes become damp and clingy when it rains, but the chill eludes me. I watch the weather forecast each day, dressing accordingly to protect myself from catching a bug. I can't afford to take sick days, I'm barely making ends meet as it is.

"Are you mad again?" Madge asks.

"No, I'm just indifferent. Frankly, I don't know you, and I'm puzzled about why you're so determined to talk to me."

"I'm a people person. And from the first time that I saw you on the subway, I thought you looked like you needed someone to talk to. A friend."

I scoff. "I don't need friends. Especially not the ones who steal my wallet. I prefer my own company."

As we approach West 50th Street, Madge pauses on the sidewalk. "Well, this is as far as I go. The voices are strong tonight and I've got messages to deliver."

Ignoring her bizarre statement, I turn and face her. "Do you live around here?"

She grins. "I live everywhere."

She reaches out to touch my arm, but I flinch away. Who knows what other tricks Mad Madge has up her sleeve. The last thing I want is to get home and find that she's pilfered my wallet again. Next time, I probably wouldn't be lucky enough to get it back.

Madge offers an indifferent shrug before turning and heading up West 50th Street. When she reaches the midpoint of the block, she pauses, casts a brief glance in my direction, and waves before vanishing into an alleyway.

I shake my head and turn towards home, but the peculiar encounter sticks in my mind. Madge is as crazy as a shithouse rat and for the life of me, I can't understand why she singled me out.

* * *

Following a brief interaction with Mr. Wong, my landlord and the owner of the Chinese restaurant downstairs, I retreat to my apartment, shutting the door behind me and withdrawing from the outside world.

Each wall in the small suite is decorated with vibrant graffiti, evidence of the previous tenant's occupation as a freelance artist heavily inspired by Banksy. Even the toilet and bathroom floor bear painted designs. When I first moved in, my urgency for a place to live outweighed any concerns about the artwork, and I couldn't wait for Mr. Wong to have the place repainted. The graffiti doesn't bother me anymore; after all, it's not like I have guests to impress.

I slip off my jacket and casually toss it onto the kitchen chair before opening the fridge and grabbing a can of Coke for my dinner. Despite the evening spent working at the boxing gym, hunger doesn't register. Ever since Little Blue died, my appetite has dwindled, causing my weight to drop from one-ninety to one-sixty—a concern my doctor frequently raises during our visits.

Once I've guzzled my soda, I flop down on the couch, my bed when my daughter would come over. My bedroom became hers whenever she visited. At first she tried to sleep on the couch, but the incessant buzzing from Wong's neon sign, positioned right outside the living room window, disturbed her rest. She likened the noise to the buzzing of the bug zapper we used during our camping trips.

As I settle into the worn cushions of the sofa, my eyes wander to a swaying cobweb clinging to the black-oxidized strings of my ageing acoustic guitar, nestled in the corner of the room. A pang of guilt hits me as I realize it's been over two years since I played. The guitar, an old Epiphone, was a gift from my mother when I was eleven. Its sentimental significance is the sole reason I haven't parted with it, despite selling off my other guitars and gear. Normally when in dire straits, a musician will sell off maybe one or two of his axes, but I got rid of most everything, not just for financial reasons. After Little Blue's affiliation to the music industry took her from me, I vowed there wasn't a snowball's chance in hell I'd ever return to performing.

That said, there are moments when I find myself reminiscing over the thrill of being on stage, captivating a packed audience and getting lost in the music. Our band was a melting pot of musicians from diverse backgrounds, which infused our music with a unique and original sound. Zee, our bass player, hailed from Turks and Caicos, steeped in the rhythms of Reggae from an early age. Lenny, our drummer, brought a fusion influence to our ensemble. Our lead singer, Christian, started in punk before joining us. Then there was me, on lead guitar, who grew up immersed in classic rock, idolizing legendary axemen like Yngwie Malmsteen, Paul Gilbert, and Brian May.

We were in demand every weekend, booked to play at some of the hottest rock bars in New York City. Music wasn't just a passion for me; it was my destiny. Despite growing up and listening to my parents' preference for Perry Como or big band groups, I always knew that my life would be rooted in the world of rock and roll. But the day Little Blue died, I plunged into a deep depression, and my passion for music vanished.

It is only recently that I've begun to seek solace in small moments of beauty, like a flower pushing through a crack in the sidewalk or a bird perched on a nearby branch. They're minor improvements on my healing path, but improvements, nonetheless.

I take the last swill from my Coke can and get up to toss it into the garbage when I see my cell light up. *Kim Chambers* flashes on the screen.

I inhale deeply, bracing myself for a conversation I know won't be easy. Despite our lifelong bond as close friends, our fleeting interactions have been marked by awkwardness and tension ever since Little Blue's passing.

"Hi, Kim."

"Hey. How are you?" Her voice is distant and monotone.

"I'm doing well. Working a lot, no time for much else. And you?"

The last time I saw Kim was two years ago at the memorial. To be expected, she looked terrible that afternoon. Her face was ashen and drawn, and her once pretty blond hair was stringy and unkempt. Since then, I've received a couple of calls from her mother, someone I always got along with. She spoke about Kim, and how she thought her daughter was going down the wrong path, using drugs and hanging out with bad people. I tried to reassure her that Kim was strong and just needed time to deal with our daughter's death. I didn't know for sure if Kim would be okay, but I didn't want to worry her mother, knowing firsthand the pain of losing a child.

I tried to reach out to Kim, but she always brushed me off. I think I reminded her too much of Little Blue. Besides, if she had gotten into drugs, the last person she would want a lecture from is me. Kim loved to party, and I didn't want our daughter around anyone who was drunk or stoned. Needless to say, we'd definitely had our share of arguments over the years. Still, I always loved her as a close friend and respected her.

After a brief pause, Kim responds, her voice devoid of enthusiasm. "What can I tell you? I'm good, too."

"Are you sure, Kim?"

She scoffs. "Let's just say I'm still working things through and leave it at that."

"Fair enough."

"I'm calling because I've been searching for Little Blue's necklace—a locket on a chain. It had a picture of her and me in it. Did she leave it at your place?"

I glance over to the small shelf under the window, where our daughter kept her keepsakes in a shoebox. I've never mustered the strength to open it. "I'm not sure. I haven't gone into any of her things since she—"

"Well, if you could take time out of your busy schedule to look, I would appreciate it."

I'm momentarily stunned by her abruptness. Kim had always been known for her gentleness. Now, her voice carries cold impatience, a noticeable departure from the girl I knew as a youth.

"I'm not really ready to go through her—"

"Jude, I haven't asked you for anything since she died. I have been going crazy looking for the necklace, and I'm asking you to look through whatever you have of hers. Is that so hard?"

I sigh and look back to the shoebox on the stand. "Just give me a minute."

I walk over and grab the cardboard box, then sit on the sofa while I cradle the phone between my shoulder and my ear. I hate being forced to do this. I'm not ready. But Kim is right. She hasn't asked me for anything since our daughter died. The least I can do is put my issues aside and take a quick look for the necklace.

I use my sleeve to wipe away the dust from the top of the box, then draw in a deep breath as I lift the lid. Immediately, I'm overwhelmed by a rush of emotion triggered by the sight of the first item inside: a picture of Little Blue and me. She looks so young, maybe seven or eight years old. It's a snapshot from our day at Coney Island, her smiling brightly while clutching the large pink unicorn stuffy I won for her at the water pistol game. It was a perfect father-daughter day, and evidently, she thought so too.

A lump forms in my throat as I struggle to hold back tears. I set the picture aside and resume my search for the necklace.

"Are you still there?" Kim's voice comes from the phone.

"Still looking. Hold on."

My fingers sift through colorful keychains, rock band pins, and a few guitar pics with my name on them. I sigh. Little

Blue was always so proud of the fact that her dad was a guitar player in a rock band. In fact, she made me promise that when she was older, I'd invite her up on stage at one of the clubs I played at, and we would perform a song together. As much as I was against her getting into the music biz at such a young age, the thought of us performing live together, father and daughter, gave me great joy. I grin slightly and a tear escapes my eye.

"Well?" Kim prods.

I rummage through the remainder of the box, looking for the shine of a chain, but there's nothing. As much as I wouldn't want to part with anything that belonged to my daughter, I wish the necklace was here. Maybe having the locket would give Kim some peace.

I sigh. "I'm sorry, Kim. It's not here."

There's a brief pause. "Yeah, I thought you'd say that."

"What's that supposed to mean?"

"You literally took two minutes to look through Little Blue's stuff. I don't think you were trying too hard to find the necklace."

I take a slow breath as my nerves crackle. "I went through the only box she left here. There's no necklace."

"Whatever."

I do my best to diffuse her frustration. "Kim, you're welcome to come and search my apartment if it will make you feel better."

"As if I would do that. Besides, if you wanted to keep the locket, you would hide it before I got there. It's pointless."

My hair stands up on the back of my neck and I can no longer deflect her attitude. "Are you saying I'm lying? Why the hell are you spewing such hatred toward me?"

"Pfft. Gee, I don't know, Jude. Maybe it's because after our daughter died, I was left to deal with everything myself while you were hiding in your apartment, licking your wounds."

I gasp, then mentally slide on the gloves. There's no way I'm letting her get away with this shit. "That's a lie, and you know it. I tried like hell to contact you after the memorial. I was fully prepared to help clean out Little Blue's room or do whatever you needed but maybe you were too busy self-medicating to call me back."

As soon as the words leave my lips, I regret them.

"What did you say?" Kim's tone is furious. "Are you kidding me? I'd rather take something to ease the pain than do what you've been doing for the past two years."

"What the hell does that mean?"

"You quit life completely, Jude. You lost the battle without trying. From what my mom told me, you sold everything—all your guitars, your gear, and even your car. You quit playing music and gave up on yourself. Our daughter would be really proud of her dad now, a night janitor at a boxing gym."

She's icy cold. I can't believe she is the same sweet woman I grew up with—the same woman who gave birth to our child. I shake my head. "That's low, Kim. No matter how shitty you feel, there's no need to come down so hard on me."

There's a prolonged silence on the line, followed by a trembling exhale. "I... I suppose that was unwarranted," she admits, her voice now quieter, more subdued. "I just can't come to terms with her being gone. She was everything to me, Jude. Without her, I feel empty. And honestly, when I see myself in the mirror, I don't see the person I used to be. I feel like I'm just a hollow shell."

I nod. She said it perfectly. I want to tell her how I feel the same way, but I can't. She needs me to be strong for her. "You know, I've been watching these videos lately about people who have had NDEs, near-death experiences. At first, I thought it was bullshit, but after listening to people who have died and come back, I'm starting to think there's some validity to their experiences."

"What are you talking about?" Kim's voice is once again sharp and defensive.

"I'm talking about how some people said they had a glimpse of the afterlife. They all confessed to having been temporarily transported to an amazing place, surrounded by an abundance of love and joy. Every one of the people stated how wonderful they felt, and they didn't want to return to their lives on Earth."

There's another long pause, and then, "What in the hell did you tell me all that for?"

I sigh, knowing my efforts have been for naught. "I was hoping you would consider the fact that even though Little Blue isn't here with us, she's probably in a place that's a hell of a lot better."

"You know what, Jude? I don't care who those people are or what they profess to have gone through. I want my child back. I want to hold her in my arms, and I want her to live out her life here as she was intended to do." Kim's voice cracks as she loses composure and starts to cry. "I'm really angry and the pain is unbearable. It never stops, Jude. It never even slows down."

"I know. It's unfair. It's hard to see purpose, but we've got to try, if for no other reason than for Little Blue. We have to do what she can't. We have to live our lives the best we can."

"Do you blame me for what happened? Do you think that I could've prevented her death that night?"

"No. Of course not. Don't be ridiculous. I know how much you loved our child."

"Well, I sometimes blame you."

"What?" My voice amps up louder than intended. "How could you blame me? I wasn't even there."

"Yeah, that's my point. You weren't there. You said you would show up, but you didn't. You were pouting because Little Blue and I opposed your views on her getting into the music business."

My ribs clench around my lungs as a lump forms in my throat. I've always felt guilty and responsible for our child's death. It's something I was in counselling for the first year after she died. "You're wrong, Kim. It's true I felt she was too young to be exposed to the music business at fourteen, but you're wrong about me not showing up because I felt defied. I never showed up because the gig I was playing went late. I tried calling when I got off stage, but you didn't answer. It was late, so I just assumed you two were in bed. But I've already told you this."

She sniffles. "See, it's those little jabs you throw that drive me nuts."

"What jabs?"

"Saying I had her out too late. That we should have been sleeping."

Though I meant nothing of the sort, my efforts to diffuse her anger are futile. She continues to rant until I tell her that I have to go. Just before we hang up, she tells me that it's both of our faults that our child is gone, not just hers.

I turn my phone off and stand at the window, looking out into the night. My heart is heavy with regret as the phone call replays in my mind.

Kim's on a fast path to nowhere. I can feel it like a speeding train toward a broken track. Still, there's nothing I can do to slow her down. Nothing I can do to make her see reason.

Then again, who am I to help anyone? Like Kim said on the phone, I gave up on life and am now just existing. I have no answers, even for myself. All I have is questions.

Deep in my soul, I know the only way out of this mental hell is to find out the truth about what happened to Little Blue in that penthouse apartment two years ago. So far, all my attempts at getting information from the cops have been futile. Considering the music execs who attended the celebration and their high rank, any chance that I'll discover the truth is wasted because money usually means the powerbrokers can get away with anything—even murder.

# Chapter 2

It's midnight and even after laboring through my shift at Skully's and enduring the hour-long journey home, my mind stubbornly resists the possibility of sleep. Sitting on the sofa, I attempt to quiet my racing thoughts with deep breaths, a technique I learned from therapy, but Kim's voice still echoes in my mind, stirring up a mix of anxiety and guilt. As I glance at the picture resting beside me, memories flood back. My precious Little Blue.

In addition to the crushing grief that isolates me from the rest of the world, I also live with the knowledge that the person who gave my daughter drugs is still out there, walking free without a care in the world. In the past, I tried to share my suspicions with Kim, but she brushed them off, attributing my fears to the grieving process. I haven't confided in her about my beliefs since.

Finally, I succumb to the bleak reality that even though my body is exhausted, my mind is bent for torment. There's no way I'm going to get any rest sitting here in the apartment.

Sliding on my coat, I head out the door.

* * *

Confronted by the unyielding Atlantic wind, I bow my head and trudge along the dimly lit streets. Walking has always been effective at suppressing the constant cycling in my mind.

Up ahead, there's a hotdog vendor, a man with long stringy hair and a cigarette stuffed behind one ear. I remember him from two years ago. Little Blue couldn't sleep, so we went for a stroll up the street and stopped at this same guy's cart for a hotdog. On the way back to the apartment that night, Little Blue looked up at me, smiled, and said I was the coolest dad ever.

As I approach, the vendor puts condiments in his rickety red cart while a few lonely, withered-up wieners spin slowly on the grill.

He nods as I approach. "Haven't seen you in a while. You used to get a couple of dogs for you and your daughter."

I offer a polite grin.

"I've got two smokies left if you want them."

I look down at the wrinkly nitrous sticks. "It looks like they've been here for a while."

"Nah. They're just well done, is all. I'll tell you what, if you buy one, I'll throw the other one in for your daughter for free."

"Just one."

"Suit yourself." The vendor grins as he reaches into the belly of the cart for a bun. "So, how is that girl of yours? I remember her smile. How polite she was."

"Just mustard, nothing else."

The vendor stops for a moment and looks at me quizzically through a few greasy strands of hair. "Okay, man. Just mustard."

After he finishes preparing the hotdog, I slide my hands into my pocket and pull out a bill.

"This one's on me, man." He hands me my food. "You take care of yourself."

Something about the man's reaction tells me he knows what happened to my daughter. How, I don't know. Then again, faces tell stories, and a vendor would become adept at reading faces in the hustle and bustle of the city, where countless lives intersect. There's a lot of living going on in the streets of New York, but a lot of dying, too. Misery is just as easy to detect as joy.

I force a grin, nod, and grab a napkin off the cart before slowly making my way up the sidewalk. As I cross the first intersection, I take a bite of the dog, which tastes surprisingly good considering what it looked like on the grill.

Halfway up the block, I find a bus stop bench surrounded by a plexiglass shield to sit and finish the dog. Across the street is an old furniture store that's been boarded up for years. Once, it was a thriving business that sold eclectic gothic pieces from all over the world. As a young boy, I recall my mother bringing me there to browse. She always gravitated towards the most eccentric and striking pieces and told me how the different things always stand out from the predictable. Her lessons taught me the value of being authentic and unique.

I tried to encourage Little Blue to be the same way, to not worry about fitting in with the crowd, but she didn't need my input. From the time she could speak, it was obvious she was different from other children her age. Instead of crying after getting into a playground spat, she would sit quietly and try to rationalize what initiated the fight.

She was the most introspective child and never needed to be coddled or reassured. It's not that she was overly confident—she was quite the opposite, humble and approachable, but her self-worth never depended on popularity, appearance, or the other things young people worry about. Little Blue was a selfless girl whose focus was to validate others. She loved to make people feel good.

A painful wave of emotion rises from my gut and forms a ball in my throat. I sigh and look down at the last bite of hotdog. Queasy, I toss it into the small trash bin attached to the plexiglass wall.

How in the hell am I supposed to cope with the loss of my daughter? I am nothing without her. Every hope and dream for my future included Little Blue, and now that she's gone I have no purpose.

Over the past two years, I've felt like a robot completing my duties as I march from one day to the next, my only feelings being anger and pain. Maybe one day I'll work up the nerve to step off a curb and walk into traffic or take a dive off a bridge. Until then, I remain here, wallowing in misery.

I'm about to stand when a muted thud against the plexiglass catches my attention. Swiveling around, I spot a stout figure pressing against the glass: an old woman with untamed red hair and a worn, lopsided hat atop her head. It's not until the woman grins, revealing her decayed teeth, that I realize who she is: Mad Madge, the crazy woman I met on the subway.

The last time I saw her, she had wandered into an alleyway after bombarding me with a stream of nonsensical chatter while I was walking home. I found her almost unbearable then, but right now, in my hopelessness, I'm almost glad to see a familiar face—a distraction.

She makes her way around the plexiglass. "Jude, right?"

I nod. "Hello, Madge." I look down and notice a half-filled booze bottle in her hand.

"What are you doing out so late in the cold?"

I shrug. "I needed some fresh air. What about you?"

Madge cackles. "The night is young and as for the cold, I carry my own fuel to keep me warm." She raises the bottle. "If you slide over on that bench, maybe I could sit down and take a load off. I might even share some of my gin."

I slide over as far as I can on the thin bench to accommodate her size. "I quit drinking, but thanks anyway."

"You quit drinking? What a dismal reality you must live in. Not me. Any chance I get to dull the voices in my head, I take."

Even though I barely know this woman, the bits that she's shown me make it easy to conclude that she's well off her rocker. Leading me to wonder if the "voices" she's talking about are a turn of phrase or if she actually hears them.

Once she's perched solidly on the bench, she unscrews the lid from the bottle and takes a long swill. A shiver runs through me. *How can anyone chug gin? The stuff is like turpentine. Her throat must look like leather from the inside.*

"So, Jude." She caps the bottle. "What's bothering you so much that you're not in bed like a regular person at this hour? Are the voices haunting you too?"

"Something like that."

She leans in close, breathing a concentrated burst of what smells like pine floor cleaner in my face. "You know, if you hold all that darkness in, it'll eat you like cancer from the inside out. Best to spill it and release the demons." She pushes the bottle to me. "What have you got to lose, right?"

I look at the liquid in the bottle sloshing around in her hand. Screw it. Why not?

Before I know it, the rim is resting against my lips and the burning liquid is sliding down my throat.

"There ya go! That's the way!" Madge roots me on.

Unsure of how many ounces I've swallowed, I pull the bottle from my lips, cough once from the exhaust of the gin, and pass it back to Madge.

"Now, tell me about your little problem." Her eyes widen with curiosity.

I shake my head. "You first." I want to give the booze time to take effect.

"Me first? Hmm. Let me think." She taps her finger on her fuzzy chin. "Well, I could tell you about my man trouble, which is what thrust me into my depression and led to me slitting my wrists."

My eyes widen. "You slit your wrists?"

She smiles. "I did. And I didn't do it the pussy way, either. I did such a good job, there was no way the docs could save me."

"And yet, here you are."

She nods slowly. "And yet here I am."

"So, what could have been bad enough to push you to suicide?"

She chuckles, "Man troubles. I got my heart ripped out and handed back to me."

"I'm sorry to hear that." I look at the bottle resting on the bench beside her and wonder if booze played a part in the failed relationship. "So, is the guy still around?" I ask, not knowing what else to say.

Madge scoffs. "Hell no. He's been dead for years. He was my second husband."

"But you're still grieving him?"

"Not so much him as the loss of companionship."

"Can I ask what it was that ended the relationship?"

"Violence, I suppose."

"He hit you. You should feel good about not being with him anymore. I hate men who hit women. I hope you had him arrested."

Madge grimaces and looks at her feet. "Well, it wasn't him."

"What do you mean, it wasn't him? Who was it then?"

She grins mischievously.

"You?"

"Yeah. It was me."

"Was it in self-defense? Was he mentally abusing you? Pushed you to a point of no return?"

"That's exactly what happened. The bugger pushed me to a point of no return!"

"Well, that's more understandable, then."

"No. Not really." She's looking down at her feet again. "I mean, it was an incident that could've been avoided."

"Explain."

She takes a deep breath. "He'd been working the day shift at the docks, and I'd been working long afternoon shifts at a textile company. By the time I got home in the evening, he already had time to rest up. Every damn day, when I walked through the door, he started in on me about sex, how we should try role-playing. I didn't see any bloody purpose in pretending to be someone else, so I told him to go pee up a rope. But he persisted. One night, I came home after work, exhausted and wanting to put my feet up. I opened the front door to find him standing there, dressed in a mailman uniform and carrying a postal bag."

I'm trying not to laugh. "Go on."

"Well, I took one look at that scrawny bastard and knew I had to put an end to his annoying fetish idea once and for all. I went directly to my bedroom, stripped down to my birthday suit, put on my red corset and slid into my high-heeled shoes, then marched back into the front room."

"What did he say?"

Madge shrugs. "Asked me what I was dressed up as. I told him I was a dominatrix, then yanked the postal bag from his shoulder and beat the living shit out of him with it."

As hard as I try to retain my composure, I can't. I bust into laugher, all the while trying to apologize to her for being insensitive.

Thankfully, she sloughs it off and eventually cracks a subtle smile. "Now, enough about me. It's your turn to spill the beans. What's got you so down and out?"

Instantly, my smile fades. I want to give her the watered-down version, but I have a feeling she'll prod me until I tell her everything.

Madge hands me the bottle. "Here, take a swig first. It'll help jog your memory."

I grab the bottle tightly by the neck and take a big, hard swill before passing it back. "It's about my daughter—"

"Little Blue?"

Shocked, I stare at her. "How the hell do you know her name?"

Madge cackles. "Wallet, subway. Remember? I saw her picture and you had her name and the date on the back. A very sweet face for sure."

I shake my head. "I can't believe—"

"Your story," Madge urges.

"Little Blue was my fourteen-year-old daughter. Two years ago, she was taken from me."

"Taken?" Madge leans closer.

"Yes. She was at a penthouse party in Manhattan. She was drugged by someone there that night and died in the bathroom."

"My Gawd. That's the saddest thing I ever heard. No wonder you're walking around in darkness. I can imagine her mother is as well. Married or separated? And what was a kid doing at a penthouse party without a chaperone?"

"She wasn't. Her mother, Kim, was there as well."

Madge lowers her head. "I see. And this Kim...you were married at the time?"

"No. It was never like that between us. Her getting pregnant was more of an accident than anything. Kim and I never had a conventional romance—we were good friends who drank too much one night and ended up having sex in her parents' garden shed in New Jersey."

"Ah yes, I get it. If you can't sleep with your friends, who can you sleep with?"

"Not really. In fact, I wasn't remotely attracted to Kim, and I'm pretty sure she felt the same way about me. I'm not positive how we ended up doing what we did. It was definitely not planned."

"How did you meet?" Madge is focusing intently.

I tell her how our parents were friends, and that before Kim's family came into money, both our fathers worked at the same paint shop in Hell's Kitchen. How during the last two summers of high school, our families reserved adjoining campsites at Lake George in the northeastern part of the state. How Kim and I spent every day of our vacation fishing or exploring trails in the area. "As I said, I cared deeply for her as a friend, but there was never a romantic spark."

I talk about how everything changed after she became pregnant and how our parents urged Kim to consider an abortion, but neither of us felt comfortable with that option. Unfortunately, tensions soon escalated between our families, leading them to stop socializing altogether. Kim chose to stay with her parents and have the child, while I joined a band and played small gigs to earn just enough money to pay child support.

Madge thinks for a moment, then says, "I know what it's like to lose a child. I've lost two. They were younger than your daughter, but I don't want to talk about that."

I shake my head and am just about to reach out and touch her shoulder, but I change my mind when she barks, "That's all part of the past for me. What about you now?"

"Now, I live every moment of every day with the unbearable realization that every incredible aspect of my child has been reduced to ashes sitting in a black urn on her grandparents' mantle. As for her legacy, she doesn't have one. Instead, she's considered just another heartbreaking statistic among teenage overdose victims."

"But you know different." Madge concentrates on my eyes.

"Of course I do. My daughter loathed drugs. She saw the effect of what dope did to people on the street and in her school. There's no way Little Blue would ever knowingly take dope."

"Did you try to find out who was at the party?"

"Yes and no. I asked a lot of questions. The only thing I found in the police report was that only those who had signed my daughter's recording contract were officially noted as present. However, Kim recalled seeing a number of men she didn't recognize."

Madge reaches into her pocket and pulls out a frayed child's toothbrush, then begins scrubbing her filthy fingernails. "Why do you think other partygoers weren't mentioned?"

I scoff. "If there's one thing music execs are good at, it's protecting each other from controversy, especially when it comes to a teenage girl found unconscious and bleeding in a bathroom. They protect their own."

"So, there's no way for you to seek justice?"

I shake my head. "It's pretty hard to point the finger at someone if they were never there."

"That's disgusting! Dirty piggies rolling around in their stinking little pen. So, tell me, what's in store for you? Are you going to be miserable forever, or are you going to pull yourself up by your bootstraps and soldier on?"

"All I know is that I'm stuck in purgatory with no idea how to get out." I exhale deeply. "They say everything happens in life for a reason, but I find little comfort in that bullshit. My daughter was everything to me. How can there be any justification for such a senseless tragedy happening to someone so special? For two agonizing years, this question has haunted me, and the bitter truth remains: the person who drugged my child and caused her death is still free."

"That's bloody bleak," Madge says, taking the final gulp from the bottle.

"It is what it is." I'm ready to leave.

"It is what it is?" Madge repeats. "Hm. But what if things weren't that set in stone? What if there were a way for you to find answers about what happened to Little Blue?"

"What are you talking about, Madge?"

She leans in close and whispers in a gravelly voice, "What if you had a chance to see your daughter again? Would you take it?"

Her words hit me hard, freezing me in my tracks. I peer into her half-drunk red eyes. "I think you've had a bit too much of that liquid fire. It's messing with your head." I chuckle as I stand, but everything starts to spin. I must have had a few too many swigs myself. "Good night, Madge. Thanks for the company."

"Wait!" She grabs my arm. "I know someone who can help you."

"Help me what?" I pull my arm away.

"Just sit back down for a moment and hear me out. You've got nothing to lose, right?"

Right now, she's reminding me of that crazy, strange lady I first met on the subway. But I appease her and sit back down. After all, she did share her booze and offered

something I've been unknowingly missing—
someone to talk to. "Okay, what do you have
to tell me?"

With her voice low, she leans in again. "I
know a man. We call him Warlock. He has
magical powers and can help suffering
people like you."

I laugh. "Oh really? And just how does
this magical Warlock help people?"

"He has an attachment to the other
world. The spirit world. He connects people
with the dead."

A loud burst of laughter escapes my lips.
I reach over and pat Mad Madge on the leg.
"Thanks again for the drinks. But I'm not in
the mood for any magic tricks tonight."

"Are you really willing to pass up an
opportunity to see your daughter? What if
she's been waiting for you? What if she needs
you, and you won't take a chance, a leap of
faith to help her?"

I look at her in disbelief. "Madge, do you
realize how crazy you sound?"

She shrugs. "I always sound crazy. It
doesn't mean what I'm saying isn't true."
There's sincerity in her eyes now, a
desperation which hints that she made up
this whole weird story just to keep my
company. It must be a lonely existence out
here for the homeless.

I sigh. "Alright, Madge. Tell me more
about your Warlock."

She grins widely. "I can do more than
that. I can take you to him."

After a good twenty minutes of walking through a maze of concrete alleyways, we enter a dead-end narrow lane. With no streetlight in range and a dark sky above us, I strain to see what's up ahead.

"Come on. We're almost there." Madge's excited voice echoes off the buildings.

After a few more steps, I make out a fire escape with a blue dumpster underneath. "There's nothing down here, Madge. I think I'm just going to—"

"Keep walking. He's just over there." She points ahead to the dumpster.

As we near the large metal bin, I make out something lying on the ground on the other side of it. It's a thin mattress, and as we approach, I see a small figure lying on top.

Madge looks at me with widened eyes. "It's him. It's Warlock. Quick, do you have twenty bucks on you?"

Reluctantly, I reach for my wallet. I knew this was all bullshit. But whatever, I'm here now.

I hand Madge the cash and cross my arms, watching as she leans over and shakes the leg of the man, then stands back and waits. But the figure doesn't move. As I look on, I notice several scattered empty bottles on the cot beside the man.

"Warlock," she says loudly. "It's me. Madge." She leans down and again shakes his leg. "I've brought a friend, someone who needs your help." Still, there's no response. Madge looks back at me. "Maybe he's sleeping."

"Maybe he's dead. Look at all of the empty bottles around him. He probably drank himself into oblivion until his body gave out."

"Oh, he's not dead. He just works long hours and—"

I laugh. "Works long hours. Alright, enough fun and games. I'm out of here."

Just as I turn my back to head out of the lane, a croaky voice rings out, "Madge. How the hell are ya, honey?"

I turn to see a thin man sitting up on the cot, legs still covered in blankets. He looks like a gnome, with a long silver pointy beard and bushy white eyebrows.

Madge waves me over. "Come and meet Warlock."

This has got to be one of the stupidest situations I can remember being in. Unwillingly, I turn and take a few steps back to the drunk duo. I nod a quick hello. "Hey, um, Warlock? Sorry to disturb you. You can go back to sleep, and I'm going to mosey on home." I point to the entrance of the lane.

The old man stares intently at me. "What is your name?"

"Jude."

The man beckons. "Come closer, Jude."

I walk to the edge of the filthy cot. Madge stands up straight and shuffles back a few steps.

"Darkness has you in its grasp. Can you feel it?" the man says.

A cold shiver runs up my spine.

"A young girl is waiting for you on the other side. She's unable to move forward without you. You need to tell her it's okay to walk into the light."

His words pierce through me. A hard lump forms in my throat. "What are you talking about, old man?" I say, trying to interject reality into the conversation.

He pulls a small vial out of his front pocket and holds it out to me. "Here. Drink this. It will help you to find Little Blue."

"I'm not drinking that. Are you crazy? Who knows what's in it!" I turn to Madge. "And nice trick, telling him my daughter's name."

She shakes her head. "I didn't tell him anything. You were here the whole time."

I laugh without humor. "You two are running quite the scam here, aren't you? You should be ashamed of yourself, profiting off grief."

The old man keeps his eyes fixated on me. "You named her Little Blue when you first held her in your arms. You looked into her blue eyes and told her that you would always be her daddy and she would always be your Little Blue."

All the air escapes my lungs. *I never told Madge how Little Blue got her nickname.*

My eyes grow heavy with moisture. This can't be real. How the hell can this street bum have powers that would let me see my daughter? My mind tells me to turn and leave, but my heart yearns so badly for just one glimpse of my little girl.

If I drink the weird, probably toxic liquid from the vial, I might die. Then again, I'm not really living now.

"Give me the damn vial."

The gnome-like man smiles and hands me the small container. I hold up the vial and swish the rust-colored liquid around. I know if I don't swallow it now, my common sense will kick in, and I never will.

I glance over at Madge. Her smile is wide, and her eyes are eager. "Bottoms up, Jude."

I remove the small cork, tilt my head back, and pour the pungent liquid into my mouth. A strong, acrid taste reminds me of the one and only time I ate a slug, a dare in childhood that I instantly regretted.

I hear myself cough. Then, one by one, I feel my bones disappearing. Within seconds I have no strength to stand, and despite my efforts to stay upright and in control, I slowly wilt to the ground.

* * *

There's a wavy mirage in front of me, accompanied by the loud thudding of my heart in my ears. Madge and Warlock are nowhere to be seen, and as I strain to focus down the lane, the sides of the buildings move like liquid. I notice I'm sitting on the thin mat Warlock was lying on. I try to get up, but my body is weak and hollow.

Out of the corner of my eye, I catch something moving beside me—a dark pulsating mass. It takes all my energy to slide away until the side of my body is against the dumpster. I continue to gaze at the changing mass, desperately hoping it won't draw closer. When I attempt to cry out for help, my voice comes out in a faint whisper.

I think about the vial of liquid and wonder what the hell kind of toxic weirdness I swallowed. I take a deep breath and am preparing to call out, knowing I must be overdosing, realizing my only chance at getting help is making someone hear me. However, just as I open my mouth to yell, something flesh-toned slowly emerges from the center of the dark, throbbing mass beside me.

With no strength to move, I close my eyes tight, hoping that when I open them, this nightmare will have disappeared. But when my eyes open, even more of the fleshy color emerges from the twisting mass.

"Whatever you are, go away. Leave me alone!" My voice is still a whisper. With my heart still pounding like a jackhammer in my chest, I have no choice but to sit motionless and stare at the pulsating strangeness beside me.

After a few moments, what looks like thick pink worms rise from the middle, and my eyes widen in horror. Frozen in place, I have to remind myself to breathe as, bit by bit, the worms reach out of the mass. Just as I count them—five worms in total—the scene sharpens, and they come into focus. They aren't worms at all. I've been watching fingers, attached to a hand, emerge out of the darkness.

As my vision continues to sharpen, the pulsating mass also becomes clearer. I gasp when I realize the twisting blackness is made of dozens of shiny black snakes, twisting and turning in unison. Nausea rises in my gut; I detest snakes ever since I was a child and was babysat by a woman who owned a boa constrictor named George. One day, after my mother dropped me off at the sitters, I lay on the sofa only to find George squirming behind the cushions. After that, I have been petrified of the creatures.

After multiple failed attempts to crawl away, I'm stuck with the terrifying reality that if these creatures set their sights on me, I'll be vulnerable to whatever they decide to do. The strange hand is now an arm covered in a black dirt-like substance, or perhaps it could be snake excrement. My eyes stay hyper fixated, and I open my mouth, attempting to push air out in a scream.

Again, my voice is nothing more than a whisper.

Reality hits —no one is coming to rescue me. I'm existing in a nightmare where I can't move, I can't speak loudly enough for someone to hear me, and I can't—

"Help me!" A faint voice echoes up the narrow alleyway.

I strain to focus. Although the buildings are sharper than they were before, I can't make out the source of the cries.

"Daddy. Help me."

"My baby. Oh, my little girl, my precious Little Blue." My strength is restored from the moment I touch her. I feel the silkiness of her hair between my fingers as I hold her close to my chest. "You're alive," I sob. "You're alive." I kiss her forehead. "I am so sorry, baby. I am so sorry I wasn't there that night to protect you. Forgive me. But I'm here now, your daddy's here, and I promise never to let anything happen to you again."

Although I haven't stopped sobbing, I feel no moisture leave my eyes. All the suffering and pain dissipate, and joy fills my body as if I've been restored to the person I was two years ago.

I feel her hands push gently on my chest, and I loosen my hold. She tilts her head up, and I look down into her crystal blue eyes.

"Dad. Don't cry." She reaches up and gently touches my cheek. "It wasn't your fault, and I don't blame you for what happened."

I smile. "I love you so much, kiddo. You mean the world to me, and I'm never letting you go again."

Her expression quickly changes, and the corners of her mouth drop down. "But Dad, I can't stay here with you for very long."

"What do you mean? Of course you can."

"No, Dad. I'm not in your world, and you're not in mine. Right now, we're someplace in-between."

"I don't understand."

"I'm not alive. I died two years ago, and I can't go back with you. I live in the spirit world now, and you are with the living."

My joy fades. "Then how am I holding you now? If you were a spirit, a ghost, how could I feel you in my arms?"

With a gentle smile, she taps my forehead softly. "Our minds connect us here, together."

I shake my head. "No. I don't believe that. If I were dreaming, this wouldn't be so real. And I would've woken up by now." I squeeze her body tighter against mine and start to sob again, and again, my eyes remain tearless.

"Dad, I just want you to know that I didn't know I was taking drugs. I would never take drugs. You know that, don't you?"

"Of course I know that, Little Blue. But what happened? Did someone make you a drink and hand it to you?"

She slowly nods. "I wasn't going to drink it, but he said he made it special for me. He even went to the trouble of putting cherries and a little umbrella in the glass. I felt bad saying no."

I take a deep breath and exhale slowly. "Do you remember who the man was or what he looked like? Was he one of the music execs who made the contract deal with you?"

She shakes her head. "No. He was someone who came to the penthouse party. That's where I first met him."

"Can you remember his name, sweetie? Or what he looked like?"

"I used to know his name. But the longer I'm dead, the more my memory fades."

"Don't say that. Don't say that you're dead."

Little Blue sighs, then lets out a huff, the same kind she would give me when she was growing up. "I do remember one thing about the man."

My back stiffens, and my gut clenches. "What's that, sweetie?"

"The man had a snake tattoo on his left forearm. It was kind of faded."

"Okay. Good. That's good information. And there's nothing else you can recall? Did he wear cologne, or did he have an accent?"

Little Blue looks into my eyes. "I told you, Dad, the longer I'm in this world, the less I remember."

I tell her that I understand, even though I don't. "And after the man handed you the drink, did he try to take you someplace alone?"

She nods. "Yes. Well, sort of. He told me the music was too loud in the living room, and he was getting a headache. Then he asked me if I wanted to find a quiet place to talk."

My teeth grit. "And did you go with him?"

"No. I told him I needed to find my mom to see when we'd be leaving. So, I went to the outside patio where she was talking with someone, and that's when I started to feel woozy."

"Did you tell your mom?"

Little Blue shrugs. "Yeah, but she was so busy chatting up a guy that she just brushed me off."

I sigh and stroke her cheek with the back of my hand. "I'm sorry, honey. Your mom didn't know anything was wrong. Otherwise, she would never have brushed you off."

My daughter smiles. "I know that, Dad. Mom feels like crap for what happened. It took me forever to convince her it wasn't her fault."

Confused, I ask how she was able to talk to her mom.

"Mom's here, on this side, with me." Her tone is matter of fact.

"I don't understand."

"Mom is on this side with me, silly. Well, kind of with me. I can only get so close, so mostly we holler back and forth. You should see her, Dad. She looks so healthy and pretty."

"Wait. What? I don't understand how Kim can be with you. I just spoke to her a few hours ago on the phone."

"Dad. You're confusing." She giggles. Then, she stares into my eyes and fills me with warmth and love. "I've got to go now, Dad. Will you come back and see me again?"

I immediately latch onto her arm. "What do you mean? Where do you have to go?"

Little Blue leans forward, wraps her arms around my neck, and then pushes her cheek against mine. "I love you forever, Dad." I watch as she slowly gets to her feet and backs away, eyes on me.

"Wait. Little Blue. Don't go away. I'll come with you. Wait." I hold a hand outward toward her. "Stay with me. Please don't leave."

Suddenly, I feel strength come back into my legs as if my bones are quickly developing inside me. I turn onto my side and onto my knees, then grab the side of the dumpster for support and clamber to my feet. Once upright, I turn back to my child and see only a strange gray mist.

"Little Blue," I yell, surprised when I hear my voice return to full volume. "Wait. Don't leave. Wait for me." I let go of the dumpster and lunge forward, only to lose strength again and crash down on the thin, stained cot.

I raise my head and cry out for my child, only to have the thickening fog swallow my words. Sobbing uncontrollably, I grab onto the mattress and pull myself forward until my lungs fill with the thick mist, and I fade back into a weak state.

Eventually, my head drops onto the cot, and everything goes dark. The last thing I hear is a hissing sound, then a sharp stab in my ankle.

# Chapter 3

The morning sun pierces my eyelids and causes a sharp, excruciating pain to tear through my head.

I slowly move my hands in front of me, expecting to feel the fabric of Warlock's filthy cot. Instead, my fingers touch something hard and cold. A gust of crisp air brushes my cheeks, waking me further. I force my lids open and look for any sign of Little Blue.

As I wearily scan the view in front of me, I become increasingly confused. No longer am I in the dark laneway on the cot behind the dumpster. I'm instead sitting on the shiny white steps in front of an upscale high-rise apartment building. Anxiety rushes through me, followed by the heart-breaking realization that my daughter, my Little Blue, isn't here—wherever *here* is.

When I try to move my feet, a throbbing pain shoots through my right ankle. I strain to focus my eyes on my foot when I hear a woman's voice beside me. "Are you okay? Do you need some help?"

I open my mouth to tell the woman I'm fine, but only a garbled sound comes out.

"Oh my. You don't sound well. I'm going to get you some help."

The woman is right. I'm in rough shape. I can't focus properly, I'm dizzy, and I'm as weak as a baby. I close my eyes and keep them shut to help stop the spinning.

I think about the vial Warlock gave me. Maybe it was rat poison or something, and as I lie here helpless, the toxic serum is coursing through my veins and ravaging my system. Maybe I won't survive long enough to get medical attention. Maybe I'll die on this stairway, and everyone will think I was a druggie who overdosed, and that will be that. My father will get a call, but I won't be here to tell him the truth. He'll believe what he's told, not that he ever thought I'd amount to much, being a musician. Still, a druggy? The shame and disappointment will devastate him. It'll linger in his mind for the rest of his days.

Then again, if I do die, there's a chance I could reconnect with Little Blue. We could be together, always. The thought of us uniting again makes me smile inside.

I hear the faint wail of sirens in the distance, and my head grows fuzzier as I teeter on the edge of consciousness. Soon, there are voices around me; they are talking with the woman. Again, I try to speak, but my efforts are futile, and soon, I surrender to the darkness.

* * *

My body is being vibrated, jostled, and transported somewhere unknown. I'm hazy and disoriented.

Where am I? Have I died?

A pang of fear hits me, and my eyes open.

There are rows of bright lights passing overhead, reminding me of driving through the Queens–Midtown Tunnel under the East River. With all my might, I turn my head to see metal bars attached to a bedframe. I'm in a hospital, being wheeled down a sterile white corridor.

The guy pushing me has straggly brown hair and blue scrubs. He leans over and looks down at me. "We're almost there."

"Where's there?" My voice is hoarse and dry.

"You get a room now. I'll bet you'll be a lot happier than you were in Emerg all that time."

We come to a swift stop, then turn into a doorway and enter a medium-sized room with two other beds. The guy in scrubs wheels me to an empty bay and pushes the head of the bed to the wall, where all sorts of machines are on wheeled posts.

"How long have I been in the hospital?" I ask.

The orderly leans over the bed and pats my arm. "Not long. About twenty-four hours."

"Are you kidding?" My voice is louder than expected.

"That ain't long. I've seen patients in emergency be there for two or three days. You're one of the lucky ones."

I turn to make eye contact, and a wave of dizziness rushes through my head. "Am I going to be okay?"

The guy pats my shoulder. "The doctor shouldn't be long. It's probably best that you ask him that question. I'm just a low man on the totem." He smiles. "Hang tight. You shouldn't have to wait long." The guy steps out of view, and the sound of his shoes trails off as he heads down the hallway.

I take a slow breath and try to calm my building anxiety. As I lay in the deafening silence of the room, I try to piece together my memory of how I got here, but I come up blank. I can't remember a thing after waking up on those white steps.

I hear people speaking in the hallway: a loud male and a soft-voiced female. They're too far away for me to make out what they're saying. A few moments later, the voices get clearer and a tall man in a white coat and a woman with flowered scrubs approach my bed.

"You're awake," the man says without expression. He studies the clipboard in his hand.

"Why am I here, doctor? Am I alright?" My voice wavers. "What about my ankle? I'm pretty sure a snake bit me. Maybe even a poisonous one."

He looks up at me. "Your ankle has superficial wounds, probably from pebbles or a stick. As for your overall condition, you'll live, but I wouldn't say you're alright."

"What do you mean?"

"Anyone who takes drugs, especially the deadly cocktail we found in your blood, isn't *alright*. We had to stabilize you; your blood pressure was skyrocketing and your oxygen levels were low. I'd say you got lucky this time. However, if you choose to keep using, the next time may be your last."

I shake my head, becoming more alert. "Look, doc. I know what this looks like to you. But I'm not a druggy at all. It was a one-time thing—"

The physician scoffs. "You know what, man, just save it. I see drug addicts every day in here, and you all have the same story. The bottom line is, it's your life, and no one can make you change your ways. In the meantime, I'll set you up with our psychologist. She'll give you some information about where to find help."

I sigh. "Fine. Whatever. You've already made up your mind about me. I guess there's nothing left to say."

The doctor tapes the chart on the bottom of my bed, then turns and exits the room.

I wanted to tell him about Mad Madge and the vial Warlock gave me, but I could tell that he wouldn't have listened. He's been desensitized from seeing so many addicts show up in emerg, with every one of them probably professing their innocence or vying for sympathy with some big *woe is me* tale.

I sigh and look up at the ceiling. I can't believe I'm in this situation. I feel like a scumbag, a derelict, and an outcast. I'm sure anyone who comes to this place because of a drug issue feels much the same way. The only difference is I'm not an addict—I only touched the stuff so I could see my baby girl again.

Right now, in this moment, I feel too scattered to know if I really did see Little Blue or if I was just hallucinating. There's a good possibility that Madge and Warlock worked a con on me, and the vial just caused me to pass out and vividly dream about Little Blue. It would explain why both Madge and Warlock left me in the alley alone after I drank the weird potion.

I must be a total idiot to have fallen for their con. I wonder how many others have been sucked in by the gruesome twosome.

As much as I'm not a violent person, there's a small part of me that wants to share my hellish experience with Skully. There's no doubt he would call on a couple of his knuckle-dragging muscle heads from the gym to pay Warlock a visit. But I couldn't do that. As much as I hate that I was drugged and left to fend for myself, I couldn't live with myself if that disgusting old bastard was knocked around and suffered a heart attack.

The fault is mine and no one else's. I should've known better. I should've, but instead I was willing to risk it all to see my child. I sigh, picturing my daughter in my arms in that alleyway. She felt so real—the softness of her hair against my cheek, the feel of her skin on my fingertips. She even sounded real. Her tone, her expressions, the way she looked at me. She acted the same as she did when she was alive. Could I really have dreamt that up?

A cool tear runs down my face. God, I miss her so much. So much so that I actually followed some drunk hag in the middle of the night, through side roads and around dirty alleyways, to find some old lunatic in the hopes that he could help me see my dead child. I'm a pathetic mess. I almost wish that whatever crazy shit I drank had taken me out. That way, I wouldn't have to feel any more pain and depression. I feel completely defeated, and I can't imagine ever feeling better.

"You must be Jude."

I've been so preoccupied by self pity, I didn't hear the two women walk in.

"Is your name Jude Rossi?" the older of the two women says. She's an academic type with a plain complexion and salt-and-pepper hair pulled back in a tight bun.

"Yes. That's me."

"My name is Jan Oaks. I'm the psychologist here at the hospital. This is

Lauren, a psychology student. Do you mind if she's here while we talk?"

I look over at the other woman. She looks about thirty, and unlike the psychologist, she's pretty and has color and life in her face. "It makes no difference to me."

Jan and Lauren approach the side of the bed. Jan gives me a forced, sympathetic grin. "I heard that you may be having some substance abuse issues. I just wanted to find out what's going on in your life, see if there's something I may be able to help with."

I shake my head and scoff. "Like I told the doctor, I don't have a drug problem, regardless of why I was brought in here."

"Why do you think you were brought in here then?" Jan crosses her arms, suddenly annoyed.

I shrug. "Gee, I don't know. Maybe the junkies I was partying with thought they'd drop me off to see if I could score some good drugs."

Lauren lets out an accidental giggle, which causes Jan to shoot her a disapproving look. "I don't think you should be making jokes, Jude. From what I understand, you've been hooked on a cocktail of lethal street drugs. And if you ask me, I'd say that's nothing to downplay."

I take a deep breath and try to control myself from coming unleashed on the know-it-all, Jan. After taking a few moments to exhale, I grin politely. "I am only going to say this one more time. I am not an addict. The reason I ended up in the emergency department was because I foolishly drank a vial of some weird toxic shit that this old guy in an alley handed me."

Jan's eyes widen and she grins sarcastically. "And are you in the habit of drinking, as you put it, toxic shit from weird people in alleys?"

Again, I fill my lungs with air and exhale slowly before answering. "I know how ridiculous that sounds, but I was drinking and feeling low down. I met this nutso woman, and she said she could help me."

Lauren is staring at me, not in judgement, but with a look of interest and concern.

"What was the woman going to help you do? Score dope?"

"No. I mean...I guess, ultimately, that's what ended up happening, but that definitely wasn't the plan."

Jan unfolds her arms and eases her rigid stance. "What was it she said she would help you with?"

Knowing I'm going to sound like a complete nut case, I quickly try to map out what to say before answering. But after a few moments with both of them waiting for a reply, I realize that no matter what words I use, there's no way to make the choices that landed me here sound rational.

"Alright, I'll tell you, mostly because it bothers me that you've branded me a drug addict when, in fact, you couldn't be more wrong." The women wait, their eyes fixated as I find my words.

I tell them about my daughter, how losing her spun my life into a dark, depressing place, and how everything came to a head last night. I mention the walk I took to the hotdog stand and then about meeting Mad Madge at the bus stop bench. The women are quiet as I continue about how Madge said she knew this guy who connected people with the dead.

Jan's eyes widen when I uttered this part. I'm not sure if it's because she's never heard something this bizarre before or because she thinks I'm an idiot for believing Madge. But by the look on her face, I can tell she's starting to believe me.

I go through the entire events of my night. When I get to the part about how my daughter came out of the mass of snakes, Jan and Lauren exchange glances. When I talk about how incredible it felt to hold Little Blue in my arms again, Lauren's eyes tear up, and Jan's expression doesn't change—she's undoubtedly been trained not to react.

"And then, I woke up on the front steps of a high-rise apartment. A lady found me, I faded out, and the next thing I know, I'm being wheeled into this room."

Jan sighs. "Well. That's quite the story." She looks down at the floor for a moment, obviously searching for a professional response. It doesn't take her long to find it.

"Listen, Jude. I...I think no matter what the reason you ended up here, drugs or no drugs, it would be a good idea to speak to someone, long term, about your grief."

I scoff. "Yeah, I've been down that road already, and look at me now. I can't say therapy worked in my favor."

Jan explains how when people suffer a great loss, they go through stages, and sometimes, they're not ready to benefit fully from counselling. Then, she asks if she can get some numbers of councillors she recommends. Even though I'm not into going through the whole therapy thing again, I nod and comply with Jan's offer, mostly just to put an end to the meeting.

Jan smiles and excuses herself to get the information for me. Instead of following her out of the room, Lauren remains beside the bed. Once we're alone, she looks a bit awkward without Jan here directing the conversation.

"I'm sorry about your daughter," she says softly. "I can't image the horrible pain you must be in."

I shrug. "Everyone has their own tragedies to deal with."

She half grins. "I guess so."

"So, you're wanting to be a psychologist? I don't know why anyone would want to hear people's problems all day."

Lauren giggles. It makes me feel lighter.

"I don't really look at it that way," she says. "I think of psychology as a way to help people, a positive thing."

"That's a very noble perspective."

"I guess." She shrugs just as Jan's voice echoes in the hallway. Lauren looks towards the door, then quickly back at me. "Just for the record," she whispers, "I don't think you're a druggy at all."

"I'm back!" Jan boulders into the room, carrying sheets of paper. "I've got a half dozen phycologists listed here. Depending on where you live, you should be able to find someone on the list that will work for you."

She hands me the papers.

"I'll check them out," I lie. "While you were out of the room, did you happen to run into the doctor or a nurse?"

"Why? Do you need something?"

I shake my head. "I just want to know how long I'll be in the hospital for."

"When I spoke to him earlier, the doctor said you'd be staying another night. Just to make sure you're strong enough to go home."

I nod and thank her, and then look over at Lauren. For the first time, I notice how incredibly blue her eyes are.

Both women leave, and I'm left in silence to think about the chain of events that led me to this moment. Every stupid decision I made was done for the chance of seeing my child again. And as the drugs leave my system and my brain clears, I'm left with the unfortunate realization that I likely didn't see Little Blue at all. That she was just an illusion caused by the drugs.

* * *

After two days out of the hospital and enduring some nasty residual effects from the toxic serum—strange dreams where snakes surrounded me—I'm finally well enough to return to work at the boxing gym.

It's 6 PM and I'm just putting on my jacket to head out for my shift when the phone rings. I debate answering, but when I see my father's number on the screen, I feel obligated to take the call. We don't talk much since he started a new relationship with his tennis instructor, a woman half his age going through a very public divorce with her ex, a high-profile New York district attorney. The woman is built like a swimwear model with a perfect figure and a face to match. I guess I can't really blame my father for being attracted to the woman or for pouring all his affection and attention on her. After my mom died, he stayed single for years, and he only took up tennis lessons, a sport he gave up in his twenties after I paid for two sessions with his now-current girlfriend. With all the drama and baggage this woman came with, I'm surprised my father doesn't blame me for introducing them.

"Hey, Dad. I'm just heading out to work."

"Jude. How are you, son?" He sounds unusually concerned.

Oh no. He knows about my hospital stay. How the hell did he find out?

It quickly occurs to me that his name must've been in my medical chart as my next-of-kin. The hospital must've reached out to him when I was first brought in. But if that's the case, why is he contacting me two days later? I let out a sigh, and nausea rises in my gut, making it hard to swallow. This is going to be a hard one to explain, regardless of what my reasoning was for taking the drugs. The one thing I know about my father is his definite black-and-white line when it comes to dope, especially after what happened to Little Blue.

"Long time no talk. How are things?" I force the upbeat tone, hoping to sound like I have my shit together.

"I'm alright, son. I was just calling to see how you're feeling." Strangely enough, he's not yelling yet.

"I'm feeling better every day. It was a stupid thing I did, and I don't expect you to understand." I sit on the kitchen chair and ready myself for the impending fight.

"Were you ill?" He sounds surprised.

"Well, in a way, yes. Self-induced, though. As I said, I'm feeling better every day, and you don't have to worry. I'm not planning on doing something that stupid again."

"I don't understand. What did you do?"

"You can just say it, Dad. I know that you know, so you don't have to go down the whole *make me confess* road."

"Jude, what in the hell are you going on about? I called to see how you were handling the news about Kim."

"What do you mean?" Now, I was the confused one. "What happened with Kim?"

There's a long pause. "Oh dear. You haven't heard."

Suddenly, my chest constricts.

"Kim committed suicide three days ago. I just heard from her mother."

I try to say something, but I can't. I feel like I've been sucked into a tornado, and everything is spinning around me.

"Jude?" My father's voice echoes over the phone. "I'm sure this news is a big shock for you. If you need to talk, I'm here."

"Yeah. Thanks, Dad. I appreciate that. I...I should probably get to work. I'm...going to be late." I'm trying to hold it together.

"Alright, son. For what it's worth, there's nothing you could've done to help her. Apparently, she'd been going down a dark path ever since...well, you know."

"Yeah, Dad. I know." A silent tear rolls down my cheek as the clench in my stomach has now turned from discomfort to agony.

"There's a memorial service in a few days at Kim's family home in Jersey. Do you remember how to get there?"

"Yeah, of course I do. I spent a lot of time there when Kim and I were young."

"Okay. Well, I guess we'll see you there then. You should probably give Kim's mother a call. It's the right thing to do."

After we say our goodbyes, I spend the next while staring out the window, staring out at nothing, in disbelief. This can't be happening. My mind flashes back to the recent call that Kim and I had a few nights ago, the same night I drank the potion in hopes of seeing my daughter.

Then, an eerie memory slams to the front of my mind. Something Little Blue said to me, or I imagined she said to me, while I was whacked out on Warlock's potion. *"Mom is here with me."*

I put my phone down and rub my face, trying to absorb everything.

I can't believe she's gone. First my child, and now her mother, in twenty-four short months. I guess I shouldn't be surprised. No one should be. Kim had been on a destructive path ever since losing Little Blue.

I think back a few nights ago, and how messed up she sounded on the phone. Maybe I should've said something to help her straighten up, but how? Every time I opened my mouth, she ripped me apart. But still, maybe there was something I should have done differently. Get together with her, hold her and console her. I was too busy feeling sorry for myself to think about helping anyone else. I'm left with the brutal reality of knowing that I couldn't save my child, and now I've failed her mother as well.

Tears continue to flow as I look at my phone and scroll to Kim's mom's number. I take a long breath, knowing there's no good time to do this. I push the dial button and wipe my cheeks.

With each unanswered ring, I'm grateful and pray that I don't have to speak to anyone. It's too hard to know what to say in a situation like this. After four rings, I'm just about to hang up when Kim's mother answers, sounding weak and defeated. "I saw your number come up; otherwise, I wouldn't have answered." Her voice is low and gravely.

"I've just heard the news. I know your pain as a parent is greater than mine, her friend. And I feel terrible for your loss. I am so sorry." I wipe away more tears.

There's a pause on the other end of the phone, followed by the odd sniffle. "You know, Jude. I'm not sad for Kim. I'm sad for me. I will never see my daughter again. But for her, I am happy. She is with Abbigale now on the other side. That's what she's wanted ever since her child died. She lived with so much misery and darkness, the pain was unbearable for her. That's why the drugs and booze—she had to be blasted out of her mind just to function."

I listen to the pained woman talk for another ten minutes before someone on her end asks a question and diverts her attention. She quickly tells me when the memorial is and, in a soft voice, says, "You really should try to make it."

Few tragedies in life can match the profound devastation of losing a child. And because I've had the misfortune of experiencing that level of pain, my heart bleeds for Kim's mom. And even though I have my grief over Kim dying, it's nothing compared to what her family is going through. As much as I don't want to go to the memorial—I avoid them like the plague after Little Blue's service two years ago—I'm morally obligated to attend. After all, Kim and I shared a daughter, and as much as I loved Little Blue, Kim's family did too.

By the time I snap out of my daze and look at the clock, it's near 7 PM, and I'm seriously late for work. Thankfully, old Skully doesn't mind if I wander in an hour or so after I'm supposed to start. I do my job well, and he trusts me. That's all he cares about. I call a taxi, something I wouldn't normally do, but if I took public transit, I'd be a hell of a lot later.

As I leave the apartment, it occurs to me that people may see my going to work after learning my child's mother has died as heartless, but if I took the night off and stayed in my apartment alone, I know the guilt would consume me.

# Chapter 4

Minutes turn into hours, hours into days, and I find myself on the subway heading for Jersey.

Kim's parents had a lot more money than mine did, and their family home and property reflect it. A manicured lawn and landscaped greenery were the perfect setting to hold their many social events throughout the warmer months. The main building was a four-bedroom heritage house that looks more like Cape Cod than Jersey, with grid-paned windows and panelled white doors.

Kim once told me that her grandfather on her father's side made a fortune in the construction business and left everything to his twelve children. Kim liked to rib me about my family living modestly, mostly in Hell's Kitchen. She liked to try and get a rise out of me. But I had a great way of counteracting her taunts, by stating that her father was working alongside mine at the paint store in Hell's Kitchen. And how, if her grandfather hadn't provided them with a bundle of money, they'd be driving the same shitty cars as my family did.

As I approach the upper-class neighborhood, I look up the street and see at least two dozen cars parked in the wide driveway of Kim's parents' house and on either side of the street. With each step, I slow my pace, feeling the heaviness of the situation grow inside me. The last time I was here was to attend Little Blue's celebration of life. The only difference was that I was heavily medicated and driving my own car—a bad combination.

I arrive too quickly and am soon met with a familiar face. Kim's father, who is standing and greeting people, says very little to me when I pass by but nods to acknowledge my attendance.

I make my way up the front stairs to the foyer, where people are dressed in black and holding small snack plates. Primped and preened and chatting, they look more suited for an upscale Manhattan party than a memorial in Jersey. When I pass the front room, I see a number of ladies flocking around Kim's mom. I wait long enough for her to spot me, then smile. Even from the other side of the floor, I can see the suffering on her face. She looks ashen and defeated. When her gaze shifts from me to one of the women next to her, I quickly walk away.

After passing more chatty people in the hall, I spot the tall staircase to the second floor, my escape to find a quiet place until the service starts.

The upstairs is adorned with fancy pastel green wallpaper and white crown mouldings, reminiscent of a French influence. I take an immediate right toward the washroom. Just as I'm about to enter, I look across the hall and see the closed door of Kim's room.

Normally, it would be completely out of character for me to enter someone's home, even if I knew them, and open closed doors. But, considering I'm the only one on the second floor and desire to avoid social interaction, I decide to take my chances. I close the door behind me as silently as I opened it.

A double-sized canopy bed sits at the far end of the room, with a trunk at the end. I walk past a white bureau and a matching armoire before reaching the chest and sitting down. My eyes scan the feminine room as I breathe in the stale air. I've been here before, when Kim and I were in our teens. Her parents had no problems with me spending time with their daughter as long as we left all doors open.

The memory makes me snicker. Regardless of their constant efforts to keep us behaving, it was pointless. Although Kim and I abided by the house rule, it was outside in the garden shed where Kim and I had sex and had subsequently gotten pregnant. Kim told me later that cameras were installed after her parents found out, just in case she was inclined to repeat the performance with someone else. Over the years, she had many such trysts in the same shed but would cover up the cameras each time.

I shake my head. She was a wild one, a freethinker for sure. I loved her as family, especially after Little Blue came along. But where once we would randomly pick up the phone and chat for hours about love and breakups and everything else, we drifted apart due to differing opinions about raising our daughter.

The wall in front of me showcases Kim's pictures—photos from her school days at different stages and candid shots of friends and family. Turning my head, I notice a gold-framed picture of Little Blue sitting on a white-mirrored vanity.

I cross the room and pick up the picture. I have the same one at my place. It was taken when she graduated from elementary school. As pretty as she was, this picture definitely reflected her awkward stage. The horrible bob haircut she insisted on getting left her ears poking out the sides like a geeky elf. Thankfully her hair grew quickly, and she went on to style it so her ears were covered. Kim had the same ears, and from what I've seen of the rest of the family, it's a trait they all share.

I'm just about to put the picture back when I see something silver glimmering inside a slightly open drawer in the vanity. I set the frame down exactly as I found it, then glance behind me to the closed door to make sure no one is watching. Slowly, I grab the small round knob on the drawer and pull it the rest of the way open.

A small book, a diary, lies flat and alone in the drawer. Once more, I look behind me to make sure the door is still closed before picking up the book.

Just as I open the front cover and see little hearts doodled on the first page, I hear the bedroom door open and look up in the mirror at the reflection behind me. Kim's father.

"Jude. I thought I'd find you here. Still anti-social, I see." Surprisingly, he doesn't sound angry that I'm in here. His voice is void of emotion. "You should come downstairs. Your father is looking for you."

When I turn to answer, he's already gone. Without understanding my motives, I slip the book into my coat pocket.

* * *

Sitting among the mourners on the decorated lawn, on chairs arranged before the tall, narrow podium, my sadness morphs into a deep resentment. Death, tragedy, darkness...I sometimes wonder how strong we're meant to be. Every one of us has suffered, yet we are all expected to somehow overcome and prevail, dragging our fractured hearts behind us. Why are we blessed with the power to love so deeply, only to be tormented by the suffering?

81

As I look around at the sniffling mourners, I vow that no matter who I meet in the future, I will only give them a fraction of myself. The rest I will hide away and keep safe.

After the last speaker tells their heartfelt Kim story at the podium, the crowd slowly thins. I look back to the last row, where my father is immersed in deep conversation with his girlfriend. I wish I didn't have to walk past him right now. I'm feeling too out of sorts to converse, and the last thing I want is for him to contrive a speech about why I should keep my chin up and resist the temptation to fall into a depression, the same thing that happened after Little Blue died. He's one of those men with a stack of anecdotes stored in his brain for every occasion. It drives me nuts.

A lady gets up from the row behind me, heading down the aisle past my dad. I seize the opportunity and walk briskly behind her, hoping to conceal myself. No such luck. The moment the woman reaches my father's seat, she bends down to adjust one of her shoes and puts me in plain view.

Like a hawk, my father homes his gaze on me. "Jude. Come over and sit with us."

So much for a clean get-a-way. Reluctantly, I sit in the empty white chair beside my dad.

"How are you holding up?" he asks sympathetically.

"I'm alright."

He gives me a doubtful look. "You know, I'm always here to talk."

He's not, actually. Not at all. There were several times over the past two years when I could've used someone close who knew both Little Blue and me, but he was too busy with his love interest to be there. But there's not much I can do about that now. It's water under the bridge. The only thing I want is to get the hell out of here. To go home, where I can block everything out.

* * *

When we pull up to the Chinese restaurant, I hop out, thank my dad for the ride, promise to check in in a few days, and head to my apartment.

I'm relieved to be home, to have escaped the grieving faces of Kim's family and friends, as well as the constant judgment from my father, who looks at me like I'm an emotional train wreck. I pour a glass of water and stand staring out the window. I look at the clear fluid in the glass and, for a moment, wish it was alcohol.

I take off my jacket and am just about to toss it on the couch when I feel something in my inside pocket. It's the diary I stole from Kim's vanity drawer.

Setting my glass down, I pull out the book and flop out on the couch. I know I should probably feel bad about taking something private and personal of Kim's,

83

and there's that unwritten rule about respecting the dead. But if there is anything in these pages that can shine a light on what happened to my child at the penthouse that night, I'll gladly live with the bad karma.

I open the book and am just reading the first few lines when my phone rings. I slide the phone out of my pocket and answer.

"Where the hell are ya, Jude?" Skully grumbles.

"I'm at home. I left you a note on your desk saying I wouldn't be in for my shift."

"You know I never read notes. Why the hell didn't you call me instead?"

"It was late, and I just thought you'd be—"

"Never mind that," he interrupts. "I need you here. A jackass plumber came in to fix one of the toilets, and next thing I know, the whole bloody floor is flooded."

I sigh and close the book. "Alright, Skully. I'll be there."

* * *

Skully wasn't kidding. The entire ring area is glazed over with icy cold water when I arrive. Thankfully, he recruited a few of the neighborhood guys that hang out at the gym to help mop up the mess. With five of us soaking up water, it only takes a couple of hours. But for some reason, I'm exhausted, probably because of Kim's depressing memorial I attended in the first half of the

84

day, coupled with the fact that I haven't eaten today.

Just as I'm putting the mop in the storage room, Skully approaches from behind and discreetly reminds me to make sure none of the guys who helped leave with any towels. With my back to him, I nod with a smile. It's baffling how a man with his net worth can be so obsessed with old, ratty gym towels. But I guess at his age it's understandable. The guy was raised in a time when nobody had much. A towel would've been a big deal back then.

Ignoring Skully's request, I say goodnight and walk out of the gym. I respect the old man, but I'm not about to pat someone down for a towel.

A powerful Atlantic wind pushes against me as I head towards the subway. As much as I'm unfazed by temperature, I prefer cold weather to hot, when more people are roaming the streets. I'm not worried about thugs, thieves or muggers, not after growing up in Hell's Kitchen. I just don't want the hassle of maneuvering around people on the sidewalks.

I momentarily grin as I remember how Little Blue loved going for drives at night. She'd point out all the colorful and flamboyant characters on the streets. In Jersey, especially the upscale area where she spent a lot of time with her grandparents, everything was safe. Similar and sculpted— the lawns, the residents and the language.

Little Blue was like me in that she wanted to experience things and learn about different cultures, music and cuisine. Needless to say, whenever we were together, we were never bored.

By the time I reach home, my feet are sore, and all I want to do is put something easy to make in my stomach and pass out on the couch.

* * *

Jolted out of a deep sleep by a hard rapping at the door, I sit up and look over at my digital clock. It's 9 AM. I quickly slip on my jeans and slide my work hoodie over my head.

"Who is it?" I holler on my way to the door.

At first, there's no response. Then I hear the quiet, muffled voice of my landlord. Half awake, I open the door and see the older man in his work apron, holding a set of keys. "Hi, Mr. Wong."

"Jude. Sorry I woke you. I need a big favor. My wife has to be in Manhattan for a foot doctor appointment, but I have an electrician coming to fix one of our ovens. I was wondering if you would drive her." He looks desperate and worried.

I sigh. I really wanted to spend the day flipping through Kim's diary, but I did tell Wong when I moved in that if he needed me for anything, quick repairs or whatever, I'd be happy to help. Unfortunately for me, the guy has a good memory. "Sure. When is her appointment?"

Wong breathes a sigh of relief. "She doesn't have to be there for an hour and a half. You can have a shower or eat breakfast or whatever, then come down to the restaurant. She'll be ready." He passes me his car keys, then thanks me again, and I close the door.

I shake my head. It's not like I mind doing the favor, but I know my whole day will be eaten up from the drive there and back. The traffic jams, the one-way streets, and of course, the lack of parking in Manhattan are all huge time thieves.

I make my way to the bathroom, disrobe, and look in the mirror. I'm a hot mess—pale skin, stringy dark hair that falls over my gaunt face. I briefly turn to the side and catch a glimpse of ribs easily detected on my skinny frame. I've always weighed in on the thin side, but I have never been this sickly looking. Initially, the anti-depression medications made me gain weight, but once I stopped taking them and my appetite waned, it didn't take long to shed whatever weight I did have.

* * *

As the rusted orange Fiero rumbles through the streets, Mrs. Wong sits silently in the passenger seat, gazing out the window,

87

hands delicately clutching the purse in front of her. It amazes me how a man as well off as Mr. Wong would settle on this shit box car when he could easily afford a modern, road-safe vehicle. I hope to hell he didn't pay more than a couple hundred bucks for this piece of junk. As if the engine's clanging wasn't bad enough, the nifty orange paint job really tops it off. I remember hearing Mr. Wong once say, "A fool and their money are soon parted." I'm pretty sure he attributes that credo to every facet of his life.

As a rule, creative people are open and non-judgemental. It's just the way we're wired. That said, I can't help but feel like an idiot when we find ourselves on the busy Manhattan streets during the morning rush.

Once I've successfully located the foot doctor building, I pull up to the entrance and drop off Mrs. Wong. She nods and tells me she'll text when she's done.

As much as I'm not in the mood to walk anywhere this morning, I'm embarrassed to be seen longer than I have to in this eyesore. I find the nearest lot, park, and walk up to West 4th Street to find a coffee shop.

This area of the city is upscale and clean and boasts one of the best universities in the world, NYU. That being said, it doesn't have the same welcoming feel to me that other areas of New York have. Here, I'm very aware of my appearance, whereas in The Kitchen, I blend in and feel comfortable.

After walking a few blocks, I see a coffee cart near the campus with a line of students waiting. I spend fifteen long minutes listening to their unrelatable chatter before finally placing my order. Once I have my coffee in hand, I scope out a bench near neatly manicured grass where I can sit and wait for Mrs. Wong's call.

As I sip my coffee on the bench, I look at the students as they walk past, wearing headphones or with their attention on their phones. Little Blue would be sixteen now, not quite the age of these students, but close. She used to talk about going to university to pursue a career in social work and help people in the community, but then she discovered her passion for singing.

I sigh deeply as I picture Little Blue here, attending school and working toward her future, something she'll never get the chance to do. I turn my head from the entrance of the university and focus on the coffee cart, where there's still a long line of customers. A woman carrying a coffee pays the vendor, then walks up the sidewalk toward me. She's older than the average student, probably early thirties, like me. Her hair is pulled back in a tight ponytail, and she's wearing athletic wear, tights, and a form-fitting matching jacket.

As she approaches, I notice something familiar about her, but can't put my finger on what it is. I know I should look away, in case she thinks I'm a pervert, but I can't, not until

I figure out who she is and where I know her from.

She's walking quickly. Before I know it, she's approaching the bench. Briefly she glances at me, then suddenly stops. "Hi. Don't I know you?" Her voice is soft and friendly.

I smile shyly. "I was thinking the same thing."

It's obvious that I don't attend NYU. I don't fit the image. Plus, I'm at least a decade older than the average student.

"Did you used to take courses here? Maybe we were in a class together."

I shake my head. "Nope. The only education I got after high school was from playing music."

"You're a musician?"

"Was. I'm not now."

"Oh. That's a shame. I love music."

"Maybe we ran into each other at a club a while back."

"No. Unfortunately, I don't get to go to many live performances. I don't think that's where I know you from."

"My name is Jude. Does that ring a bell?"

She tilts her head in thought. Then, suddenly, her face changes into a look of astonishment. "I know where I've seen you before." She's fidgeting with the rim of the paper coffee cup. "You were at the hospital emergency ward. I was with the psychologist who spoke with you. My name is Lauren. Do you remember?"

I suddenly feel smaller and embarrassed. Lauren, the pretty psychology intern. If I could make myself disappear right now, I would.

Lauren notices my discomfort and tells me not to feel bad about being at the hospital in the shape I was in. "Sometimes we get into situations we never dreamt we'd be in. Don't worry about it."

"Well, it was definitely a new situation for me, that's for sure."

"So, what are you doing at NYU? Thinking about joining up for some courses?"

The very thought makes me snicker. "Yeah, right. I barely got through high school. I'm not what you would call an academic."

Lauren giggles. "Don't sell yourself short. I'm sure you could do anything you put your mind to."

"Thanks for the vote of confidence, but you're giving me too much credit." I tell her why I'm on campus—that I'm biding my time until I have to pick up my landlord's wife.

She tells me that she's meeting one of her old psychology professors, then looks at her watch. "Actually, I should probably get going, or I'll be late."

My heart sinks. I haven't enjoyed a conversation like I just had in ages. Lauren smiles, tells me it was nice seeing me again, then walks away.

Before I can think of what I'm doing, I call out her name. When she turns and looks back, a lump forms in my throat.

I have to say something to her. What if I never see her again? There are millions of people in New York, and the odds of my running into her were slim to none. I can't imagine another encounter happening again.

"I was just wondering...I don't know. If you might, maybe, want to go for a coffee or a drink some time." I sound like an awkward pubescent boy.

Lauren smiles, then returns to the bench. "Do you have a phone?"

I pull out my phone. She holds out her hand and I pass it over, then watch as she quickly types something. "You have my number now." She hands the phone back. "Call me and we'll figure out a time that works."

"I look forward to it."

Once she's blended in with the students entering a building, I shake my head. I must be out of my mind. As much as this girl takes my breath away, I have no business asking her out on a date. I'm broke and living above a Chinese restaurant in Hell's Kitchen.

Suddenly, my cell buzzes. I look down at the screen and see a text from Mr. Wong. "My wife has finished her appointment. Please pick her up."

* * *

The city sounds like music playing out-of-rhythm as we make the slow drive back home—horns blaring, music escaping through car windows, and the sounds of moving vehicles. Throughout the ride, I've been feeling both excited and nervous about what lies ahead with Lauren. If I take her out and she sees what a loser I am—working as a janitor at a boxing gym and barely scraping by—I'm sure she'll want nothing more to do with me. Then again, maybe we'll hit it off so well that she won't care. But honestly, I can't see it going that way. She's kind but also smart, and I can't imagine someone with their life together wanting to get involved with someone who doesn't.

Once I have Mrs. Wong home and the car is parked, she invites me into the restaurant for a complimentary dinner. Normally I would decline, but after only having one cup of coffee in my system so far, I gratefully accept and opt for a take-out combo meal.

Once I'm back in my apartment, I grab a fork and sit down on the couch to eat and pick up where I left off browsing through Kim's diary. As I stuff a forkful of egg foo Yung into my mouth, I open the book in the middle and scan the barely legible writing.

From what I can make out, Kim is writing about a male friend she was dating before Little Blue was born—not my

93

business. I flip the pages forward with my thumb until I'm two-thirds through the diary.

*"Today I took Little Blue to get her ears pierced,"* Kim wrote at the top of the page. Since there are no real dates in the book, I do my best calculations to figure out when the entry was written. I estimate that Little Blue would have been around twelve when she got her ears pierced, which means I'm still too far back in time. I flip forward through the pages to find more recent entries, stopping when I come across a sketch of a snake in the outer corner of a page.

Immediately, I flash back to that drug-induced dream or hallucination I had in that alleyway not long ago, where Little Blue appeared from the mass of churning snakes.

*"I want so much to be with my daughter, wherever she is. I don't want to be here in the world without her. I have nothing left here. If I didn't have drugs and booze to quiet the voices, I would've killed myself already."*

I shake my head and breathe in deeply, then set my food aside. Why wasn't I there for her more?

I turn the page and see the words, *"The Party"* written in bubble letters with a crying cartoon-like face drawn beside.

*"We had arrived at the posh penthouse late, around 9 PM, and there were about ten people there, all men. We had worn our best dresses, ones I charged on my father's credit*

*card without him knowing. Little Blue wore a pink dress. She looked at least five years older with the make-up I had put on her. I wanted her to feel special and important. This was her night. As for me, I had worn a long, form-fitted sequin gown with matching black sling-back heels. As soon as we walked off the penthouse elevator, all eyes were on us. Both Little Blue and I loved the attention. It was a party in her honor, and she was finally getting the attention she deserved as a singer."*

I take a deep breath and close my eyes. It's hard reading these words and picturing my child the last night she was alive. Then, I remind myself that if there's a clue pointing to the person who'd drugged my daughter, I want to know. Opening my eyes, I slowly scan the words, almost speed reading, looking for names or titles of the men who were there.

My eyes stop on the word *snake*, and I slow my pace. *"While I was outside on the patio, getting maybe a bit too friendly with the music producer, Little Blue walked out and asked to speak to me alone. I looked at the handsome guy in front of me and rolled my eyes. Why did I do that? I should've been more sensitive to her needs than worried about paying attention to some guy I just met. I hate myself for that. Little Blue and me walked inside and stood near one of the floor-to-ceiling windows. She told me she wanted to go home because she was feeling woozy, an excuse she'd used before when she was tired or bored. I told her to grow up and relish the moment, as not every singer gets a party thrown in their honor. Then, Little Blue shrugged and said this guy kept harassing her, something I should've investigated. But I was too selfish. I didn't want to stop talking to the hot guy I was flirting with, a decision that eats me up every moment of every day. Though, I did glance over at Little Blue a few times after that. She was talking with a husky grey-haired guy and a musician. Though I didn't recognize him at the time, I later found out who the musician was—the singer for Electric Snake, a huge rockstar that packs a lot of punch in the industry. I have no idea who the grey-haired guy was. All I remember is that there were more older guys than younger ones at the party that night."*

I hold the book open and glance up at the wall. Kim wrote that Little Blue had been talking to Chad Michaels, the famous singer from Electric Snake. And why am I only finding out about his presence at the party now, two years later?

When Little Blue died, I spoke with the police, and they told me the only people at the party were music execs who had been working with Kim and Little Blue and a few of their associates. It seems incredibly odd that someone as famous as Chad Michaels would have slipped under the police's radar.

Why wasn't he mentioned before? Was he hiding something or being protected?

Sickening scenarios play out in my mind. Maybe Chad was seen giving Little Blue drugs and the execs are protecting him. Or maybe he drugged my daughter, brought her into the bathroom, and took off after she hit her head. Either way, he wasn't on the police report, and that alone raises huge flags.

As for Kim, why the hell didn't she tell me a huge rock star was there? Did they pay her off? Did she know something about what happened that she kept from me?

A wave of nausea rises in my gut. I set the book down, pick up my food and go to the sink to splash cold water on my face, discarding the half-eaten Chinese food in the trash on my way.

After drying my face with the small rag I keep on the oven door, I take a deep breath and try to center my thoughts. I have so many questions after reading Kim's diary. Questions that need answers. I wish I could ask Kim. Unfortunately, other than what's in her diary, she took the truth with her to the grave.

As I wipe a rogue bead of water from my chin, I notice my hand is shaking. As much as I want to continue reading the diary, I need to have a clear mind so I can process every bit of information. I look over at the clock. I've got a half hour before I have to leave for my shift at Skully's. The book isn't going anywhere. I'll wait to read more when I get home from work tonight.

# Chapter 5

My journey to work is a blur as my thoughts focus on the police report and what was mentioned—or, more importantly, what wasn't. Aside from the recording execs familiar to Kim and a few of the host's friends, no suspicious individuals were present. I smell a rat! For years, I've heard about the way music moguls are protected by dirty cops, judges, and anyone else they pay off to keep their secrets swept under the rug.

As I enter the building, Skully peeks his head out of his office. "Jude. Come here for a minute. I need to talk to you."

I walk into the small office and can't help thinking, *please don't let this be about his damn towels again.*

Skully sits behind his cluttered desk, hands folded in front of him, as I hunt for one of the few chairs not buried under stacks of papers. As soon as I'm seated, he says, "You know, Jude, I think the world of ya. And even though you only came to work for me two years ago, I feel closer to you than any of my other employees."

"Thanks, Skully. I appreciate everything you've done for me."

"Well, don't be too quick to thank me yet." His brow furrows. "Times have been tough at the gym lately. It's because of all the newer, bigger joints that opened up in the area. Because of this, I've had to let the front desk kid go and two trainers who've been with me for five years."

My chest tightens, but I force air into my lungs and straighten up to take the blow. "Are you firing me, Skully?"

He shakes his head. "No. I ain't firing ya. But I have to cut your hours back some. I'll be covering the front desk during the day and will be here to lock up at night. I need to cut two of your shifts a week. We'll stick to that schedule until business picks up."

Skully looks distraught. Despite the fact that cutting my hours would devastate my already paltry income—I'm struggling to pay rent as it is—I can't help but feel sorry for the old man.

I sigh. "Don't worry about it, Skully. You have to do what's best for the business. I get that. I'll work with your situation and look for a part-time job to help make ends meet until things get better here."

"Alright. Then it's settled. You can go." His tone returns to its normal gruffness as he motions to the door.

Typical Skully—tough as nails on the outside but a softie at heart.

For the rest of the night I clean the gym while the light from Skully's office glows under his door. I should be worrying about how I'll get by until I find a second job, but instead, my mind is consumed with what I read in Kim's journal about Chad Michaels and how he eluded police detection at the penthouse party two years ago. I need to come up with a plan to track him down. His address in New York is likely hidden, making him nearly unreachable to the public. I wish I had deep connections in the music industry, but I don't. Rockstars like Michaels are on a completely different level from a former bar band musician. Nevertheless, I'm determined to find him. Once I do, I'll do whatever it takes to uncover the truth. And when I have that truth, I won't rely on our slow-moving judicial system to hold him accountable; I'll take justice into my own hands.

"Jude, you ready to shut 'er down for the night?" Skully hollers from behind his door.

"All set."

"Okay. Make sure you do a towel check, and I'll meet you at the back to lock up."

* * *

An angry wind howls up the street as I walk close to the storefronts for shelter on my way to the subway. My mind wanders back to a time when store owners would post *Help Wanted* signs in their front windows if they had a position open. Now, the merchants use the internet, making the information available to everyone in Hell's Kitchen and beyond. Before, by walking in and meeting a potential employer, you had a chance to shake their hand and leave a good impression. Now, with everything online, you're nothing more than a 2D digital applicant. I miss the old ways of doing things. More personal.

It's late, and all the office workers have gone home, leaving the night to be inhabited by the more eccentric and colorful characters. I remember something my father said to me when I sold my car to cover my bills: "Now you're left to walk the streets with all of the freaks and geeks." A shallow comment from a man who is in a relationship with a woman half his age and has more baggage than a garbage truck. It's always seemed funny to me how the people with so much drama are the first to judge everyone else.

* * *

The subway is only a third full, a far cry from how many foot passengers it sees during the day. I look to the rear seats, where nobody is sitting, and make my way down the aisle. Once seated, I watch the other passengers. A young guy with headphones gently rocks his head to the beat of whatever he's listening to. Next to him is a girl with neck tattoos and two lip rings, reading a comic book and chewing gum loudly. The remaining passengers are the typical late-night subway commuters—older individuals who sit silently, their faces blank as they quietly endure the ride.

I tap my fingers on my knees, not to make a beat, but to burn off some of the nervous energy I've accumulated through the night, anxiously waiting to get home and dive into more of Kim's diary entries.

The subway halts one stop before mine, and I barely notice who's boarding until I hear a familiar cackle. Looking up, I spot the unmistakable red frizzy hair peeking out from beneath a green camo hat.

When Mad Madge turns and looks at me, my chest fills with rage. As she maneuvers around the other passengers with her sights locked on me, I turn my attention to the window in hopes of discouraging her. It doesn't work. A moment later I hear the strained breath of the overweight woman.

"Looky, looky. It's Mr. Rossi. This must be fate." She sits beside me.

I shake my head in disgust and do my best to control my temper. "There are other unoccupied seats. I'd appreciate it if you chose another one."

"Nah, I'm just fine here. Plus, it's been a while since we talked. We can get caught up."

After everything she's put me through and now her casual attitude, my resentment boils over. "Listen, Mad Madge. The sight of you makes me sick to my stomach. You're a thief, a liar, and a con artist. Your ass should be in jail, along with your weird alley dweller cohort."

Madge looks at me. Tears well up in her eyes, and my guilt is instant.

I exhale loudly. "Hey, don't cry. I shouldn't have gone off on you. You're obviously mentally unstable and—"

Madge bursts out in maniacal laughter. "Gotcha!"

The subway comes to an abrupt halt at my stop. I stand. "Move, please."

Madge shuffles her weight in the seat, then grunts and gets up. "This is my stop as well."

She deliberately ambles as slowly as a turtle in front of me, then steps off the subway onto the platform. When I'm able, I veer around her and make my way to the stairs.

"Jude, wait," Madge bellows from behind.

Without turning around, I stick up a middle finger and keep moving.

"You know, you cast me in an unfair light, considering you're a bigger thief than I am." Her words are quietening from the distance.

*Go to hell, you crazy old bat!*

Once I reach the bottom of the stairs, I see an older man pushing a small cart with a basket on the front. A tall, awkward bag sways on top of the cart. I'm just about to pass when the bag topples over and several apples roll onto the pavement. The man is feeble, and his hand shakes as he reaches for the fruit.

"Let me help you." I quickly scramble to gather the fruit.

Once I have the apples back in the basket, I position the bag so it won't fall over again. The old man grins with a full set of brownish dentures. "Thank you, son. Just stay right there. I have something for you."

"No need, sir. I'm happy to help."

"Just hang on, I've got it right here." He slowly rummages through his front pocket.

I look behind me on the staircase, hoping Madge hasn't gained speed and caught up to me, but thankfully she's nowhere in sight.

After a few long moments, the old guy pulls something out of his pocket and then opens his hand to reveal a shiny quarter. "Take it! You've more than earned it."

I snicker inside. "No, sir. Really. It's fine. Keep your money."

The man looks offended as his brows furrow. "Are you afraid I have dirty hands? Is that why you won't take my money?"

"No. Of course not."

"Then, take it, boy!"

I reach out and take the quarter. "Thanks. That's nice of—"

"I really got to get back into yoga. I'm out of shape." Madge's irritating voice rings out.

I can't believe it. I glance behind me, and she's standing there.

"You asking this poor old guy for cash? Gee. If I knew you were that broke, I would've gone through my pockets for loose change."

I roll my eyes and then direct my attention back to the man. "Take care, sir." And I start walking.

"Wait up, Jude."

I scoff and keep moving.

Just my luck, I need to cross the street, but the walk light is red. Sure enough, Mad Madge approaches and stands next to me. "Y'know, the way you're acting, I'm starting to get the feeling you're not happy to see me." She cackles.

"You've got a warped sense of humor, lady."

"Oh, c'mon. After everything I've done for you, you're spitting venom at me?"

I turn to face her. "Are you out of your mind? You could've killed me that night. I ended up in emergency because of that poisonous crap you gave me."

Madge suddenly looks serious, and she holds her hands out in front of her. "Whoa. There, you're wrong. I didn't give you anything. Let's get that straight right now. Besides, you weren't the only one that woke up sick."

"Pfft. Is that right? You took the potion too?"

"Hell no! But Warlock bought us a bottle with your twenty bucks and instead of getting the good wine, he opted for a couple of bottles of cheap stuff. I swear, I was sick for a good couple days after that."

"You're too much. Just stay away from me. Far away."

To my relief, the light turns green and the walk sign lights up. Speed walking, I'm halfway across the street when I hear, "I thought you handled those nasty snakes well."

Her words stop me in my tracks. How the hell did she know what I hallucinated? Maybe seeing snakes is a side effect of the drugs they gave me.

The walk light begins to flash, warning it will soon turn red. I collect my wits and make my way to the other side of the street.

Just as I start heading up 52nd Street, I hear Madge yell out in fear. I turn to see her stuck in the middle of the road with cars whizzing past.

I don't believe this. Reluctantly, I turn back, hold my hand out to oncoming vehicles and venture into busy traffic to rescue Mad Madge.

"Come on, dammit!" I grab onto her dirty coat sleeve and walk her to safety.

As soon as we reach the sidewalk, Madge leans over, putting her hands on her knees as she gasps for breath. "That was so scary. I thought for sure I was going to be killed." She giggles.

"Nope. You're fine. And I'm leaving!" I let go of her sleeve and continue on.

"You know, you have me made out to be a villain, but the truth is, you're worse than me."

A burst of laughter escapes my lips. *Convince yourself of whatever you like, lady. I don't care.*

"I may have stolen your wallet a while back but I returned it. Whereas the diary you stole, you have no intention of putting it back," she says.

I stop walking just before the bus stop, my head spinning with confusion. I turn to see Madge smiling and walking my way. "What did you say?"

"Ahh. I've got your attention now."

"How did you know about the diary?"

Madge shrugs coyly. "I know lots of things about lots of folks."

"Are you going to tell me or just play games?" A thought occurs to me. "Did you break into my apartment when I wasn't there?"

"Don't be ridiculous."

"Then how?"

"Jude, I understand that you are confused about me and what happened that night in the alleyway." Her voice is suddenly sincere. "I'm sorry that you got sick and ended up in the hospital, but wasn't that a small price to pay for seeing Little Blue again?"

As I stare at her, my words stifle. I have no idea what to think. Before, I had the truth of knowing that she and Warlock were crooks, preying on people who are grieving and making a profit. Now, with what she's just told me about the diary, the snakes, and my reunion with my child, I'm completely baffled. "Come clean with me. You owe me that."

"I don't owe you nuthin', Jude. In fact, I think it's the other way around. Do you think everyone who loses a loved one gets to see them again? Without me, you would never have known about Warlock." Her tone is bordering on anger.

I'm not sure if it's because of the sincere look on her face combined with the information she had about me, but I believe her. I guess Warlock must've really had some weird connection to the dead, and I must've really seen Little Blue. Still, one question rises above the others. "How did you know about the diary?"

Madge shrugs. I can tell she's still stewing over me being disrespectful and calling her names.

Just then, a transit bus pulls up beside us, and three people get off. Madge smiles. "A storm is comin', and it's comin' fast. You'd best prepare yourself. Why don't you spend the next few days thinking about how to adjust your attitude? Then, just maybe, I'll answer your question."

And before I can say a word, the bus doors close and she's gone.

* * *

The walk is a blur, my mind jumping between disbelief and belief. Madge knew too much about my apparent hallucinations after I drank the potion. And the diary. There's no way she could know about that. Unless...unless she followed me home, then when I went to work, broke into my place and found the diary. That's the only thing that makes sense.

With this scenario in mind, I quickly pick up the pace until I'm speed walking. If I get home and find the diary is either stolen or in a different place than where I left it, I'll know that Madge is playing with me.

When I arrive at Wong's restaurant, the place is dark and there are no cars out front. Standing on the street, I look up the long metal staircase to my apartment on the second floor. An eerie shiver runs through me. I swear, if that crazy old woman has been in my place, I will seek her out and have her arrested. Though, a small part of me does hope she's broken in. It would explain how she knew about the diary. I remember telling her who Kim was, so Madge mentioning her by name isn't a surprise.

Grabbing onto the rickety railing, I slowly make my ascent, holding my breath for what I may find when get inside the apartment.

I turn the handle and slowly push against the paint-peeled door, but it doesn't open. Still locked. I put my key in, turn it, then open the door.

A red hue from Wong's restaurant sign floods the apartment as I slowly scan the front room, looking for signs of an intruder. So far, everything seems to be in place. My guitar with the spider web attached sits in the exact same position in the corner. My laptop is folded shut on the end table, the same way I left it. And lastly, I spot the most important thing, the thing that, if missing or moved, would explain Madge's in-depth knowledge of my theft. As I stare at the small book sitting where I laid it on the edge of the couch, a cold chill runs up my spine.

*How the hell did Madge know about the diary if she didn't break in and find it?*

In trance-like confusion, I walk through the rest of the apartment, noting only that nothing is disturbed before returning to the living room.

I've never believed in the supernatural. It all seemed like rubbish to me. But there are things Madge couldn't have known about my experience in the alleyway with Little Blue. How could she have known about the black snakes unless she has some strange powers that open her mind to another realm?

I rub my face, then shake my head. I feel like I'm going mad. And no matter what reasoning I come up with to explain the old woman's insights, nothing fits. The only explanation that makes sense, in a nonsensical way, is that I did see Little Blue after drinking the potion. I did pull her out of a mass of snakes.

The threat of a headache manifests as a dull pressure behind my eyes. This is all too much for my head. I grab a pillow from the bedroom, return to the couch, and close my eyes.

# Chapter 6

The orange glow of morning floods through the kitchen window and leaves brush strokes of color across the wood floor. I sit up and catch my bearings before going to the kitchen to make coffee.

As I wait for the small machine to percolate, a noisy beep comes from my cell phone. It's a text message from my father, asking me to go to lunch today. With unfocused eyes I type a message back that kindly refuses his offer, informing him that I have to work today. I don't, but after my bizarre night, I don't need the stress of interacting with him. The more my father treats me like a mindless loser, the weaker I feel, and I can barely muster the strength to get through each day as it is.

I sit at the table and glance at the diary on the arm of the couch. Immediately, I think of Chad Michaels—the bastard who might be behind Little Blue's death. Undoubtedly there are more clues in the diary. Then my mind reflects on last night and the confusing issue of Madge and what is real and what isn't about what she told me. Both issues require my undivided attention, which I'm feeling too scattered to do now.

Instead, I open my laptop and search the employment columns and scroll down the short list of jobs I'm obviously unqualified for—accounting, heavy duty mechanic, and dental hygienist. There are other sites where I can search for work, but the more I read, the more defeated I feel.

When I was a boy, whenever I was confused about something, I'd go for a stroll outside to clear my head. With my mind so tangled right now, I decide to get dressed and take a walk.

I am just sliding on my trainers when my cell rings. I don't recognize the number, but for some reason, I feel compelled to answer. "Hello."

There's a soft giggle on the other end. "You don't sound very enthused to talk to me."

It takes a quick moment before I realize that it's Lauren. "I'm sorry. I just wasn't sure who was calling."

"Who did you think would be calling? A psycho ex who was disguising their number? Or maybe a loan shark that you owe thousands of dollars to?"

I chuckle. "None of the above."

We talk for a few moments, discussing everyday things like how our jobs are going and the weather. She's just what I need right now, a distraction from my tangled thoughts. After a few more moments of talking, she asks me if I have any plans for the next few hours as she doesn't have to be at the hospital for her shift until this evening.

"What do you have in mind?"

"I'm not sure. If you're up for grabbing a coffee somewhere, if that doesn't sound too mundane?"

"I can do mundane. Where would you like to meet?"

"You live in Hell's Kitchen, right? Why don't I drive over and meet you at a coffee place close to you?"

"Sounds good." I quickly try and picture where there's a coffee place nearby that won't take too long to get to on foot. "What about Jake's Java Joint on 52nd Street?"

"Never heard of it, but I'll punch it into my maps and meet you there. How does forty minutes sound?

# Chapter 7

Jake's Java Joint is one of Hell's Kitchen's most popular coffee bars, thanks to its nostalgic charm dating back to the 1970s. Known for its 'authentic' Italian coffee, the café has attracted numerous celebrity customers over the years. Many of these stars leave signed photos proudly displayed throughout the funky little shop.

Thankfully, I arrive before her and manage to secure a small table at the back of the room underneath a black and white signed picture of Joe Lynn Turner, debatably one of the greatest rock vocalists in the world. I quickly pull out my wallet to make sure I have enough cash to treat Lauren to one of Jake's gourmet drinks. Thankfully, I have a twenty-dollar bill and some loose change in my pocket.

I'm down to my last few bucks. It's a good thing Lauren didn't suggest we go to lunch, or I'd have to fake an illness or an injury to get out of it. I've never been embarrassed by having no cash when taking a woman out, and regardless of my circumstances now, I don't plan on experiencing that humiliation.

It's been a long while since I was out with a lady. The last one I met at a gig, and back then I had plenty of cash to afford a nice bottle of wine and dinner at an upscale restaurant. How things have changed.

* * *

Her hair moves with her steps as she makes her way toward me, removing her aviator sunglasses and smiling as she arrives at the table. "Jude. I'm sorry I'm a few minutes late. Traffic. Have you ordered already?"

I return the smile. "I just got here, and no, I haven't ordered yet. You have a seat, and I'll get the drinks."

"Nope. I invited you for coffee, so I pay. That's how it works."

"I'm kind of used to paying," I say, keeping within the male role.

"I'll tell you what. If you ask me to meet you next time, it'll be up to you to grab the tab."

Even though I don't know Lauren well yet, I can tell she has her mind made up.

I tell her I'd like a latte, and she sets her glasses on the table and heads toward the counter. I notice how her body moves in her tight blue jeans and how her fitted coat accentuates her tiny waist. It's been a long time since I've looked at a woman this way.

117

Over the past two years, I'd thought I'd become numb to any kind of passion.

I watch how she interacts with the barista, playful, pleasant and kind. A girl like her must not be jaded yet from being a psychology student. Working in the emergency department would be a crazy experience, especially when dealing with the riffraff off the street. Yet here she is, bubbly and animated with no signs of being cynical. So far, she's a great distraction.

When she returns carrying the drinks, I stand up and help her set them down.

"Parking was interesting, that's for sure. The lot outside is tiny and full of cars."

"Yeah. If we were here any later, we would've never found a table. This place gets busy."

Lauren takes a sip of her coffee and looks around at the celebrity photos and memorabilia on the walls. She tells me that I made a good choice of where to meet and then asks me if I've ever seen a famous person in here before.

I shrug. "There was this one time about ten years ago when I thought I saw Clinger from M.A.S.H, but it turned out to be just some guy with an extraordinarily large nose."

Lauren giggles and tells me how she used to watch reruns of the show with her grandfather.

"Do you have a close-knit family?" I ask.

She thinks for a moment. "Unfortunately, not anymore. When we lived in Maine, where I went to school until I was ten, we were surrounded by relatives, but since we moved to Manhattan, it seems like the only blood relatives nearby are my parents and my sister. And what about you? Big family?"

I shake my head, then tell her how my mother died years ago and then share the story of my dad and his complicated girlfriend. "No siblings. No living grandparents."

"Well, if it's any comfort, I don't see my family much anymore, even though we all live in the same city."

"Because of your schedule?"

"Not really. It's more because of class distinction, I guess."

"What do you mean?"

"My father is a big-shot entertainment lawyer, which is why we originally moved to the city. He opened his firm here twenty years ago. Anyway, when he started to add some high-profile clients to his roster, he changed and became focused on things that I found shallow and irrelevant."

"Like?"

"Like what kind of car he drove and where he bought his suits and what parties he was invited to—it's ridiculous."

"And your mom?"

Lauren laughs. "My mother settled very nicely into his world and now considers herself among the other rich socialites who live on the Upper East Side.”

“And that’s not the lifestyle you wanted? I know a lot of women who would jump at the chance to experience that way of life.”

“Well, they can have it. I couldn’t bear to live that shallowly. My focus is on more important things. That’s why I want to become a psychologist. There are too many lost souls that need help. So, instead of worrying if I’m wearing the right designer label or having my hair done at the best salon, I prefer to do something more impacting and meaningful with my life.”

She catches me with a frozen grin. “Why are you smiling at me?”

I shrug and put my hands around my cup. “I don’t know. I guess because I’ve never met anyone like you before. You’re a breath of fresh air, to say the least.”

“Nah. I’m not doing anything so special. Maybe one day I’ll be able to make a significant difference, but for now, I’m still learning and doing a lot of grunt work.”

“Why did I expect you to downplay the fact that you’re a good person?” We both laugh. “I am sorry that you don’t have a relationship with your family, though.”

“Oh, I do. It’s just not a regular get-together kind of family thing. I might see them once every couple of months. It’s not like I’ve eradicated them from my life completely or anything. I just don’t get involved with how they live their lives.”

"And how do they feel about your career direction and purpose?"

She scoffs. "Let's just say that I'm a growing concern in their eyes."

We slowly sip our drinks as we effortlessly delve into different aspects of our lives. When she asks me about my work, I'm honest. I talk about my old band, how we made it into the A club circuit, and how I walked away from everything music-related when I lost my daughter two years ago. I even tell her about Wong's Chinese Restaurant and my modest apartment above it. For some reason, I feel like I can talk to this girl without feeling self-conscious or ashamed.

"Don't you miss performing? I once saw an interview where a musician was talking about how true musicians don't have a choice. If they don't play, they quickly fade into a dark place. Is that true?"

"Well, looking at my life now, I'd say that was a fair assumption."

"You should think about playing again. I bet you are a great player."

"Was a great player. I'm sure whatever talent I did have is long gone. If you don't use it, you lose it, so they say."

"I bet you'd surprise yourself on how much you'd remember if you picked it up again. I'd love to hear you play."

The words all musicians like to hear. "So, you work today?" I change the subject.

Lauren nods, then glances at her watch. "Yeah. And I've got laundry to do before then."

"That's okay. Since my hours have been recently knocked back, I've got to find a part-time job. So, I should probably be on my way too."

Her smile seems to fade, and the corners of her mouth slant downward. "I wish we could stay and chat more, I've really enjoyed this."

If only she knew how spending this time has helped me. Since she walked into this place, both my anxiety and confusion have subsided, and I feel stronger and more focused.

"When can I see you again?" I surprise myself with the question.

She smiles. "When?"

"Five minutes after you leave." We laugh.

"I'd like to see you again, too. Actually, I'm off tomorrow if you want to come to my apartment for dinner and maybe a movie? Or is that rushing things?" she says.

"Do you always invite strange men to your apartment? I mean, we barely know each other." I wink.

"Never. But I have a way of reading people, and so far, I haven't seen any psycho warning signs in you."

"Good. And yes, I'd love to come over."

Lauren grabs our empty cups from the table, walks over to the trash and drops them in. I walk up behind her and thank her for the coffee, then hold open the front door. In the parking lot, I walk with her to her car and smile when I see its make and condition. It is a twenty-year-old Chevy HHR with dents on the corner panel and rust spots on the bottom of the body. She looks at me and grins sheepishly. "This is my beast. I named her Hope."

"Why is that?"

"Because when I'm driving and she makes strange noises, I hope I make it to where I'm going."

I laugh and tell her not to feel bad about her junker. At least she has a car.

Lauren smiles, looks around the lot, and then back at me. "So, you didn't drive here?"

I shake my head. "Nope! My only modes of transportation are the subway or the loser cruiser."

She giggles. "Loser cruiser?"

"The bus."

She offers me a ride home. Normally, I would be horrified to let a female see where I live, especially one as beautiful and smart as her, but for some reason, I feel safe with her, safe to let her see the real me.

En route to my apartment, I notice a sticker on the dash. "EAT THE RICH," not what I'd expect from a girl who grew up on the posh side of the tracks. She is full of surprises, including her piece of crap car. I'm sure with a rich daddy, she could be driving her choice of shiny vehicles. But, as she stated back at the coffee joint, she's not about the money. She's a real person who wants to make her way in life and not on the backs of her parents. How incredible. She is definitely like no one else I've ever met.

The drive to Wong's goes by too quickly, as all I want to do is stay in her company. She pulls up in front of the restaurant, and we say goodbye. I glance one more time into her alluring eyes and then shut the door. I stand and watch while she makes a quick U-turn and then drives back down the street. I fumble for my keys and pull them from my pocket, noticing that my hands are trembling. Walking up the stairs, I experience a sensation I haven't felt in ages—a euphoric buzz that leaves me light-headed and exhilarated.

* * *

As I enter the apartment, the remainder of my joy drains from my body, pushed out as the weight of my burdens returns.

I look at the diary on the edge of the couch, and guilt hits me. How could I have felt happy seeing Lauren when I haven't yet solved what I now believe to be my daughter's murder? I sigh deeply. I've been selfish today. Instead of going out, I should've been here reading the remaining pages of Kim's diary for clues.

My shoulders tense, my stomach clenches, and I realize that while I was with Lauren, I was relaxed. But as much as her presence affected me in a positive way, I need to put my affection for her aside and focus my attention where it belongs.

# Chapter 8

Immersed in the diary, it quickly becomes apparent to me that drugs, drinking and hooking up with random guys seemed to be how Kim spent the last months of her life. She mentioned being destitute a few times, how she reluctantly moved back in with her parents, and how they nagged her constantly about her reckless lifestyle. As I read on, I can't help but wonder if she was irresponsible prior to our daughter's death, and if so, how much of her wild lifestyle did Little Blue see? On the days Little Blue stayed with me, she never spoke ill of her mother. She adored Kim and was loyal to her.

Hours pass as I sit unmoved on the couch, reading the words in the diary intently. Finally, I lay my head back and sigh when I finally reach the last entry. I wish I knew how bad off Kim was. I just assumed her wild behaviour and substance issues were a way to self-medicate after our daughter died, but now I believe Kim was on some kind of suicide mission long before that fateful day. And even though I could find no more information regarding the penthouse party, I think it was a good thing I took the diary out of Kim's vanity drawer. Her parents are emotionally ruined by her death; they don't need to find the diary and read about all the bad choices that led to Kim's passing.

Steaming hot water sprays over my numb skin as I reflect on Kim's diary in the shower. When the temperature starts to turn cold, I shut off the taps just as my cell I placed on the bathroom counter buzzes.

I can't imagine Skully calling this late, or for that matter calling at all. Maybe it's because I haven't responded to his message about my not coming in for a couple of nights. He's more of a text person, something I painstakingly tried to teach him over many months. He fashions himself as being *tech-tarded*, a term he coined for himself. *"There's something to be said for the old way of communicating, when people actually had to meet in person to discuss things."*

Even though I was born in the computer generation, I understand where he's coming from. These days, everyone hides behind their devices, and genuine social skills seem to be fading. Playing in bars for years forced me to become approachable and diplomatic, but after Little Blue passed away, my desire to interact with others vanished.

I grab a towel from the rack and dry off while I look down at my cell. I recognize Lauren's number just before the phone goes silent.

I'm not sure if it's the cold air on my wet skin or the excitement of knowing she called, but the hairs on my arms are standing on end. I'm quick to finish drying off, then I slip into my sweats and hurry to the living room. Sitting on the couch, I dial her back.

"Hello." Her voice is a bit tired but sweet and sounds like music to my ears.

"Sorry, I was just getting out of the shower. How was your shift?"

"It was a trying night. I'm not sure what kind of weird energy blew into the emergency ward, but I felt more and more exhausted for every patient we spoke to."

"That makes sense. You're dealing with people who have emotional issues, I'm sure they are tough nuts to crack. Pardon the choice of words."

"I think the worst part is knowing we'll only see them for one short visit. So, the impact we have is minimal. After that, they're given numbers to mental health resources with long wait lists. I just hate to see patients struggling with their inner demons. I wish there were a faster solution for these people, instead of suffering out there on the streets. It's no wonder a lot of them choose drugs to numb their pain."

Her passionate tone shows how much she cares. She is truly an incredible person. I love people who lead with their hearts—they are a rare breed.

Without breaching any confidentiality rules, Lauren gives me a few brief scenarios about how the troubled patients were brought into the emergency. In one particular case, a man had witnessed a dog getting kicked in the park and got into a physical confrontation with the abusive guy to make him stop. Lauren told me that the man defending the animal was arrested and brought into the hospital with his hands and feet shackled. "How's that for an injustice!"

"Unfortunately, there will probably always be those cases—where they've been treated unfairly. I'm sure it's frustrating to witness. I guess that's why I'm surprised you'd choose to work in that environment. It would be too hard to see day after day."

Without missing a beat, she tells me that her frustration is her issue, not the patients', and that she feels fortunate to make a difference in these peoples' lives. "Sometimes all they really need is someone to listen."

Feeling as though my comment could've sounded insensitive, I agree with her. "My hermit lifestyle has made me a bit calloused."

"I don't find you calloused. You've just been sleepwalking for a couple of years." There's a pause. "What were you like before Little Blue died?"

"I had a more open perspective on the world. I was never given any reason not to."

"Did you try and fight the darkness, your depression initially?"

I think about her question honestly. "I don't think I did. From what I can remember, I felt like I was being sucked into a black hole, and because I couldn't imagine anything more important than my daughter to live for, I had no purpose making me want to fight."

Lauren sighs. "I'm sorry I didn't know you then. Even though I'm new at what I do, I could've been there to listen. I could've been a shoulder to lean on."

"That's very sweet, Lauren, but I'm glad you weren't around then. I wasn't a very nice person. I was drowning my sorrows in booze and angry at the world."

"That's understandable." Her voice is remorseful and heartfelt.

We talk about Little Blue for a while, and then eventually, I describe my interlude with the crazy lady on the subway, and Lauren lets out a giggle. "I'm sorry, Jude, I shouldn't laugh, but picturing the old woman saying those inappropriate things is so crazy, it's funny."

I laugh with her. "Oh, sure. It was a real riot. I felt like crawling under my seat."

She giggles. "Were the other passengers shocked at the old woman's behaviour?"

I scoff. "On the subway, at night, in New York? No one batted an eye. The crazy lady stole my wallet, too, all without me noticing. She might be crazy, but she's damn clever."

I go on to tell Lauren that my mind-blowing experience with Madge didn't end there—she was behind me as I walked home from the subway and claimed to have lived in the time of Clara Barton, the nurse who started The Red Cross.

"Wait, what? Wasn't that sometime in the mid-eighteen hundreds?"

"Yep. Now you know just how deranged Madge is."

"So, let me get this straight. When I met you that night in emerg, you said that a crazy lady had lured you into an alleyway, then gave you drugs with the promise of reconnecting with your daughter in the spiritual world. Was that the same woman?"

Hearing the words aloud, I feel ridiculous and ashamed. "Yes. The same woman." I want to clarify that it was Warlock who gave me the serum, not Madge, but I already feel stupid enough.

"I get it. It's not hard for grieving people to be lured in by the promise of seeing a loved one again, especially their child.."

I can tell by the compassion in her tone that she's picking up on my embarrassment. "Have you seen her after that?"

"Briefly, yes."

"And what happened?"

I take a deep breath and close my eyes. I don't want to tell her about my latest encounter with Madge—she's going to think

I'm addicted to the nutty woman—but for some reason, I can't *not* answer her. She's honest and open with me, so as much as I don't want to answer, I feel I owe her the same respect. "I was furious with her. I accused her of taking advantage of my grief and urging me to drink the toxic serum her cohort sold me."

Lauren scoffs. "I bet she had a million excuses."

"No. She didn't. Instead, she blew my mind. She mentioned things I saw after I drank the serum and then blacked out in the alleyway."

There's a pause at the other end of the phone. "Really? Like what?"

"Like the mass of snakes I saw my daughter come out of."

"Wow! This woman is good."

I just about added that Madge also knew about the diary I took from Kim's parents, but I stop myself. As much as I want to be open with her, I can't be on this. She would immediately peg me as a thief, and all of my excuses wouldn't gain her respect back.

"Can I ask you something, Jude? And don't be afraid to be honest with me. I have no judgement."

"Okay. What's your question?"

"When Madge told you about the snakes that you saw while under the influence of whatever you drank, did you believe that maybe your encounter with your daughter wasn't a hallucination, and it really happened?"

I take a moment, even though I know the answer. I don't want to sound gullible. "Let's just say that her words made me think twice."

"I bet. Can I maybe play devil's advocate for a minute?"

"Why not."

"Okay. Just hear me out. You told this Madge woman about your daughter dying, Then, she takes you to someone…"

"Warlock."

"Ok. Warlock. She takes you to him and charges you money for some sort of potion. Am I right so far?"

"Right. Yes."

"Then, after you drink what turns out to be a dangerous cocktail of drugs, you pass out and think you see your daughter covered in snakes, yes?"

"Yes." I nod, even though she can't see me.

"Jude. What if, while you were in a drugged-out stupor, this Madge *told* you there was a mass of snakes beside you? What if she added the whole interaction with Little Blue? The power of suggestion is an incredible thing. I studied the subject at university. Haven't you ever seen a hypnotist put on a stage show? It's the same kind of principle."

"Yeah, years ago. The guy made people cluck like chickens and run around."

"Exactly. In all likelihood, that's the same kind of thing Madge and her partner in crime did to you that night."

Her explanation makes sense, a lot more sense than drinking a vial of spiked liquid and seeing snakes and a spirit.

"I know you want to have hope that you did connect with your child. I would, too, without question. But I don't want a couple of con artists to pull the wool over your eyes again. I'm telling you, it's far more likely they worked a scam on you."

I want to believe her rationale—I really do—but all I can think of is the book. How did Madge know about it, unless she was somehow connected to the afterworld?

I'm not sure if that makes Madge's claims about everything legit, but until I see the old crazy woman again and she can convince me further, I'm not ruling out any possibility.

"I hear you, Lauren. I see things from your perspective, believe me. No matter what head space I'm in, Madge won't be able to snow me again. You can trust that."

Thankfully, the conversation veers away from me and onto other things, like our tastes in movies, music and food. All of them meant a lot to me at one time, but not now. I don't watch TV, I never listen to music anymore—it only reminds me what the music industry took from me—and though I was once a dedicated foodie, trying new recipes every chance I had, I now only eat because I have to.

After what seem like moments but was actually hours, Lauren remarks, "Oh wow, have you seen the time? It's 2 AM, and I've got an early morning appointment." She giggles. "I had no idea we were chatting for this long."

We say a long goodbye, arrange a time she can pick me up to watch a movie at her place the next night, then hang up.

As I lie on the couch and stare at the ceiling, I think about Lauren and how I'm transported somewhere else when I speak to her. For that time I'm focused on nothing else but the sound of her voice. I barely know her, but what I do know, I like. A lot.

* * *

A thunderous crash echoes through the front room, making me jump up and look around. After a few disoriented seconds, I glance out the kitchen window and spot a garbage truck on the street, its hydraulic arm appearing to have come unhooked.

I rub my eyes and look back at the clock. 10 AM. I can't believe I got a full eight hours of sleep—something I haven't gotten in what feels like forever.

I make coffee and stand at the machine until it percolates enough for the first cup. Then I resume my position at the window and stare down at the incapacitated garbage truck. The driver, a round-bellied guy about sixty, has placed orange pylons around the truck's perimeter to avert traffic. Passing cars honk at the driver and yell, a typical New York reaction to road obstructions.

Soon, a city pilot car pulls up with his amber lights flashing. A man gets out and approaches the truck driver. Soon, the two men stand in conference, scratching their heads, determining a plan of attack. I open the window to let fresh air in and hear music escaping from the open window of a passing car. It takes me a minute to place the song until finally I remember "Play it Hard," a filler tune from the best-selling album Shake Me by none other than Chad Micheals.

My stomach tightens, and a dull pain grows behind my eyes. I close the window and set down my coffee. Michaels is heavy on my mind. While I suffer from losing my child, he takes everything from me and reaps the rewards of being a rock star. It isn't fair. He needs to be stopped. He needs to pay for what he did.

I sit at the table and open my laptop, my hands trembling as I again search his name. I scroll through dozens of mainstream magazines featuring interviews with Michaels, hoping to find one crumb of personal information, anything that I can go on to find the sonofabitch.

Hours pass, and the dull ache behind my eyes has now turned into a full-fledged headache. I close the laptop and go to the bathroom, where I take two aspirin and run cold water over a facecloth. Lying on the couch, I place the cloth over my eyes and take slow, methodical breaths.

I lie motionless, trying to think of places Michaels would frequent—a hot spot club on the weekends, his favorite restaurant, or maybe he has children or family in the public spectrum. After waiting for the aspirin to take effect, I return to the table and resume searching, this time changing my search request to Chad Michaels' family.

Hopeful, I scan through dozens of images of Michaels pictured with other people, all selfies with fans or pictures with various musicians. Does this guy not have any family or what? This is ridiculous. You'd think he'd have an ex-wife, children, or at least siblings, but nothing is coming up.

I sit back and rethink my search. I've got to refine it. I tap my fingers on the table until it occurs to me. I punch in, *Chad Michaels Insider*. This ought to bring something up.

A top-rock magazine article immediately pops up on the screen. "Chad Michaels Revealed." I grin and slowly scroll through the interview, reading each word like a hungry hawk scanning the landscape for food.

*Chad Michaels is known for keeping his personal life out of the tabloids. When he's not taking center stage, he's a dedicated father to an unconfirmed number of children. Today, Michaels has a proposed* *net worth of $250 million and boasts homes on both coasts, along with a recording studio and a penthouse in one of New York's most sought-after areas, Tribeca.*

"Tribeca!" I whisper. "Gotcha!"

The rest of the interview mentions Michaels up-and-coming overseas dates on his upcoming tour. Later on in the piece, there is a mention of the cars Michaels has been spotted driving around the city in: an Astin Martin DB12, a McLaren F1, and a Bugatti Divo, their price tags adding up to millions in machinery. It makes me sick. You could feed a third-world village for a year on what it costs for even one of these cars.

Tribeca's penthouses and lavish apartments cater to the elite, from top celebrities to wealthy executives. I remember seeing pictures online of some of the area's most-recognized celebrity residents strolling through the neighborhood and nearby parks, walking their dogs, or jogging. I wonder if Chad Michaels has a dog.

There's a loud screech of tires; I jump up and look out the window. The two city workers are shaking their fists at the rear-end of a speeding SUV. I shake my head and wonder how more public servicemen aren't killed on these streets. I check the time. 11 AM. Still morning.

I grab my phone and text Lauren about what time she wants to get together tonight.

She quickly responds and suggests five, then follows up with, "Should I pick you up?"

If I make my way to Tribeca on the off chance of running into Chad Michaels, or at least familiarizing myself with the area, I can navigate my way to Lauren's afterwards. "What's your address? I'll be there," I text.

"399 East 68th Street, buzz #935, see you at 5."

I sit back down at the laptop and search for directions to Tribeca. It won't take long to get there via the subway. Then, I look up the distance from Tribeca to Lauren's place. It's about a half-hour bus ride, give or take.

I stand up to get a fresh cup of coffee, and the room spins. I grab the table and take deep breaths in and out. Why am I dizzy?

It's rare that I feel this lightheaded. I try to figure out what could be wrong until I remember I haven't eaten anything for quite a while. While trying to compose myself, I see an incoming call and wince. It's my father.

I answer, hoping he won't be able to talk long. "Hi."

"Jude, you're awake. What a surprise."

"What's up, Dad?"

"I thought if you were going to be around in an hour, I could stop by for a quick chat."

"You never come to my place. Why now?"

"I have news that I know will have great meaning to you."

I sigh. "Can't it wait? I actually have a lot to do today."

I can hear the instead edge of frustration in his voice. "No. And trust me, put off whatever you're doing. This is far more important."

My father thinks everything involving him is far more important than whatever I have going on in my life. It's a character trait that has always been a bone of contention with me. "Fine, come over, but I really don't have long to visit because—"

I hear the deadness on the other end. He hung up on me. I don't believe it. The man has no grasp of how rude he is.

Without knowing exactly how much time I have before he arrives, I quickly get up and start tidying the place, shoving dirty cups in the cupboards and sticking magazines and old newspapers into the oven. I see a few dirty t-shirts hanging off the couch, which I grab and toss onto my bed, then close the door. In the bathroom, I rinse dried toothpaste from the sink and pull the shower curtain closed to hide my collection of empty shampoo bottles mixed with new ones.

I'm just closing the bathroom door when there's a loud rap on the front door. There's no way he could've got here this quickly. Then it hits me—he was already here when he called. I shake my head. He has zero respect for my space.

I open the door to my father leaning against the doorway and smiling.

I force a polite grin. "Come in." As soon as I turn from the doorway, my eyes catch something on the arm of the couch. Kim's diary.

My eyes widen, and a wave of anxiety rushes over me. I direct my father to the table and pour him a cup of coffee, then make a beeline to the couch and shove the diary between the cushions.

Back in the kitchen, I pour myself a coffee, then sit across from him at the table. "So, what was so important?"

"Well, it's quite a remarkable story, actually. I was on the phone with Kim's father. We were talking about the memorial, and how many people attended. Then he told me about how he and his wife were heading to France for a month to clear their heads. It really is beautiful there this time of year—"

"Dad," I sigh. "Get on with it."

"Right. Anyway, the subject came up about Little Blue's ashes, and he said that since Kim is no longer around, the rightful place for the urn is with you."

I suddenly perk up. "I finally get to have my daughter's remains?"

My father nods.

My eyes well up. Because Kim had primary custody and because she couldn't part with our daughter's ashes, I never pushed the issue. But now that she's gone, I can finally keep what is left of Little Blue with me forever. A hot tear runs down my face.

"We can drive to Jersey now to pick up the urn," Dad says. "I know you said you're busy today, but I thought this takes precedence over everything else."

I smile, then reach out and touch my dad's hand. "Of course it does. Thank you."

Immediately, I feel an urgency to get on the road. It's an hour-and-a-half drive, and knowing Kim's parents and the grief they're in, they could easily change their minds. For some reason unknown to me, I always felt like they wished I would fade out of the picture so Kim could meet a 'normal' guy—one with a career who could assume the daddy role to my daughter. I was never going to let that happen.

I think it was my rock and roll affiliation that bothered them. A lot of academic types don't relate to the whole rocker vibe. That being said, my parents never came to see me play live. As much as my mom loved to hear me sing and play while I was at home, she claimed my persona changed once I was playing in clubs. I tried unsuccessfully to explain that frontmen have to exude a party vibe to draw the crowd in, but she would shake her head and insist I shouldn't pretend to be any other character than myself. I quit trying to convince her after that.

* * *

The afternoon wind whips my hair around my face and into my eyes. I nudge my father and point upward, hinting that he should put the roof up. He laughs and yells over the street noise, "If you had short hair, you wouldn't have to worry about it."

I gather my hair in a ponytail and hold it in place. Since my father fell in love with his tennis instructor, his musical tastes have entered a strange and unfamiliar realm. While I was growing up, he was into classic rock and rock-a-billy, and now he has top forty pop songs blasting through the car speakers. It's obvious his girlfriend is a fan of the genre. I never understood how some people in new relationships change their tastes to match their partners. I never had—I always thought that diversity and individuality were far more beneficial and interesting in a relationship—but I noticed how past girlfriends would lose their own identities and start mirroring mine. I found it boring, and the relationship would fizzle out.

But if my dad is happy becoming the male version of his girlfriend, then so be it. I just hope he's not too wounded when she gets bored with his ass-kissing ways and moves on to the next poor sucker.

* * *

Brilliant hues of crimson and amber line each side of the interstate. The landscape in

New Jersey in the fall is stunningly beautiful. I'm not sure why I'm noticing it today and not when I recently took the transit to Kim's memorial. Maybe it's because I'm happy about getting Little Blue's ashes. Maybe it's because of my positive interactions with Lauren. Whatever the reason, I'm happy for my returned desire to take in the beauty around me.

I think about Lauren and wonder if she's spent much time in Jersey this time of year. If she hasn't, maybe I'll ask if she wants to take a trip out here one day. Of course, she'll have to drive—I can't see her wanting to ride the loser cruiser with me.

Then, it hits me. Lauren. 5 PM in Manhattan.

I glance at the time on my phone screen. By the time my father drives to and from Jersey, adding time to talk with Kim's folks, it will be at least 4 PM, which means there's no way I'll have time to stop in Tribeca before Lauren's. As much as I want to familiarize myself with the layout in Tribeca so I can find Chad Michaels, it will have to wait until tomorrow. Besides, I can't think of anything more important right now than getting Little Blue's ashes and finally bringing them home with me, where they belong.

"Do you want to stop for a drink?" my father yells over the rushing wind.

I shake my head and motion my finger forward. *I don't want to waste any time. Just get us there.*

Regardless of my father's heavy foot on the gas, it seems to take forever before we finally pull up to the property. All traces of the extravagant memorial have vanished—the tents, the carefully arranged flower stands, the elaborate lawn decorations. Now there are two storage trucks pulled up to the entrance and men in blue uniforms meandering about.

"Maybe it's best if you stay in the car, son. I think seeing you will be hard for Kim's parents."

I shrug. I really don't want to see them, especially after stealing Kim's diary from their house. I have one of those faces that shows guilt like a badge of dishonor. "I have no problem with that."

I watch as my dad walks up to the house and rings the bell. A moment later, Kim's father opens the door, and the two men disappear inside.

I close my eyes and pray. *Please don't let them change their minds about the urn.* Grief can do funny things to people, making them act erratically.

I watch the workers pack what looks to be wrapped frames into their vehicles. My guess is that Kim's parents want their expensive artwork to be secure while they're away. The art on their walls was a lot of landscapes, flowers and abstract pieces. Not really my style, but I'm sure some were investment pieces, painted by a well-known artist and accumulating worth year by year.

I remember visiting Kim here when we were young. She would catch shit after throwing a ball in the house or exhibiting any other reckless behaviour that could potentially damage the pictures. I never had to worry about that kind of stress at home. Other than a torn-out page from a Norman Rockwell magazine my mother had framed and a few of my school pictures, the walls in our small home were bare.

I hear the distant voice of my father as he steps out of the front door, carrying a blue bag that doesn't look big enough to hold the urn. He turns back to the door and briefly waves, then walks to the car. I close my eyes again. Please let my child's ashes be with him.

I open my eyes just as he approaches the car. "Here, take this." He passes me the bag.

It's heavier than it looks. I open the straps and look inside. The first thing I see is the shiny black lacquer of the vase. I tip it back and read the words, *Abbigale Kimberly Rossi. Forever young and will forever live on in our hearts.*

A shiver runs through me, and my eyes well up. "Thank you, Dad."

My father pats me twice on the leg, then starts the car. "Now, let's get the hell out of here before they have a change of heart." He steps on the gas, flips a U-turn, and heads away from the house.

With my hair flying wildly in my face, I press the urn to my chest. I know she's gone, but somehow, inside my hands, I feel her closer.

# Chapter 9

It's 4 PM on the nose when we pull up to Wong's restaurant. I quickly glance in the side view mirror. My hair looks wild and tangled like it's been backcombed with a rake. My father looks at me and grins. "Nice lid, kid."

I chuckle. "Yeah, courtesy of your damn convertible."

He pats the bag. "I hope you feel better in some small way."

I think of all the times I thought of my father as self-serving. "Thanks again, Dad. I can't believe you did this for me." My eyes well up again. "You don't know what this means."

"I'm a parent, I can well imagine. And don't forget, she was my granddaughter. It's good to see her ashes are where they should be."

I sniff up tears and get out of the car. My first instinct is to keep walking, but I stop, turn, and look back. "You have time for lunch or something in the near future?"

"Sure. I'll be in touch." He smiles, then pulls away from the curb.

Keeping the urn pressed firmly to my chest, I walk up the stairs to my apartment. Once inside, I scan the room for a good place. I finally settle on the corner shelf above my guitar. The only option, considering Little Blue loved to sit for hours and listen to me play.

Once the urn is safely positioned, I step back to get a clearer look. "You're home again, sweetheart, with your dad. Where you belong."

I wipe the tears. I know I can't have her back, but at least what is left is here with me. I look around the room, and for the first time since she died, the space feels bright and warm.

After taking a while to sit with the urn, I realize I only have a half hour to make myself presentable and catch the M11 bus to Lauren's.

It takes a good ten minutes to get my wind-swept hair brushed and in order. I brush my teeth and take one last look in the mirror before heading to the bus stop. I wanted to pick up some flowers or a bottle of wine en route, but there's no way I'll have the time. And truth be told, I can't really afford it right now.

Tomorrow, I have to put some time into looking for a part-time job. Rent day comes around fast.

* * *

Lauren radiates when she answers the door in a short, flowy cotton dress, bare feet with her toenails painted, and her hair in loose curls that frame her pretty face. I feel almost boy-like shy while I stand in front of her, trembling inside and trying my hardest to make eye contact.

Once inside, I kick off my shoes and follow her to a small but stylish room. As I look around at the furniture and décor, it strikes me as funny that although her apartment is located in one of the pricier areas of Manhattan, the furniture and decorations look casual and inexpensive. The loveseat and matching chair look at least thirty years old, and the small wooden coffee table has chips and coffee mug stains. There aren't many pictures on the walls, other than a few framed collages of people. Near the front window, a dusty fake plant stands five feet tall in a pot with a huge crack. There's a modest-sized flatscreen on the wall in front of the sofa, with an old-fashioned turntable and records on a short cabinet just off to the side.

She sees me looking and laughs. "I know. The outside of the building doesn't really match the inside of my apartment, does it?"

"It's great. It's a lot nicer than my place, that's for sure."

"It's home. Plus, I don't spend much time here. I mostly come here to sleep and eat, then I'm out the door to work and repeat. Why don't you take off your jacket, and I'll give you the grand tour?"

Lauren grabs my jacket from me and tosses it onto the back of the loveseat. I follow her down a short hallway off the living room, where the light from two rooms casts a glow on the wooden floor. When we approach the first doorway, she stops. "This is the bathroom, a three-piece with the noisiest pipes in the world."

We then move to the last doorway. "This is my bedroom. Believe it or not, it's the biggest room in the apartment. Not a great floor plan for a person who lives alone."

I step into the room, which features a large, wrought-iron, four-poster bed. Next to it is a tall mahogany armoire with more scratches and dents. Beside the armoire is a matching vanity with just as many flaws. "My bedroom furniture was handed down to me from my mother. I could have refurbished everything, but I kind of like broken things. They have more character."

"Is that why you like me?"

"No. And for the record, I don't think you're broken, crazy, or a lost cause, regardless how we first met."

"Yeah, right. Are you forgetting the condition I was in that day? I was a hot mess."

She giggles shyly. "Well, regardless of your condition, I did kinda think you were hot."

"You've got to set your standards higher, girl."

"There's nothing wrong with you, Jude. You're a grieving father, and it's expected that you would have repercussions from that, emotionally or otherwise."

"Those are the words of a doctor."

Lauren shakes her head. "I'm not a doctor. I'm at the bottom stage of learning. But I do know crazy, and you're not it."

"How do you know for sure?" I grin. "Maybe crazy runs in my family."

"Well, if that's the case, I'm in big trouble. Crazy goes way back on my father's side, all the way to the mid-1800s."

"That's a long time ago. Are you sure someone in your family isn't pulling your leg?"

"This wasn't the icebreaker I had planned, but now that we've arrived on the subject of crazy, I'll show you."

Intrigued, I sit on the edge of her bed and fold my arms.

I watch as Lauren goes into her armoire, rummaging around in a narrow drawer before straightening up with a Ziplock bag of papers in hand. She sits beside me, opens the bag, and gently pulls out the folded papers. Once they're on the bed, I notice the three sheets are quite brown, with the edges torn or crumbled away. "Wow. These look very old."

Lauren nods. "All the way back to the 1800s." She slowly unfolds each of the three pages and lays them between us on the bed. "The print has faded, but I'll try to make out the important parts."

She gently picks up the first piece of paper with an easy-to-read heading, The New York Ledger.

July 6th– Pittsford Village Tragedy: Marjorie Gamble Banks Murders Husband, William Banks.

The words underneath are a lot smaller and less legible.

Lauren clears her throat and squints at the page.

*"In the village of Pittsford, on the evening of July 6th, Marjorie Banks tragically lost her reason and took the life of her husband, the esteemed William Banks. Armed with a hunting rifle, Mrs. Banks entered the Wine Without Reason Tavern around 7 p.m., where she found her unarmed husband and fatally shot him. Patrons of the tavern, familiar with the Banks's as regular patrons, were stunned by the cold-blooded act. Following the murder, Mrs. Banks calmly seated herself at her husband's table, finished his drink, and awaited the arrival of the sheriff."*

"Wow. That's wild. And who was this murderess to you?"

"She would be my great, great grandmother on my father's side."

"That's quite the family connection you have. And after a hundred and fifty-four years, it's amazing that you have these newspaper clippings."

"Yeah. I know. They were passed down to me from my grandma, who I was very close with. They probably belong in a museum, but I just haven't been able to part with them."

"I get it. If I had something as cool as these, I wouldn't want to give them up either. So, what ended up happening to this woman? Let me guess, she was hanged or drawn and quartered or something gruesome like that?"

Lauren laughs. "No. Actually, her story gets progressively more bizarre."

"How so?"

Lauren picks up the second piece of paper and strains to read a faded column. "It says here that there was a trial, but because she was well respected in the community—she often fed the homeless and made blankets for them—anyway, because people held her in high regard, a lot of villagers came forward at her trial and spoke to her good character. So, instead of getting hung—drawn and quartered was a punishment that ended with its last victim in 1782 in Portsmouth, England—Marjorie was sent to Utica Insane Asylum."

"That's heavy. But at least she lived."

"One would think that would be a better alternative, but while I was in university, I had access to endless historical archives. And, when I wasn't studying, I did some digging on Utica. Let's just say that the methods to treat the mentally ill then wouldn't be happening today, that's for sure."

"That bad?"

"Unfortunately, a lot of their practices didn't end well."

I almost ask her to elaborate, then quickly change my mind as flashes of horror movies I've seen send shivers up my spine. The night is young, and I don't know if I could shake the horrible images from stories of inhumane treatment of patients. "Dare I ask, what ended up happening to the murderess, Marjorie?"

"She actually made it out of there."

My eyes widen. "You're kidding? Let me guess, her brain was fried and she lived out her days as a vegetable?"

"You have a vivid imagination, my friend. But thankfully, you're wrong. From the meager accounts documented about her, after a couple of years, she attended a panel meeting with psychiatrists and asylum heads and was deemed mentally sound."

I feel a burst of relief. "And was she able to go back to her family afterwards?"

She shakes her head, and the edges of her mouth turn downward. "That part is probably the saddest. At the time of the murder, she had two children. Boys. I read they were seven and nine. They were transferred to an orphanage in The Bronx, and Marjorie never saw them again. So, we can only assume the boys lived out their days without parents in a time that didn't embrace orphans. They were seen as the lowest cast in society and probably went through hell."

I sigh. "Was there ever any mention of why Marjorie killed her husband?"

Lauren picks up the last brown page on the bed and moves closer to me. "This was a picture taken of Marjorie Gamble some years later when she advocated for change regarding the mechanical restraints used on patients in Utica."

"Didn't the newspaper clipping say her last name was Banks?"

Lauren nods. "Yeah. Gamble was her maiden name, and she dropped the Banks part when she was admitted to Utica."

The image is grainy and hard to make out. I move my face closer. She was a portly woman, dressed in a matronly high-collared, long-sleeved dress with a scarf draped over her neck and her hair fashioned in a tight bun atop her head. Then I notice the eyes, which are like many other historical portraits I've seen: light, almost non-existent pupils giving the subject a ghost-like appearance. I look away and sit back. "She didn't look like a killer per se. More like a housewife, or a schoolteacher."

Lauren smiles. "It's ironic, really. By all accounts, she wasn't a stupid woman. To answer your earlier question, when she spoke at her trial, Marjorie said the reason she shot her husband was to remove the demon from her family.”

“She thought he was a demon. That does sound a bit crazy, actually.”

“Not really. Allegedly, William Banks took liberties with young girls. It was said that one of them, a milkmaid at their farm, came forward and confided in Majorie. Rumor had it that this wasn’t the first time he had abused his power on a young employee. Marjorie felt she was doing the right thing by taking the guy out.”

I grin. “Good for her, but what a hefty price to pay. Her whole life was destroyed for one act of justice.”

“Yes. I agree.” Lauren carefully folds the papers and puts them back into the bag. “During spring break, I went on a road trip to Portsmouth and found Marjorie’s grave.”

“You did? How interesting. What did the headstone say?”

“Her name, the dates she lived and died, and the words *Head for the Hills*. Whatever that means.”

I let out a breath. “I don’t think Marjorie was crazy at all. In fact, I think she was a hero.”

Lauren smiles in agreement. “A vigilante.”

When the papers are safely returned to the armoire, Lauren leads me back to the front room, then walks into the kitchen, a small alcove off the living room.

"You have a lot of records. A hobby of yours?"

"Kind of. Sometimes, on a Sunday, I'll hit the flea markets and go on a treasure hunt for albums." She rummages through a cupboard.

I walk over to the record stand and thumb through the jackets. Expecting to see modern pop stars, I'm dumbfounded to find Foghat, Cream, The Doors, and other iconic artists from the early 70s.

Lauren walks up behind me with a drink in each hand. "Hot Toddy?" She holds out a cup.

"Thanks. These records…"

"I know they're kind of outdated. But I've never related much to the contemporary stuff."

I laugh. "Girl after my own heart." I follow her to the loveseat.

Once seated, she gives me a long look over the rim of her cup. "You should play again, Jude."

I shrug. "Nah. I don't think so."

"I'm not talking about gigs. Not right away. Just picking a guitar up when you're alone and getting the feel for it again. You can't tell me that you never think about it."

"Sometimes, I guess. I'll be walking to the subway, and a melody will hit me. But I've trained myself to push it out of my head."

"Music can be therapeutic. Did you know that?"

"Yes. I knew a couple of musicians who were music therapists. They'd play in senior care homes. They said it was amazing how some patients would positively respond, even people who seemed catatonic."

"Absolutely. But I won't push the issue...too much." She giggles, then gently elbows me. "Just promise me you'll open your mind to it."

I nod, to end the subject. "So, what movie are we watching?"

"Well, you've seen how nostalgic I am when it comes to music. My movie choices fall into the same genre. I hope that's okay."

"More than. I prefer old flicks, too."

She grabs the remote and scans through her Netflix saved folder before selecting *Trading Places*, one of my favorites—a legendary comedy starring Eddie Murphy and Dan Ackroyd.

"Great choice."

As we watch the movie, our bodies gradually shift closer to each other until I can feel the heat from Lauren's leg against mine. We laugh at the same scenes. As we watch, I can't help but feel incredibly lucky that a girl as seemingly perfect as Lauren would want to spend time with me, a guy well beneath her class.

It's about 8 PM when Lauren gets up, saying she picked up a lasagna for dinner. After she warms the meal in the oven, I help her set the small table.

Lauren selects a record: *Tommy*, one of my favorite albums from The Who. We talk about her work, hobbies, and opinions on politics and social issues through dinner. When she turns the table and asks me to divulge, I reciprocate and discuss what life was like growing up, my relationship with my dad, and how one day I hope to have a better-paying job.

But in everything I'm sharing, I neglect to mention my most recent bit of good fortune in getting Little Blue's urn. I'm not sure why I don't. I guess because I don't want the conversation to go in a depressing direction. At least not tonight, while everything feels so upbeat.

When the clock on the wall reaches midnight, Lauren and I are shocked at how many hours have passed while we have been locked in conversation.

"I really should get going," I say. "Besides, I'm sure you have to get up early tomorrow to get to work."

Her eyes turn coy. "Don't go. Unless, of course, you have to be up early."

"I don't, really. I mean, I do need to get on the job hunt tomorrow, but I don't have a set time to do it."

"So, you'll stay?"

I grin. "If you'd like me to." I look at the small loveseat, then at the chair in the corner. "Are you sure you have room for me?"

"You can sleep in my bed with me, if you like. Without any funny stuff, of course."

I laugh. I wouldn't think of pushing my luck. Lauren isn't the type to engage in a one-night stand. Then again, neither am I, not anymore. I've been out of action for what seems like forever. Besides, as much as I'm attracted to Lauren, I wouldn't disrespect her by making a pass. It's too soon.

* * *

The morning sun shines through the fine linen curtains, creating a subtle pattern on the walls. I glance down to see a mess of Lauren's hair nestled on my chest and my arms wrapped around her.

Warm contentment fills me as I purposely control my breathing so as not to wake her. Here, at this moment, all the painful things that have hindered me for the past two years are gone. At this moment, all I feel is a sense of peace.

Moments pass in silence while my mind opens doors to possibilities that have been closed for me for so long. Maybe I should pick up my guitar, not for any other reason than to create music again. Maybe I should set my job goals higher than a janitor position at a boxing gym and look for work that gives me purpose.

Lauren shifts, then brings her hand up and rests it on my chest. A moment later, she yawns, then slowly looks up at me and rubs her eye. "Good morning, Jude. Don't look at me, I'm a broom rider in the morning." She giggles.

But she's wrong. In fact, she looks more beautiful now, with no make-up and tousled hair, than she did when she was made-up.

"You can go ahead and have a shower first, and I'll make coffee."

I watch her get out of bed. When the sun hits her, I can see the silhouette of her perfect body under the long white t-shirt she's wearing.

The difference between the water pressure here and in my micro apartment in Hell's Kitchen is significant. My nozzle only releases a meager amount of water, whereas here, the water pressure is immense. I try to hurry, taking just long enough to soap down and rinse off in case Lauren is in a hurry to get to work.

Once I'm back in my clothes with my hair brushed and tied back, I head to the kitchen to see Lauren dancing to a classic rock song while making toast. When she feels my presence, she turns and blushes. "That was the fastest shower in history." She turns down the music and passes me a coffee. "You know, I was thinking about something you mentioned last night, about finding a part-time job."

I nod, wondering what she's thinking.

"Well," she says, running her fingers over her cup awkwardly, "the last time I spoke to my father, he mentioned that his firm had some minor repairs that needed fixing. Panels replaced and bathroom faucets fixed, that kind of stuff. Anyway, I don't know if he's hired someone already, but if you like, I can ask him. I'm sure he'd pay well. He pays all of his employees well."

"I wasn't expecting you to say that. Jobs are hard to come by nowadays. If you're sure it won't be an inconvenience—"

"Of course not. It would give me a reason to call him. Even though I don't see eye to eye with him about most things, he's still my dad, and I've got to put more effort into reaching out once in a while."

"That would be great. Just don't go to too much trouble for me."

"It's just a phone call, Jude." She smiles. "I can't make any promises, but it's worth a shot."

"Regardless if it amounts to anything, I think you're really sweet for thinking of me. Also, thanks for last night." I take a sip of my coffee. "It was a nice distraction from my usually dull routine."

"Same here. It felt great to have someone to talk to outside work."

"Maybe we can get together again."

"Sure. We can go to your place next time."

A lump forms in my throat and makes me clear it. "My place really isn't what you'd call entertainment-friendly. I don't even have a stereo."

"Okay. If you're not comfortable, you're welcome to come back here again."

"I'd like that." I feel like I just dodged a bullet. As down to earth as Lauren is, I think it would be hard for her to hide her disappointment after seeing my shabby apartment.

Lauren takes a shower while I finish my coffee. By the time she comes out, she's dressed and has her face and hair perfectly done. When she's ready, I walk her downstairs. She gives me a peck on the cheek and tells me she'll call me later.

On the walk to the bus stop, I'm euphoric and whimsical, remembering my night with Lauren. God knows why she's taken an interest in me, but I'm sure glad she has.

I sit on the bench next to an elderly man reading a newspaper. When he turns the page, I see the headline: "Chad Michaels to Perform in Times Square."

Instantly my joy drains away, replaced by a deep sense of bitterness. I wish I hadn't seen it, but now that I have, I can't shake off my disdain. The beautiful image of Lauren fades from my mind, now filled with Michaels' revolting face.

It's early, and not that far to Tribeca from here. A half hour tops by bus. Even though I probably won't find Michaels, at least I'll get familiar with the area, so I'll have a better idea of the layout later. Once I find out where the popular drinking joints are, I could start asking around about Michaels.

When people know information about a rockstar, they like to talk about it.

* * *

The trip to Tribeca goes faster than anticipated, with minimal waits at each stop and not a lot of passengers getting on or off the bus. I hop off at 11ᵗʰ Avenue, across from Hudson River Park. The area is impeccable, manicured and clean, with eye-catching real estate and colorful walkways along the Hudson River. It's easy to see why the rich choose to live here.

As I walk toward the entrance of the park, my eyes are drawn upward to the many shiny, tall buildings, every one of them with a penthouse—perfect nesting spots for a rockstar. I catch the scent of freshly made bagels at a pink food stand and stop to order a cinnamon and raisin treat before continuing my stroll. I can't believe I'm actually hungry, a sensation I've been unfamiliar with for the past two years. Once I reach the entrance, I notice how fitness-minded the locals are, with bikers, joggers, and rollerbladers in a constant stream in and out. I spot an empty bench where I can sit and watch the fitness freaks as I eat my warm, high-in-carbs bagel smothered in creamy butter.

After I've finished eating, I stand and look toward the nearest apartment tower, where a black town car is pulling up. A suited

165

man in a hat gets out of the driver's side and opens the rear passenger door. I shake my head, pondering whether these well-to-do passengers earned their fortune through hard work or inherited it from wealthy parents.

A man in dark pants, a black t-shirt, and a red baseball hat with matching trainers is the first to get out of the car. As soon as I get a clear look at his face, I'm gobsmacked. It's Chad Michaels. Directly behind him, a small child hops out of the car.

She's young, no more than five, but looks like she just walked off a catalogue page. She's wearing a perfectly pressed red dress with a little black bow in the back and shiny black shoes with small red ribbons on the toes. As soon as the town car pulls away from the curb, Michaels crosses the road toward the park without holding onto his child's hand for safety.

I never thought it possible, but seeing the lack of care he has for his daughter makes me hate him even more. I turn my head as he slowly passes in front of the bench I'm sitting on.

He's starting on the park path when, out of nowhere, a man with a camera approaches him. "I don't believe it, Chad Micheals." I hear the man's excitement.

When Micheals stops to talk to the man, the little girl crosses her arms and sticks out her bottom lip. "Daddy, let's go. I want to walk in the park."

But Micheals is so engaged with his admirer, he doesn't acknowledge his kid. I shake my head in disgust. Mr. Rockstar needs a hard reality check, and I'm hell-bent to be the one to give it to him.

"Daddy, if you don't hurry up, I'm going to scuff my shoes on purpose." The little girl begins stomping the toes of her shoes into the cement. I silently chuckle as I root for the child.

Michaels poses for a couple of pictures with his fan, which further annoys his daughter. "Daddy, I'm not kidding. If you don't listen to me, I'm going to run down the path and hide. Is that what you want me to do?"

Still, Michaels doesn't acknowledge her.

I scoff a little louder than intended, and the little girl turns her eyes sharply to me. I grin, sympathetically. But instead of doing what most children would do when a stranger looked at them—grab onto her father's hand and turn away—she turns her back on her father and walks to me, eyes fixated on mine.

I'm not sure what to do. If her father does take a second to look at his daughter, he'll see her talking to a strange man on a park bench, not a good scenario. Plus, I don't want Michaels to get a look at my face, not yet. I need to get him alone and vulnerable first.

I shift my gaze from the girl to the passing cars on the street, hoping she'll change her direction. But in my peripheral view, I can see her getting closer.

Shit. What do I do? Should I get up and walk away? If I do, Micheals will definitely notice me sitting here. *Go away, little girl. Go back to your Daddy.*

Soon enough, I hear the sound of her breathing, and I have no choice but to turn and face her.

"Hi. My name is Claire. What's yours?" Her eyes are the darkest brown I have ever seen and up close, her skin is almost porcelain, pale and flawless, not even a freckle. She reminds me of a doll in a toy store.

"Sweetie, you should stay close to your dad. It's not safe to wander around by yourself."

She looks almost angry by my words. "I can do whatever I want. My daddy doesn't care. See?" She points at Michaels behind her.

"Of course he cares. He's just busy talking to that man. That's why you should go and stand with him. He'll be worried if he can't see you."

"Sometimes I try and make him mad just so he'll look at me, but he doesn't."

I feel bad for the kid, but unfortunately there's nothing I can do to make her father give a shit. The only time he'll ever stop to care is when he's old, and there's no one around; his kids will have grown up without the love and attention they need. They'll be bitter and want nothing to do with their father, even if he was a rockstar.

The man with the camera shakes Michaels' hand and walks away.

"Look, Claire. Your dad is finished talking to that man now. You should hurry and go back over there."

"Yeah, I guess so." She grins. "But I know something you should do, too."

What a curious little girl. "What's that?"

"You should—"

Before she has a chance to finish her words, Michaels starts down the park path away from us. Claire looks at him, then briefly back at me and smiles. "Goodbye."

Then, she runs quickly until she resumes her place in his shadow.

* * *

My apartment feels smaller and more outdated than it did yesterday. After spending the night at Lauren's, the contrast has made my place seem even more run-down. As I sit down on the couch, I realize something else is missing: the presence of another person to talk to and laugh with.

My epiphany is short-lived as my mind focuses on Chad Michaels and the neglectful way he treated his daughter, Claire. The next time I see that son of a bitch, I'll wait until he's alone, and then I'll get the truth out of him about what happened the night Little Blue died. He's guilty, he has to be. Why else would he be ushered out of the penthouse once my daughter was found in the bathroom?

It's obvious he was the one who drugged her, and whoever kept his name off the police report is just as guilty as Michaels is. An image of his daughter, Claire, enters my mind.

Claire will be better off without a father like that; it's not like he gives a shit about her anyway. It's so unfair that he has a beautiful child but doesn't give a shit about her, whereas what's left of my daughter sits on my shelf in an urn, and I would give anything to have her back again.

But at least I know which area the bastard lives in, which is a lot more than I knew when I woke up this morning.

My phone buzzes as a text message comes in. It's Skully letting me know that he needs me to work tomorrow night. Then, I turn my attention to my laptop and sigh. I guess I should search up help wanted postings. If I don't get off my ass, I'll be screwed once rent day comes.

As soon as I start scrolling down the job postings, I can tell I'm in trouble. Once again, there are only postings for professionals and apprentices needed, both of which require prior training, which I don't have. What the hell am I going to do?

My phone buzzes and I sigh. I'm in no mood to speak with anyone right now, I glance at the screen, purely expecting to ignore the call. But when I see Lauren's number, I have an immediate change of heart.

"Hello." I do my best to sound upbeat.

"Hey, handsome. What are you up to?" Her voice immediately pulls me out of my dark mood.

"I'm reminiscing about the time we spent together and how much I enjoyed it. I'm also looking for a part-time job, which is so far proving futile."

Lauren giggles. "I had a good time last night as well. And as for your job search, I may have some good news."

"Great! I could use some positivity right now."

Lauren explains how her father returned her call about the handy man job, and said that they had just hired someone.

I sigh. "Well, thanks anyway. It was kind of you to reach out to him."

"Let me finish. My father said that although they just hired someone, the person is proving to be useless. So, if you want the job, I can give you his work address, and you can meet him at his office tomorrow morning. Eight-thirty."

"Really?" I'm unable to hide my excitement. "You're the best. I appreciate this more than you know."

"It was nothing, really." It's obvious she doesn't take compliments easily.

"I wish there was something I could do to repay you."

Lauren hums and haws playfully. "There is something you can do for me."

"Uh oh. Here we go. A pint of blood?"

"Naw. Nothing that bad."

"I'm ready. Whatever it is."

"I want you to pick up your guitar again. You don't have to play it long. Just pick it up."

I sigh audibly. "You're a real brat."

She giggles. "I know."

I let a few moments pass. Then, I say that I'll do it for her, and not because it's something I'm into doing yet.

"That's okay. Whatever the reason, as long as you do it."

"Fine. I'll do it."

We hang up soon after—Lauren had to return to work—and I turn to gaze at my dusty old guitar in the corner. "Shit."

I promised myself that I'd never play again. Not after Blue. But now I'd promised Lauren, so I don't have a choice.

# Chapter 10

I slowly turn the guitar and pick off all of the cobwebs. The strings are black with carbon, and it hasn't been in tune for two years.

I pick it up and settle onto the couch. The riff I used to warm up with before live performances was from Van Halen's 'You Really Got Me.' After years of warmups I could almost play it in my sleep. I take a deep breath and hope it'll come easy.

After a few tries, it's obvious that not only won't my fingers cooperate, but I'm struggling to remember the chords. I promised Lauren I would try, so I don't give up. Finally, after a half dozen feeble attempts, I get it right, but it sounds like crap. It's amazing how much muscle memory can fade in just two short years.

I keep playing until my now black fingers start to throb. If I do decide to play again, it'll be a long time to get back to where I was, if ever.

When I put the guitar away, I look up at the urn. "I wish you were here, Little Blue. I wish we were singing and playing together like we used to."

I spend the rest of the evening getting my clothes ready to meet Lauren's father about the job. All the while, I keep glancing at my phone, hoping I'll get a message from Lauren. But I don't. She must be having a busy night at the hospital.

Just before I retire for the night, I send her another thank-you message.

She responds with a happy face, and the information and address to her dad's work: Lawrence Banks, Banks and Associates, 140 Broadway 44th Floor.

Underneath, she writes, "Call me when you're through, and I'll pick you up. I want to hear how it went."

* * *

The large plaque above the glass front entrance reads '140 Broadway, The Banks Tower' in gold lettering. *Does he own the entire building?*

The doors feature gold handles and matching handrails. As I walk in, a doorman greets me with a look that suggests he's not used to seeing my kind around here. Class distinction and prejudice are two things that curdle my stomach. As a musician, I've experienced definite discrimination from people outside of the working class, an issue artists have had to deal with for centuries. Because of this, I've built up a thick skin.

Across the white marble foyer, a gold concierge desk stands by a bank of elevators.

A thin, aged gentleman behind the counter nods as I approach. "How may I help you?" He looks past me and exchanges a glance with the doorman.

I straighten my posture. "I have an appointment with Lawrence Banks."

The man's eyes widen, then he picks up the phone. "And your name?"

"Jude Rossi."

After punching in a few numbers, the man directs me to the elevators. "You'll want to get off on the 44th floor, sir."

*Oh. Now I'm a sir?* I grin and thank him.

After a quick ascent, the bell chimes, and the doors open to a large open floor with offices separated by glass walls. I make my way across the floor to a long horseshoe desk, where a kindly-looking older lady talks on the phone. With the receiver tucked into her neck, she meets my eye, smiles, and then holds up one finger.

I turn and look around the expansive office at the framed artwork on the walls. Red leather couches and a tall, stainless steel water cooler are on one end of the room.

The secretary hangs up. "Mister Rossi?"

I turn toward her. "Yeah. I'm here to see Lawrence—"

A grey-haired man wearing a long-sleeved white shirt, khaki pants, and sporting a sculpted gray beard walks into the room. "Jude. Hi, come with me."

I follow him around a corner and into the only office without glass. Lawrence—or Mr. Banks, I'm not sure which to call him yet—directs me to a cushy chair on the opposite side of a large mahogany desk.

He leans back and folds his hands. "So, you're a friend of my daughter."

I grin nervously and hope to hell that Lauren hasn't mentioned where we originally met. "Yes. Lauren is an amazing person."

He stares at me, studying me for what feels like forever. All the air seems to dissolve from the room, making breathing hard. If I could disappear right now, I would.

"What are you looking for, full-time or part-time work?"

"Part-time for now, Mr. Banks."

He leans forward. "Call me Lawrence. Lauren said you work at a boxing gym?"

I nod. "Skully's Gym, yes. It's in Hell's Kitchen. I work evenings as a janitor."

"I hope you carry a gun on your way home. I bet there are a lot of lowlifes lurking around after the sun goes down."

Typical upper-class attitude. It makes me sick. They turn their noses down at anyone who doesn't fall into their class.

"So, when can you start?" he continues.

"I guess anytime." I smile. "Can I ask you a question?" *How do you manage to sit down with that giant pole up your ass?*

"Go ahead."

"What exactly will I be doing here? I only ask to make sure I have the skill set required for the job."

Lawrence smirks. "Can you change a lightbulb and fix small appliances and run errands?"

"Of course, yes."

"Then you've got the skillset."

"That's great. I really appreciate this, Lawrence."

He forces a grin. "I'll walk you out so I can get you set up with a door fob at the front desk."

As we're exiting his office, a door opens across the hall and a young blonde walks out, dabbing a tissue on her eyes. She sniffs, looks up at us, and then swiftly walks toward the elevator. As soon as she's out of earshot, Lawrence whispers, "Grieving widow. There's only one thing to do to help that situation."

"What's that?" I ask.

"A good boning to take her mind off of things."

I can't believe he just said that. If I didn't need the job, I would call him a heartless pig and leave, but I can't, so I pretend like I didn't hear him.

"Mabel, get a fob set up for our new employee, Jude." When Lawrence looks at me this time, every flaw on his face becomes glaringly apparent: a small scar above one eye, pockmarks his facial hair doesn't cover, and dark, unsettling eyes that remind me of a reptile. The only thing missing are scales, which, after hearing his comments about that girl, I suspect might be hiding under his clothes.

"Alright. Mabel will take care of you," he says, slapping me once on the back, then disappearing down the hallway.

I should feel happy knowing that I've found another job, one that probably pays a hell of a lot better than working at Skully's, but I'm not. In a way, I feel like a sell-out. Working for a heartless chauvinist isn't a position I would normally put myself in. And it's not like I have much of a choice right now. Otherwise, I won't be able to cover rent and pay bills.

Then, there's the whole Lauren issue. I like the girl, even though I just met her. I like everything about her, especially the way she feels in my arms. It's because of her that I got this job, and if I don't take it, she will be disappointed.

I'll work here until I find something else. Until then, I won't tell Lauren what her father said or what a waste of skin I think he is.

Once Mabel gets my information and sets up the fob, I get into the elevator and text Lauren, forcing as much enthusiasm into my words as possible: "Great interview. Got the job. You're the best! I'm just on my way down the elevator. Are you en route?"

I watch the light move through the numbers until my phone beeps with

Lauren's reply. "Jude. I am so sorry. Was on the way to pick you up when I got a call from Jan. I've got to go in, it's an emergency. Call you later."

My heart sinks. The thing I was looking forward to the most today was seeing her.

* * *

Every public transit ride in New York has a distinctive odor that's uniquely its own—a mix of take-out food blended with alcohol. Add to that the scent of cheap perfume from nose-blind older folks who can't tell how much they're applying, and you've got the unmistakable aroma of the city.

I sit in the aisle seat across from two women about my age. Both are heavily tattooed and wearing enough makeup to compete with a Sephora display. Little Blue once dragged me into the make-up shop with her to buy lip gloss. Thankfully, she was never into wearing a lot of clown paint, something I dissuaded her from until she was older. I see too many pre-teens walking around trying to look older. I always felt it was unsafe. A lot of good my protectiveness did for my daughter, who ended up paying the ultimate price by falling prey to a ruthless predator.

"Do you want to go out this weekend?" one woman says to the other. "There's a rave at my buddy's place."

179

"No way! Look at what just came up on my newsfeed," her friend says. "Chad Michaels was just in a bad car accident in Tribeca."

I freeze in place and lean in to hear more.

"Did the news article say how badly he was injured?" the other says. Then, just as the first opens her mouth, the bus jerks to a halt. Both women stand, grab their things, and shuffle past me.

Chad Michaels was in a car wreck.

My first reaction is fierce joy. Then it transforms into dismay as I realize what this could mean.

If the sonofabitch dies, the truth about what happened to Little Blue will be lost. I need to confront him and find out what happened. I need to look into his eyes and tell him who my daughter was and what he took from me. I need to make him pay for his crime. An eye for an eye.

*I need to find out where he is and if he's alive.*

The hospital he's been transported to is one of the most modern in New York. I think hard about how to find out where he's being kept. He's a celebrity, and if someone saw me prowling the hallways and looking into each room, I'd probably get thrown out. I need a way to blend in.

I remember the thrift store a few blocks from home. I've seen scrubs in there before. I reach into my pocket and open my wallet; I've got ten bucks left after the bus fare. If the scrubs are too much money, I'll have no choice but to steal them.

The thought of sinking to a criminal level makes me uneasy and ashamed, but what choice do I have? Chad's daughter saved him from me last time—I couldn't confront him while she was there watching—but I can't let him get away again. I might not have another opportunity, especially if the bastard decides to die.

I open the door to the small thrift boutique. An older woman with a messy bun and horned-rimmed glasses barely looks up as I head to the back of the store.

Sifting through racks of old man pajamas, dated button-up paisley and striped shirts, I hit pay dirt and see three or four scrub separates. The first pair of pants is a mile wide and looks like it would come to my knees. The next pair has a stain on the back that has a brownish hue—a hard pass. The two remaining options look about right. I pick the pants that have a matching top and then take them to the register.

"How much for these?" I ask the woman.

"Are they pajamas?" Her voice is thin and raspy.

"They're technically scrubs, but they were on the pajama rack," I say, hoping pajamas are cheaper than street wear.

"Well, if they were on the same rack, they're fifty cents each."

I breathe a sigh of relief and pay the lady.

* * *

Work ethics run strong in my family; my mother always impressed upon me just how important it was to fulfil our obligations. My father was the same. Even on the days he felt ill, that man worked his shifts. With this in mind, I feel pangs of guilt as I call Skully to cancel my shift tonight. He's a miserable old codger, but he's always been fair, and regardless of my reason for needing to get tonight off, I feel like crap bailing on him.

"Hello." His voice is tired-sounding and shaky.

"Skully, it's Jude," I say in a raised voice so he can hear.

"I'm glad you called. I was going to call you anyway. I'm not gonna need you tonight after all. We haven't had a lot of business today, so there's nothing urgent that needs to be done. And I counted all the towels myself, so that's done, too."

I snicker under my breath.

"Okay. I won't plan on coming in then," I say, feeling relieved.

"I'm sorry about that, son. I know you're probably counting on a regular paycheck this month, but she's gonna be a bit skint. If you come up short for living expenses, you let me know."

I don't know what I did to deserve a friend like Skully. He's always been kind to me.

I tell him about the job I landed today in the city, and he sounds genuinely thrilled at first, then tells me not to quit at the gym because I'm the best worker he has. I reassure him that I won't leave him high and dry and that I'll put in the odd shift no matter what. I say goodbye and am just about to hang up when Skully remembers something, "I sent you a little cash in case you were out. I did it through email like you showed me before."

I'm not only overwhelmed by his generosity, but I'm shocked that the old boy remembered how to send a money transfer, something I showed him how to do months ago when he needed to pay tradesmen. He bitched the whole time and stated that he prefers to write checks to anything electronic, so I'm blown away that he actually figured it out alone.

* * *

The internet is flooded with news about Michaels. The latest report claims that Chad suffered a broken arm and three broken ribs, but no head trauma, or anything else life-threatening. Good! He'll be coherent when I confront him, providing I can BS my way into the ward. Even better, the article mentions the hospital—Tribeca General.

# Chapter 11

Pressed between medical staff and visitors in the elevator, I keep my head down. After numerous unsuccessful attempts to get Michaels' room number from the hospital, I decided to disguise my voice as an elderly man and convinced the operator that I was a relative, which allowed me to obtain the room number 411.

As the elevator doors open, the smells and sounds fill my mind with vivid memories of that fateful night two years ago, when I watched my child leave this world. I take a deep breath and pull up the face mask I picked up from the dispensary after changing into the scrubs in the bathroom.

I follow a group of people out of the elevator, trying to blend in. I scan the hall back and forth until I see an overhead sign that reads *rooms 400-420*. I follow the sign and turn down the hallway, immediately noticing an unattended housekeeping cart. It's a perfect prop to get me where I need to go without being questioned.

I briskly push the cart up the long hallway, reading the room numbers. Once I reach the 407 mark, I look up the hall at the nearby nursing station and realize in dismay that Michaels' room is directly across from a group of nurses chatting behind the desk. Considering that Michaels is a celebrity, I'm sure the medical staff is under strict instruction not to let anyone enter his room.

With only a few steps to go, I create a short script for when I'm stopped. I eye the exit, a door to the stairwell at the end of the hall. If a staff member asks for my I.D, I'll have to make a run for it. I arrive at the nursing station, nod at the women, then turn to room 411 and see the name, *Michaels, Chad* written on a small piece of cardstock on the door.

The nurses barely notice me, and I feel home free as I push the cart against the wall and grab a stack of towels. However, just as I'm about to push the door open, the sharp voice of a nurse rings out, "Excuse me."

Heart hammering, I turn to see the woman in pink scrubs. "Yes?"

"Be quiet when you're going in there," she demands. "The patient is sleeping."

It's obvious she's a Chad Michaels fan. I nod and give her a thumbs-up as I enter the room.

Without the name on the door, I wouldn't recognize him—his hair is flat and stringy, his face ashen and hollow. A far cry from the handsome image presented in the media, the big celebrity I'd watched taking pictures with a fan.

Knowing I have only minutes, I swiftly approach the side of the bed. His arm is encased in a sling, and there are bandages wrapped around his bare torso, with his uninjured arm hooked up to an IV. A monitor is attached to his finger, and my gaze follows the line up to a large grey machine with a digital readout—identical to the one that flatlined the night Little Blue died.

My eyes scan his bare arm, looking for the snake Little Blue had described, but there's only a thin tattoo of barbed wire around his exposed bicep. The snake must be under the sling on his other arm.

A wave of rage hits me. I want to hurt him.

I take a deep breath and lean in close to Chad's, pressing my mouth to his ear. Through gritted teeth, I whisper, "Wake up."

He groans and slowly turns his head toward me, his eyes fluttering open. It takes him a moment to focus. "Are you a nurse?" he mumbles.

I offer a cold smile and shake my head.

"Then who are you?" His tone sharpens with sudden awareness.

"I'm the one who's going to make you pay."

Chad's expression quickly changes from curiosity to fear. "I don't know what you're talking about—"

"I'm making you pay for what you did to that young girl in that penthouse two years ago."

He winces in pain as he tries to sit up. "Who the hell are you? And how did you get in here?"

"I'm the father of Abbigale, the fourteen-year-old girl you drugged and left for dead in that bathroom."

His eyes widen. "Look, man. You've obviously got the wrong guy. I didn't hurt anyone, especially a child."

My eyes shift to his splinted arm. "Tell me about the snake tattoo. The one under that splint, on your forearm."

Chad shakes his head in confusion. "All I have is my daughter's name on my wrist. I swear it. You've got the wrong guy."

"The night you drugged my daughter, you were ushered out of the penthouse before the cops got there. You are guilty as hell. Admit it. I want to hear you fucking say it!"

His eyes dart around, looking for help. "Look, man. I was at a penthouse party a couple years ago where a girl died, but I heard about it later. I'd left long before any of that went down."

"What a convenient answer. You actually think I believe you?"

"It's true. I had an emergency. I had to leave."

"So, why wasn't your name on the police report if you had nothing to hide?"

Chad shakes his head, "I guess my lawyer didn't feel the need to drag my name into it, considering I wasn't there at the time of the incident."

"Let me see your forearm."

Michaels turns his arm with the I.V.

"The one in the sling."

"My arm is fractured. I can't take it off."

I grin, "I can."

I catch him glancing at the call buzzer on his bed and quickly push it out of his reach.

"Fine. But I need help removing it. After you see my arm, you have to leave, deal?"

"I don't make deals with people like you."

He sighs, "Go ahead. Take it off."

I untie the sling and then unwrap the elastic bandage until I see his swollen, bruised arm inside the rigid plastic splint.

Every few moments, I look at the door. I know I don't have much time.

I command him to lift his arm, and then I carefully remove the brace. Examining both the inner and outer forearm, I scan past the bruises for the snake tattoo. But aside from the name 'Claire,' etched into his wrist, I find nothing.

"Now do you believe me?"

"I don't know what to believe anymore." I focus on his scared face. "Tell me why you left my daughter's party that night."

Micheals turns his head away. "It doesn't matter why I left."

"It does to me," I say, gripping hard onto his injured arm.

"Okay. Okay," he groans. "I left to see my daughter, Claire. She was sick in the hospital."

"Considering how you treat her, I find it hard to believe you'd leave a party just because she was sick."

Chad's expression morphs from fear to anger. "You don't know what the hell you're talking about."

"Don't I? I saw you at the park the other day. You ignored your little girl like she was a piece of garbage, an annoyance rather than your child. You make me sick."

Chad glares at me with a sudden hatred. "My daughter passed away from leukemia one day after I went to that penthouse party."

I want to laugh at this blatant lie. "Nice try. I met your daughter recently. She spoke to me while you were signing an autograph in Hudson River Park."

Chad shakes his head, as though clearing it. "I...I was in the park the other day, and I did sign an autograph for a guy, but how the hell do you know that?" His eyes are confused. "And how did you know my little girl's name? We never released any information about her to the media."

"I know her name because she talked to me in the park while you were playing rockstar, not caring if she lived or died—"

Suddenly, he lunges forward, and his fist connects with my jaw. The IV rips from his vein, sending fluid and blood all over the white hospital blanket.

An alarm goes off. A moment later, the door opens and a nurse hurries inside.

I quickly pull up my mask and make a beeline past her, my jaw throbbing in pain. I slam through the doors to the stairs and use the rails to fly down the steps until I'm on the main floor, where I find the bathroom, retrieve my clothes from the garbage, change, and speed out of the building.

My adrenaline is pumping a lot harder now than it was in Michaels' room. My situation is hitting me. I'm in big shit for doing what I did. I impersonated hospital personnel and accosted Chad Michaels. I pretty much threatened his life while he was in a hospital bed. There's not a judge in the state who wouldn't throw the book at me.

My insides are trembling as much as my hands. I need to plan my next move to avoid getting picked up by the cops. I see the bus to Hell's Kitchen ahead and, for a moment, debate catching it. But I'm afraid to go home in case the cops show up, which I'm sure they will. Michaels probably called 911 and reported me before I was even out of the hospital. I told him my daughter's name. It won't be hard for the cops to figure out who I am and where I live.

I can't go to my father's; his girl friend wouldn't permit it. Besides, the cops will no doubt call him and ask about me.

As soon as I see the entrance to the Hudson River Park, I speed up my pace. Once I'm out of plain view and seated on a bench nestled between full bushes, I dial Lauren. She answers the phone on the first ring. "Hi. Where are you?"

I tell her I'm in Tribeca; she asks why, and I tell her that I had to see someone in the hospital. Thankfully, she doesn't ask me more questions, and I don't have to lie.

"Do you work tonight at the boxing gym?"

When I tell her that I'm off tonight, she offers to pick me up. As much as I want to be with Lauren, I feel too paranoid to be good company. That being said, I can't go home, and the cops don't know about Lauren. "Sure. That would be great."

* * *

When her car pulls up, I quickly jump in. It's only when I'm putting on my seatbelt that I look at her. She's more beautiful than before; her hair is styled in loose curls, and she has just enough makeup to accentuate her pretty eyes and full lips. "You look great." I'm suddenly aware of how dishevelled and freaked out I must appear.

She smiles sweetly. "Were you jogging or something? You look a bit spent."

"No. I've just had a crazy day so far."

She asks if I'd like to come to her place, and I quickly agree; it's a safe space where I can figure out my next step. That said, keeping up my fake cheerful demeanor is going to be challenging.

Just as Lauren parks the car, her cell phone beeps, and she looks at the screen. "It's my father. He wants you to start work in a couple of days. He said that he texted you but got no response."

I quickly check my texts messages. In the craziness of the day, I must've missed my message alerts. I quickly reply, saying I'll be at the firm at 8 AM sharp the day after tomorrow.

"It's funny that he's dealing with you directly. Usually, he'd have the office manager take care of scheduling trades and stuff." She shrugs. "I guess his hands-on approach is because you're my friend. Could be his way of trying to get closer to me."

Given the mess I'm in, the last thing I want is to be out in public. But since I'm probably a wanted man, working at a law office might be a smart move. No way they'd think to look for me there.

Skully's Gym, however, is a different story. If the cops go to my apartment and I'm not home, all they have to do is go downstairs to the Chinese restaurant and speak with Mr. Wong to find out where I work. Thankfully, I never told Wong about my new job at the law firm.

Lauren makes us a sandwich, and we sit on the loveseat. She asks what we should do, and I suggest watching a movie. She looks at me oddly for a moment, then shrugs. "Sure," she says, grabbing the remote and turning on the TV.

As we finish our food—a painful process considering my tied-up stomach—Lauren flips through the channels. She stops scrolling when a picture of Chad Michaels appears on a local news station.

Lauren turns up the volume as the newscaster reports, "Chad Michaels was in a car accident yesterday, but his publicist has stated that he is expected to make a full recovery."

I cough, my stomach twisting. Watching, unable to breathe, I wait for additional news about a crazy man sneaking into the rockstar's room and threatening his life, but it doesn't come. I draw in a tight breath and exhale hard.

"Are you okay?" Lauren asks.

"Food went down the wrong way."

"That's sad about Chad Micheals." Lauren turns the channel. "He's one of my father's celebrity clients. I only met him once, but he was really nice."

I look at her. "What? Your dad represents Michaels? For how long?"

She shrugs. "I don't know exactly, I'd say about five years now."

"Is your father the only lawyer who represents Chad?"

"No. I mean, there are other lawyers in the firm who know Mr. Michaels a lot better than my father. I think a few of them even go to parties and play golf with the guy. It's all hobnobbing and ass-kissing, if you ask me."

"I see."

"Too bad about the accident, though. The guy's sure had his share of heartache; I feel sorry for him."

I put the rest of my sandwich on the saucer. "What do you mean?"

Lauren contemplates for a moment, then says she's probably not supposed to say anything, but she trusts me. "Their little girl died of leukemia. She was only five."

"How many kids does he have?"

"Only one, as far as I know."

The room starts to shrink and my head is buzzing. "How long ago did his little girl die?"

"It would be about two years ago now. And shortly after, his wife, Emily, left him, which surprised everyone. My mother said that anytime she'd bump into them, they always seemed deeply in love."

Immediately, I reflect on what Michaels said about his daughter. But I saw her, as plain as day. I could feel her breath in front of me and hear her shoes on the pavement and the way she tried noisily to get her father's attention.

But, she couldn't get his attention. Why wasn't he paying attention to her? Maybe, just maybe, it wasn't that he didn't want to see her. What if he couldn't see her?

A chill runs up the back of my neck. I sit frozen, trying to make sense of everything, but I can't. It's all too much to process.

"Jude? Is everything okay?" Lauren sounds concerned.

All of a sudden my stomach springs my food up my throat. I cover my mouth and run to the washroom.

I barely close the door behind me when everything I just ate spews into the toilet. I wait until I'm sure that nothing still lurks in my gut, waiting to follow the same road as my sandwich. When the threat is gone, I wash my face with cold water and try to settle my nerves before returning to the living room, where I'll have to convince Lauren that I'm completely fine, and that the food she fed me didn't cause my episode.

As soon as I open the door, I see Lauren in front of me, looking confused and worried. "Are you okay, Jude?"

"Totally fine. I just had a queasy stomach."

There's doubt in her eyes. "Something else is going on, isn't it? You don't look ill, and the only other reason you'd be throwing up is if you're upset or worried. Is that it?"

I reassure her that my nerves are just fine, and all I need to do is take it easy for a while. We don't know each other very well—even though I feel a deep connection to her already, she doesn't know if I'm the type of person who has a fragile gut.

I'm hoping this will occur to her, but after fifteen minutes of sitting quietly on the sofa together, she looks at my hands and notices I'm shaking. "Look, Jude. You can talk to me openly. I'm not here to judge you, and it's obvious that something happened to really upset you. Enough to make you throw up."

Her eyes are real, and she seems genuine and trustworthy. Even though we haven't known each other long, I really believe she's exactly who she appears to be—a kind-hearted, authentic person who genuinely wants to make the world better by helping others. I could see that the day I met her at the hospital—she was compassionate and didn't jump to conclusions like her boss did.

"Tell me, Jude. What is going on? Maybe I can help."

I drop my shoulders. "I've done something reckless. Something you're probably not going to understand. In fact, you'll probably never want to speak to me again if I tell you. Are you sure you want to know?"

Lauren pauses for a moment. "Honestly, after everything I've seen and heard working at the hospital, I don't think much can surprise me."

"I hope you're right."

Lauren gets up, pours me a glass of water, and settles back down next to me on the loveseat. I take a few sips, then a deep breath, and then lay out the story. I tell her how I dressed up as a hospital employee to get into the ward where Chad Michaels was. I recount my encounter with the rockstar and how I was so furious I wanted to end his miserable life but couldn't after he raised doubt.

I can tell she's trying to suppress her shock as she asks how I managed to escape after Michaels ripped out his IV and set off the alarm.

"I got the hell out of there. As fast as I could."

She's quiet for a long moment. Then: "Okay. Wow. I'm not going to lie, that's intense news. But I mean...it could be worse."

I scoff. "How? I bet half the police force is looking for me right now."

"With respect to you and how worried you're feeling, I highly doubt that half of the force is actively hunting you. This is New York. Unless you showed up at the hospital with a bomb strapped to your chest and carrying an AK47, the police aren't going to give you high priority. You didn't hurt him, right?"

I shake my head. "I threatened Michaels. Who knows how badly he's embellished what happened."

"I don't know. I never got the troublemaker vibe off him. He struck me as a more honest, linear type. My father said that out of all the celebrities he's worked for, Chad's the most honorable and respectful."

"How can you say that after what he may have done to my child?"

"Jude, this man was a father. I'm not sure if you know this, but he donates his time to charities like inner-city youth programs and actively advocates against drugs. I'm not saying that he's a saint, but I'd be hard-pressed to believe that he's responsible for what happened to your daughter. If he did have something to hide, especially a penchant for drugging or messing with young girls, somehow, somewhere, it would've come out in the press. Sickos always reveal themselves, no pun intended." She puts her hand on my leg. "Also, you have to remember what he was going through two years ago. His little girl was terminally ill. I'm not saying you shouldn't be upset over what happened to Little Blue—of course, you should be, and you should definitely seek out the truth—I'm just trying to give you some insight into who Chad is and, more importantly, who he's not."

I put my hands over my face. "I don't know what to believe anymore. Since Little Blue died, everything has been going so slow. Now everything is going so fast—too fast. I'm making crazy decisions without thinking and messing everything up." I take my hands from my face and look at Lauren. "And you. How can I do this to someone so incredible and kind?"

"What are you talking about? You haven't done anything to me."

"Yes, I have. Your father is a big-time lawyer, and you're hanging out with a criminal. I shouldn't have come here."

She sighs. "We don't know each other well yet, Jude. But I feel a strong connection to you. It's the strangest thing that I've never felt before. As for my father, of course, I love him, but we're not close. We don't look at things the same way. That being said, if you are in legal trouble, I'll do what I can to get his advice."

"Why would you do that for me?"

She smiles. "I'm a sucker for a nice guy."

I feel the same magnetic pull toward her. I lean in and hug her tightly. I've got nobody else I can confide in my life. Skully is great, and my father did get me Little Blue's urn, but both men are older and wrapped up in their own affairs. They have no time for my drama.

Lauren tells me she has a great idea, and I should stay the week at her place, which is close to her father's firm. "At least until we know if the cops are searching for you."

We spend the rest of the night snuggled together on the loveseat, and as the hours slip by with her in my arms, the chaos of my reality melts away. When we retire for the night, we talk for a while, and then I drift off to sleep, wrapped in the warmth of her embrace.

# Chapter 12

The rhythmic buzz of Lauren's alarm wakes us, and before I can say good morning, she's up and in the kitchen making coffee. I roll onto my side and stretch my fingers across the warm sheets where she had been. I'm reluctant to get up, dreading the return of reality and the anxiety of my situation. I wish she would forget about the coffee and come back to bed—having her next to me is the only thing that can ease the growing pressure inside me.

A few minutes later, Lauren walks in, carrying a cup of coffee for me. She places it on the bedside table. "I love sleeping with you. I feel like I've known you forever." She sits on the bed next to me. "I'm happy you're staying for a while. It'll give us a chance to get to know each other better."

I sit up and grab the coffee. "We're kind of doing it backwards, don't you think? Aren't we supposed to get to know each other and then sleep in the same bed?"

Lauren shrugs. "I'm not really a traditional girl. That being said, you're the second guy that's stayed in this apartment since I moved in."

"Oh oh, competition?" I snicker.

She shakes her head, "Not likely. My cousin stayed with me a year ago for about a week when his wife kicked him out."

"So, what happened after he left? Did his wife take him back?"

"Yeah, but I don't know why. He was a slob. He never cleaned up after himself."

I make a mental note to be diligent about tidiness while I'm here.

"I have to leave soon. What are you going to do today? Maybe you should just lay low and watch TV. Let things blow over for a while."

"I'd love to believe me. But I need to get a change of clothes and some incidentals for when I start work tomorrow. I can't show up wearing a t-shirt and wrinkly jeans I've slept in. I need to make a good impression."

She tells me to be careful if I plan on going to my place and to not stick around long in case the cops have knowledge of where I live. I couldn't agree with her more. Plus, if I get busted, I have no money to bail myself out, and I certainly couldn't call my father for help. I'd never hear the end of it.

Lauren suggests I wait for her to finish her shift, and then she can drive me to my apartment, but I don't want to risk getting busted while she's with me. She's got too much going for her with her work, not to mention the fallout that would happen from her father if he found out.

She looks at her clock on the bedside table, then leans over and, for the first time, kisses me on the lips. "I've got to take a shower and get ready," she says, then turns and walks into the bathroom.

My life has been turned upside down, but at least I have this beautiful creature who, for some reason, thinks I'm worthy of her attention.

After Lauren finishes in the shower, I make myself get out of bed. When she steps past me with her wet hair clinging to her sculpted body, wearing nothing more than a towel, I get a sudden urge to pick her up and carry her to the bed, but I resist. She'll let me know when she's ready to take that step.

When she dressed and we both had a piece of toast and a coffee refill, she cautions me again to be careful when I go home to get some things. After a quick goodbye kiss, she hands me the key to her place, and we head out.

* * *

An eerie darkness looms over the street as I make my way to my apartment. I am overcome by heightened paranoia as I focus on every parked car as I walk.

To keep my visit brief, I make a mental list of everything to grab as I climb the stairs—my toothbrush, shaving gear, a few changes of clothes, Little Blue's urn, and Kim's diary. As much as I don't need it, I wouldn't want someone coming in and taking it.

As I quickly sprint from room to room, filling the leather backpack Little Blue had bought me a couple Christmas's ago, I hear a car door shut down on the street. I hurry to the kitchen window and peer down to the entrance of Wong's restaurant, where I see a small car pulled up in front of the building. It's probably just an Uber; the Chinese restaurant is a common place for people to get dropped off. Relieved, I resume gathering my things.

It only takes me five minutes to grab and pack everything. Before taking off, I decide to change my trainers. Sitting on the couch, I kick off my shoes and slip on the others. I stand up, grab the shoes I just took off, and toss them into my room when there is a sudden knock on the door.

I freeze in place, my mind racing with thoughts of impending doom. That hard rap on the door was purposeful, unlike when Mr. or Mrs. Wong have come upstairs.

Maybe if I stay completely still and don't make a sound, they'll think no one is home, and they'll go away. Then, I remind myself that I'm in New York, and if the cops want to get in, they will. I have no chance but to answer the door and face my fate.

My heart pounds like a runaway train, threatening to burst through my chest. My knees nearly give out as I cross the living room. Taking a deep breath—likely the last free one I'll have before they lock me up—I grasp the handle and slowly open the door.

It takes me a moment to process who is standing in front of me. "Michaels. What are you doing here?"

Chad Michaels is holding his slinged arm to his chest, the hospital band still on his wrist. I'm not sure if it's because of the dim lighting outside or because he's out of his hospital bed, but his face looks healthier, less ashen than when I saw him last.

He tilts his head upward until his eyes meet mine from under the rim of his baseball cap. "I need to talk to you, Jude."

I step closer to him, then look down the stairwell at the street.

"Don't worry, I didn't bring the cops with me."

"Why are you here then?"

"It's about my daughter."

I'm unsure what his motives are, but I've got nothing to lose. I move aside and motion to the living room.

When I watch him walk past me, I notice a slight limp. I know instinctively that he checked himself out of the hospital against the doctor's advice.

"Mind if I sit?" Michaels makes his slow way to the couch.

I close the door, then walk over and stand in front of the couch. "How did you know where I lived?"

I can't tell if it's a sarcastic grin on his face in response, or a grimace from the pain he's in. "Well, you kind of told me who you were after you snuck into my hospital room. Once I had that information, you weren't hard to track down."

"Why aren't the cops with you? Are they waiting outside somewhere?"

"No. I'm not here to get you busted. Like I said when you opened the door, I want to talk about my daughter."

"You mean Claire."

He nods.

"I told you everything already, when I saw her and what she was doing."

"I know. That's what's messing me up. She's been dead for two years now. Technically, you couldn't have seen her, right?"

"I don't know. I mean, I understand that she's passed on. All I know is that I saw what I saw. I don't know what else to tell you."

"It's not that I think you're lying, not after what's happened to me. It's just that I'm confused about it all."

"What do you mean by what has happened to you? Did you see her, too?"

"No." His voice is low. "But I wish I had. I guess it's the reason I came and found you. I need to know if you really did interact with my little girl or if you're just screwing with me because you thought I had something to do with your child's death."

"I wouldn't mess with you or anyone like that. I'd never make up a story about a loved one, especially a child. I know how badly it hurts when you lose a child."

"I felt her presence. Often. And strange things would happen while I was at home."

"What things?"

Michaels shakes his head. "At first, I thought I was seeing things or losing my mind. I would be working in my studio for hours, and when I would come out, there would be small indentations in the carpet, like shoe prints walking down the hall. I would be in the living room or the kitchen and hear doors opening and closing. At first, I dismissed the noises, but after they continued to happen, I thought about Claire and how she would always do disruptive things to get my attention. She was headstrong. A pest." Michaels smiles as tears drip from his eyes. "She had no patience, and if you weren't paying attention to her, look out."

"The shoes," I mutter under my breath.

"What?" Michaels wipes his eyes and looks up at me.

I tell Michaels about Claire's threat with her red-bowed, shiny black shoes. "She threatened to scuff them on the cement when you wouldn't pay attention."

"Her favorite shoes." Michaels stares at me through fresh tears.

I walk over and sit beside him on the sofa. "I don't know how all this is happening or what it means. I don't even believe in spirits and ghosts. But I know what I saw and heard in the park that day. And I'm beginning to think that I had an interaction with my daughter's ghost, too."

His eyes widen. "You were able to see your girl?"

I nod, then tell him the whole story about Mad Madge, Warlock, and getting to hold and talk with Little Blue.

Michaels doesn't seem as shocked or disbelieving as I would be if someone told me this story. Instead, he stares at me in silence, tears still running down his cheeks. "Do you think this Madge person could help me see my Claire? I'd give anything just to talk to her again."

"I don't know, Chad. But I can't even say for sure that I did see Little Blue. Don't forget, I was drugged out of my mind. The only thing that makes me think it could be true is Madge. I saw her after that night, and she knew things, things she couldn't have known. Not unless she was there and observed what I was seeing."

"See? Then it must've really happened. Please, Jude. Can't you take me to her? I'll give you anything you want."

"I don't want anything from you, Chad. Except maybe for you to call off the cops."

"What cops? I never called the cops on you. In fact, when the nurses ran into the room after I pulled out my I.V., I told them that you were a fan."

I breathe a sigh of relief and the clenching in my gut starts to loosen. "Why didn't you tell them the truth?"

"I don't know. I guess because you mentioned Claire, and somewhere in the back of my mind, I wanted to believe you."

I nod, understanding his desperation. It was the same desperation that made me go along with Madge in the first place.

"So, what about it? Are you going to take me to meet this Madge woman?"

I tell him that I'll do my best, but that I have no idea where to look. "She's a street person, a nomad, and she shows up at the most unexpected times. But yeah, I mean, I owe you one. After all, you could've had my ass thrown in jail."

"I don't care about any of that. I just want to see my kid again."

I have no idea what to do next or where to start looking for Madge. Maybe she's not around anymore. It's not like she gave me an address where I can find her. As far as I know, she lives in alleyways and spends her time on the subway, picking pockets.

That's it! The subway.

Michaels is in no shape to walk the streets, but maybe if I take him on the same route where I first met the crazy old woman, we'll get lucky. But first, before we go anywhere, I have to ask him one thing, just in case something happens and I don't get the chance to talk to him again.

"Chad, I need to ask you something before we leave to look for Mad Madge."

"What is it?"

"You admitted to being at the penthouse party the night my daughter died. Can you tell me who else was there?"

He becomes quiet and taps his free hand on his knee. "Your daughter and her mother. My lawyer, a record producer, an engineer, an agent, and there may have been someone else, but I don't really remember. I wasn't there very long before I got the call about Claire being taken to the hospital, so a lot of what happened is kind of a blur now."

"Do you remember the names of any of the guys there?"

He shakes his head. "Not really, just my lawyer, but I already mentioned this to you in the hospital. I think he goes to a lot of gatherings—he's the one who invited me that night. Because of my name, he thought it would be a good way to socialize and meet new clients."

"You never told me his name. Is it Lawrence Banks?"

Michaels looks surprised. "How did you know that?"

"It's a long story."

I can tell he's trying to make sense of what I've told him but can't.

"Does Banks have a tattoo on his forearm?"

"A tattoo? I have no idea. He's always in a suit. But I doubt it. He's not the tattoo type.

The other men at the party were younger. I'm sure some of them had ink, but I didn't notice."

"Can you do me a favor and get me the names of everyone at the party? I already know a few from the police report, but not all."

"Sure, man."

I nod and then look at his arm. "I'll take you for a subway ride, and maybe we can drive around for a bit and look for Mad Madge, but if we don't spot her, there's not much more I can do."

Michaels grunts as he rises from the couch. "Thank you, Jude."

* * *

The pain was too great for Michaels to drive, so he'd taken an Uber to my place. He pays for the ride to the subway. I stand behind him in case he falls. He slowly grits his teeth through the pain and makes it up the stairs to the platform. It's midday, and there are a lot of people ambling to get on and off the subways over the lunch hour. When it comes time to board, I grab onto Michael's arm and lead him down the aisle.

Remembering where I first met Madge, we make our way to the back row. Thankfully, the other passengers see the shape that Michaels is in and move out of our way. The glasses and baseball cap he's wearing act as a disguise and so far, no one has recognised him. Once we're seated, I set my sights on the doorways, ready to identify Madge.

"I don't remember the last time I took public transportation." Michaels chuckles. "I forgot how many colorful characters ride these things."

He goes on to tell me how he was raised poor in Hell's Kitchen by working-class parents—a story similar to my own—and how, after his father passed away, his mother relied on the subway to get to her cleaning jobs, where she took him with her.

The subway stops to let people off and on as I carefully watch for the stout woman with the fiery red hair, but so far no one fits the description. After an hour of riding around, it's obvious that Mad Madge isn't going to make an appearance. Then again, it was nighttime when I first met her.

Michaels turns to me. "You mentioned someone named Warlock. Since this Madge woman isn't showing up, why don't we try to find him?"

I shrug. "Not a bad idea if I knew where to look. Madge did tell me that he moves around all the time, so I don't know how successful we'll be, but it's worth a shot. But how are we going to get around?"

Michaels grins. "Do you have a licence?"

* * *

To automobile aficionados, the Astin Martin DB12 is the fastest, classiest, meanest piece of machinery, with Dual Twin Turbochargers and a 4.0-litre twin-turbo V8, and here I am sitting in the driver's seat of a slick silver one. I look over at Michaels and grin. "You gotta be kidding me."

He shrugs. "It's just a car."

"No. My last shit box set of wheels was 'just a car.' This is arguably the best sports automobile made today."

"Maybe you should apply to be a salesman for the company." He chuckles. "Just don't get us into a wreck. I've already had one of those this week, and I can tell you—it hurts. So, be careful. The slightest tap on the gas and this thing takes off like a rocket."

"I'll drive responsibly."

Once we're buckled in, I gently touch the gas and the car springs ahead. Michaels gives me a look. "I told ya, this thing has a lot of power."

I've read about these cars; they have an eight-speed automatic transmission and an electronic rear differential. So, as Julia Roberts once referred to the Lotus Esprit, the car corners like it's on rails. That being said, if you give the DB12 too much power, it won't mean a lick of difference about the differential—you'll be an uncontrolled rocket on wheels.

I hit the gas again, but this time gradually. Still, the car is led by the nose, and I feel myself being pushed back into the seat.

We head Southwest on West Broadway and make a right on Chambers Street. At every stoplight, I see crossing pedestrians noticing the car. When I turn onto 9A North, I tell Michaels to keep an eye out for Madge, a portly old lady with the bushiest red hair who may or may not be wearing her bra on the outside of her clothes.

After another few miles, we're back in Hell's Kitchen.

My excitement over my undoubtedly once-in-a-lifetime opportunity to drive this stellar car fades as I remember my purpose for being here. I need to somehow locate either Mad Madge or Warlock. The only problem is, that it was late when the crazy woman led me through a maze of alleyways, and I haven't the slightest idea where we ended up. I was probably aware at the time of street signs or distinctive buildings we passed, but the drugs I took that night robbed my mind of that now invaluable information.

I retrace as much of my midnight journey with Madge as possible. I take a few quick turns of where I remember walking with her, and then everything goes blank.

As I drive, I tell Michaels about Warlock. "He's a skinny old guy with a grey beard. He was lying on a thin, filthy cot behind a dumpster. That much I remember."

We roll down what seems like a dozen alleyways and slow down when we pass every dumpster but can't find the old codger anywhere. We cruise the back of buildings and sides of the road, and after asking a dozen homeless people—all having no idea who Madge or Warlock are—Michaels' pain eventually gets the best of him, and he tells me to take him home.

Since we're in Hell's Kitchen, it would save me a lot of time dropping by my place before I take him and his car back to Tribeca, but with all the groans he's been making, I don't suggest it.

On the way to his place, I thank him again for not calling the cops and apologize for not being able to find Mad Madge or Warlock. "You know, Chad. There's a huge likelihood that the two of them are scammers and have fled to find a new area with fresh people to prey on."

He shakes his head. "You're a logical guy, Jude, and I believe what you said about seeing my daughter. I also believe that if this crazy Madge lady told you things about the night you saw your Little Blue, she could not have known unless she could see the dead. I agree that this whole spirit-sighting topic is a little hard to get your head around, but if there is a smidgeon of hope that I can see my little girl again, I want to try my hardest to make that happen."

I sigh. "I know. I just don't want you to get discouraged."

"I passed *discouraged* a long time ago. Even though I still walk through my life and act like the star I was created to be, inside I feel dead and without purpose."

It's like he's reading my mind. Everything he feels, I have felt and am feeling.

When we get to his place, and I park the car, he asks me to do him a favor—that if I see Madge, to ask her if she will help him the same way she helped me. "Money is no object. I don't care what it costs."

I toss him his keys, and he asks me to enter his number into my phone. "Please, call me if you hear or see anything."

I agree, then shake his hand and cross the street to walk to the bus stop.

Sitting down and looking at my phone, I scroll to Michaels' name and number. How many women in the world would give just about anything to have the rock star's digits? I'm just about to slide the phone into my pocket when I get a text message from Skully: "Are you doing okay, son? Give me a call so we can chat."

Since there is no bus in sight and no other people waiting, I dial Skully.

He answers on the fourth ring, just before the call goes to messages. "Jude. That you?" he grumbles.

"How are you?"

"Dealing with a bit of a boost in business actually. We had a good day at the gym. Signed two eight-week training contracts—

one for a boy's club and the other for a women's self-defence organization. Looks like we're back to where we were before I had to cut your hours. You can come back full-time now."

"That's great news, Skully. I didn't think it would take too long for things to improve, but I never imagined it would be this fast."

"Yeah. I'm happy about the change, that's for sure. It was almost a perfect day."

"Almost?"

"If it weren't for that kid boxer I had to put the run on."

"That doesn't sound good. What happened?" As soon as the words leave my lips, I regret them. "Please don't say this had something to do with your damn towels."

"Yeah. The little shit finished working out in the ring, and after he had a shower, he got dressed and headed for the door. I had one of those uneasy feelings about the guy, so I stopped him, made him open up his gym bag, and guess what I found?"

I bite my lip to keep from laughing. "One of your towels?"

"You bet your ass I did. So, I took what was mine, gave him a slap upside the ear, and told him never to come back."

I look up to see the bus coming down the street. "I've got to go, Skully. I'll give you a shout as soon as I can."

As I watch out the window, I can't help but feel sorry for Michaels. He's just as lost over his daughter's passing as I am about

Blue. I'm not sure if it's easier to lose a child to cancer or to have a child that I would define as murdered.

I guess either way, loss is loss. Regardless of what caused the death, the deep grieving of a parent debilitates us all.

The twenty-minute ride seems to pass quickly, with my mind busy thinking about Chad Michaels, starting work tomorrow at the firm, and, of course, Lauren. I want to tell her that I no longer need to stay away from my apartment, but if she knows I'm not a wanted man, there'd be no reason for me to crash at her place, which is the only good thing that's happened to me in two years. But I can't lie to her about it. I have to let her know.

Once I'm back home, I sit on the couch and tap out a message to Lauren.

"Hello beautiful. I hope your day is going well. Mine has been full of surprises, all of which I will tell you about later. Also, it turns out that I don't have heat on my tail after all. So, I guess you're free from having to put up with me for a week."

It takes a few minutes before she replies. "I'm happy for you. What a relief. A little bummed out that you won't be staying with me, though. I never realized how much I appreciated the company until you stayed over."

I smile as I read her words. "If you like, I can pretend that it's not safe for me to stay at my apartment right now." When I send the message, I get a wave of regret. What if Lauren thinks I'm trying to freeload off of her or, worse, wanting to get into her pants?

Another message comes through. "Bring your guitar."

I exhale a long breath. *Thank God.*

It's five. I have two hours to go before my shift starts at Skully's gym. After the scare of the 'cops' banging on the door, the shock of seeing Michaels, and driving around on a mad quest to find Madge, my brain is feeling the impact. I'm feeling mentally drained, and desperately need a nap. But on the off chance I don't wake up in time for work, I decide to pick up my guitar and play for a while. If Lauren wants me to bring it, I don't want to look like a fool because I can't remember how to play properly.

As I play through scales, trying to limber up my fingers, I stare at Little Blue's urn.

*I swore off playing music when you died, a decision I know you would have opposed. So, now I'm playing again, sweetie, and it's thanks to this wonderful lady I met. I know you would have really liked her. I miss you, Little Blue, and I will until my last breath.*

Tears well in my eyes, and I'm just reaching up to brush them away when a crash comes from the bathroom.

I quickly set the guitar down on the couch and sprint to the bathroom, where I notice the toothbrush holder on the floor. Granted, the ledge around the sink is narrow, but never has the cup fallen in the whole time I've lived here.

I'm just about to bend down when, out of my peripheral vision, I catch something in the mirror. There's a spot of steam, despite my not having showered recently, and something is drawn in the center. I move closer and see a shape that resembles a snake.

I jump back and rub my eyes, and when I open them, both the steam imprint and the shape inside have vanished.

A cold shiver runs up the back of my neck, and I exit the room and return to the couch, where I rub my face with my hands. What the hell is happening to me? I feel like I'm losing it. Maybe all of the spirit/ghost talk I had with Michaels has my mind playing tricks on me.

I pick up my guitar but don't resume playing. I'm feeling creeped out, and I want to be quiet so I can hear if anything else happens.

I look at the time on my phone. I've still got an hour before I would normally be leaving for work but given my strange experience—or overactive imagination—I decide to leave now. My hairbrush is in the bathroom, so instead of chancing another weird steam image on the mirror, I grab my baseball hat from beside the door, zip my guitar into a gig bag, put on my jacket, and sling my packsack over one shoulder before heading out.

It feels strange bringing my guitar out of the apartment. The last time I had it out was when I played the gig in Jersey, the same night Little Blue died.

# Chapter 13

The night wind is usually a strong force in the fall months as I walk up 52nd Street toward the subway station, but not tonight. Tonight, the air has an eerie stillness, making the atmosphere heavy and noticeable with each breath. But at least I'm not in my apartment where whatever I saw (or didn't see) could happen again. I put my still-shaking hands in my pockets and my head down and focus on the sidewalk as I try to clear my mind.

Two guys, both around twenty, are walking towards me. I catch their eyes, and they share a look that sends a shiver down my spine. New York's a fantastic city, but when night falls, and you're on your own, you've got to be on high alert.

As they get closer, one of them slips his hand into his pocket, and my mind races—could it be a knife? Or a gun? I hold my breath as they pass by.

Once they're out of sight, I turn to keep an eye on them. I've heard the stories—how criminals often walk past you first, then wait for you to let your guard down before they attack from behind.

Then, I see a cop car slowly driving towards me. My chest tightens, and my hands tremble briefly until I remember that I'm in the clear since Michaels covered for me. The cruiser rolls past and stops alongside the two young men. I hear car doors and the authoritative voices of the cops, but I don't turn around.

* * *

Skully is waiting at the door when I arrive, looking more decrepit and aged compared to when I saw him last, just days ago. "You doing alright?" I ask.

He scowls. "What are you, my wife? Mind your own damn business."

I grin, and he chuckles. Then I head down the hallway, hang my jacket on the usual hook in the storeroom, and walk out to the gym to check out the mess.

As I walk past Skully's office to grab the broom and mop, I spot a clipboard stuck to the door. In huge, dramatic red letters, it reads, "Towel Sign-out." I can't help but chuckle. He must be the laughingstock of every member here. But as quirky as the old grump is, he's shown me a lot of kindness for the past two years. Maybe someday I can bring Lauren here, show her the historic gym, and introduce her to Skully—after giving her a heads-up about his gruff demeanor, of course.

The evening unfolds just like any other: I'm in the gym, sweeping, mopping, and tidying up, while Skully is holed up in his office with the light glowing under his closed door. Once I'm ready to leave, I meet Skully in the hallway, and we say goodnight as we lock up for the night. With my backpack over my shoulder and my guitar case in hand, I head into the cool night.

As I walk toward the subway station, I give Lauren a call. Her voice is tired, but she sounds happy to hear from me. I let her know I'll be there in about half an hour. I'm excited to see her—I can hardly wait—but I also feel a huge relief knowing I won't be heading back to my apartment tonight, especially after that strange bathroom mirror incident. I still feel creeped out even if I imagined seeing what I did.

Buskers and artisans are just packing up as I step onto the platform, where a half-dozen people are waiting to board. The subway isn't due to arrive for another ten minutes, so I walk to the back of the gathering and rest my back against the tiled graffiti wall.

I've always found the residents and store owners across New York's five boroughs friendly and chatty. But on public transit, it's a whole different story. As I stand alone and people-watch, it's rare to see anyone talking to each other. Most people either wait silently for the train or are glued to their phones. Maybe it's a safety thing—they feel more secure by keeping to themselves.

Finally, the train arrives and the doors open. After throngs of passengers get off, I stand behind the growing crowd to board. Waiting for my turn to get on, I feel a sudden pressure on my shoulder. Thinking it's probably another passenger getting pushy, I turn around and scowl. I am shocked when I see Mad Madge standing directly behind me. She's wearing a lopsided purple fedora on top of her trademark flaming red hair. She has a freakish amount of dark make-up on her pale skin, making her appear almost ghoulish. "Hello, stranger. Did ya miss me?" she cackles through her broken teeth.

"We've been looking for you."

"We? Who is we? Do ya got worms?"

The subway door alarms chime as a warning.

"Are you getting on?" I say, pointing to the train.

She stares at me without responding. I back away from the doors as the last people get on. Soon, the train moves down the track, and Madge and I are the only ones left on the platform.

"Let me guess, you want something from me, don't you?"

I nod.

"Ha! You have a short memory, Jude! Did you forget what happened at our last meeting and what I told you? You were rude to me, calling me a scammer and a fraud."

"I remember, Madge. And I'm sorry. I just—"

"Do you remember the last thing I said to you then?"

I shake my head.

"I told you to think about how you could make things up to me. Does that ring a bell?"

"Okay. Sure. I remember," I lie.

"Well then, what have you come up with?"

I ask her what she's hinting at when a homeless man staggers down the platform stairs carrying a bottle in a brown paper bag.

Madge grins. "For starters, you can get me that bottle."

Confused, I ask her if I can give her the money to buy a new bottle, but she refuses. "I want that bottle."

From what I know about the nutty woman, there's no way I'm going to be able to dissuade her. I reach into my pocket, pull out a twenty-dollar bill and approach the drunk man. "Hello. Listen, I'm not sure what you've got in your bottle or how much is left, but is there any chance you'd consider selling it to me?"

The old codger laughs, revealing a mostly toothless grin in likeness to Madge's. "You thirsty? Cuz I can give you a swill, and I won't even charge ya."

"No, thank you. It's not for me. It's for her." I point behind me.

"Who's her?" The old guy says looking around me. "I'm legally blind. Tell her to come here."

I turn around and motion for Madge, who now has her arms crossed impatiently. She shakes her head slowly.

"She doesn't want to. So, how about that bottle? Is it worth twenty bucks to you?"

The old guy thinks for a moment, then shrugs. "Why the hell not."

I hand him the money, and he passes me the bottle. Then he turns around and goes back the way he came, most likely to find the closest liquor store.

I head back to Madge. "Here's your damn bottle. Are we square now?"

Madge opens the bag and laughs. "You got taken for a ride, Jude. It's the cheapest vodka on the market."

Before I can respond, she has the cap off and takes a long, hard drink from the bottle. Afterwards, she stuffs the bag into the side pocket of her ripped and tattered jacket. "So, tell me, what is it I can do for you? You want to take another walk like before and find your daughter again? Is that it? But I thought you didn't believe you even made contact."

"To be honest with you, Madge, I don't know what I believe. All I know is that no matter how you do it, I need to try to connect with her. I have important questions. Plus, there's another issue I need to ask you about."

She looks at me with curiosity. "Interesting. Walk with me, and you can tell me all about it."

As we make our way down the stairs, the wind has picked up, blowing a cloud of fine debris into my face. "Look, is there somewhere we can go and talk? A restaurant or a bar?"

She laughs. "Oh, you want to wine and dine me? No thanks. You're not really my type. But I'll tell you what—follow me, and I'll take you to a cozy place out of the weather. I think you'll like it."

Red flags immediately go up when, at the bottom of the stairs, she takes the first alleyway off the sidewalk. I stop and stare down the dark lane.

"Come on, you pussy. No one's going to bite you, except maybe me." She cackles.

Michaels and I couldn't find her driving for most of a day. If I don't throw caution to the wind and follow her, I may never get the chance to ask her the questions I so desperately need the answers to. Also, I need to find out if she can help connect Michaels to Claire.

I only take a few steps before I trip on God knows what in the dark alley. Madge hears my feet scuffle on the ground, then she takes a few steps back, grabs onto my arm, and leads me further into the darkness. "We're almost there."

A thought enters my mind. What if Mad Madge is leading me to street thugs who'll steal my wallet and beat the shit out of me? It's not like Madge has proven herself to be a trustworthy person, and she has proven to be a thief. This was a bad idea.

"Mind your step," Madge says, then leads me up three short stairs. I have no clue how she's managing to navigate through the darkness because I can't see a thing right now. Then I hear the creak of a doorknob turning, followed by the groan of the door opening and a faint, flickering glow of light spills through the doorway.

The first thing I see is a burner, a large upright grate, and a heater of sorts in the middle of a large trash-filled cement space.

"What is this place?"

"The bottom floor of an old building."

"Close the door." A raspy voice echoes across the room.

I push the door shut and follow Madge toward the light. As I walk, I glance at the walls. On either side of me are people sitting or curled up, with blankets or clothing covering them.

"Do these people live here?" I whisper.

"Some do when security isn't around."

Madge walks over to an old woman sitting not far from the heater. She's just as outlandishly dressed as Madge and around the same age—ancient. Madge holds up the bottle in the paper bag and offers it to the woman.

A few feet over, there's a free space where we sit down. "You see that old broad I gave my booze to?" Madge whispers. "Her name is Lilbit. You could say that she's my student. I'm teaching her how to get a man and how to act and dress."

"Your student?" I say in disbelief.

Madge nods. "Soon, I could have any of the guys in this room eating out of her hand."

I shake off the weirdness. "I only came here with you because I have some questions I need the answers to."

Madge reaches into her pocket and pulls out a McDonald's wrapper with half a cheeseburger in it. But instead of eating it herself, she leans over to the man sitting nearby and hands him the food, then turns her focus back to me. "What do you want to ask me?"

"How did you know what I saw in that alleyway after I drank Warlock's serum, and how did you know about the diary?"

"That's two questions, my friend. Not one. But since I'm in a charitable mood, I will make an exception. The answer to your first question is easy. I see things, and I know things. That's it."

"What do you mean? How is that possible?"

Madge laughs and taps her finger on my temple. "You've got to open your mind without using your brain. As for the second question, a thief always recognizes another thief."

"I'm no thief!"

She smiles. "Did you ask to take that diary, or did you pinch it and hide it in your dirty pockets when no one was looking?"

"That's different than being a thief. I took the damn book because I wanted to see if Kim wrote about the night my daughter died."

"And asking to borrow the diary wasn't an option?"

"You know what, Madge, you're nothing but a—"

Her brows furrow as she speaks through pursed lips, "Be careful, Jude."

I force in a deep breath and count to ten. "I apologize."

"That's better. My answer to your second question is the same one I gave you for your first one. I see things and I know things."

"I did see Little Blue that night, didn't I?"

"Your heart saw her, not your eyes."

"But how could I feel her skin and her hair and hear her speak?"

Madge taps on my temple again.

"Can I see her again? Or, however you want to put it."

Madge smiles. "Yes. But her time is running out, and soon the door will be closed. I do not have the power to connect you to the other world like Warlock does, and he's not always easy to find."

"But you said yourself that you see things and you know things. Can't you connect me to Little Blue?"

Madge shakes her head, "No. Warlock is the portal. It is with his method that the door gets temporarily opened."

"You mean the drugs he uses?"

"The serum is to help you achieve a semi-level of consciousness so that your mind is open to all possibilities, but it's his gift that connects you."

I rub my face and shake my head. If any normal person were overhearing this conversation, they would think I was as nuts as Madge.

"I have one more question for you." I tell her about Chad Michaels and how I met his daughter in the park. Then, I tell her how, two years before that day, I learned that Claire had passed away.

Madge cackles, "You've got it now, boy! I don't know this Claire, but it sounds like she came through the portal at the same time Little Blue did. And from my experience, she will stay near you until she finds the answers she's looking for."

"How is this possible?"

Madge points at her temple and smiles. "Have you seen or heard anything you can't explain since meeting the child in the park?"

I shake my head, then I remember. "I thought maybe I was seeing things."

Madge's eyes widen with interest. "Go on."

I tell her about what I saw in the bathroom mirror, the steam and the shape.

"It's common for spirits to use steam to write or draw messages. She was probably trying to tell you something."

"Tell me something by drawing a snake? How the hell am I supposed to figure out what it means?"

"That's not my problem." She shrugs. "But, if you want to see Little Blue again, I will take you, but I can't guarantee this won't be the last time. And make sure you've got a twenty to give Warlock."

* * *

Once we've navigated out of the dark alley, Madge leads me back to the subway, and after a short ride, we get off at the 52nd Street stop. It's windy, an icy wind that chills my bones for the first time in two years.

I stuff my hands in my pockets and walk in stride with Madge.

"So, Madge. Do you think there's any chance of connecting Chad Michaels with his daughter? He's desperate to see her, and I know he would pay."

"That's not a question for me."

"Maybe I could call Chad now, and he could meet—"

Madge stops walking. "You'll do no such thing. I agreed to help you. I never agreed to help anyone else, so don't push your luck or I'll change my mind."

We walk in silence for three long blocks, giving me time to sort through everything in my head. Madge's mention of seeing and hearing 'things' has stuck with me. For some reason, I believe her. Even though I've been sceptical since that hallucination in the alley, knowing that I did see her and the idea of seeing her again is overwhelming.

We turn down West 50th Street and walk about half a block before turning down an alley. Thankfully, there's a small amount of light shining down from nearby streetlights, and I can see where I'm walking.

Halfway down the alleyway, Madge turns up a narrow cement lane that's only wide enough for us. I look up at the tall brick walls to the sliver of sky above. "How do you know Warlock will be here?"

"Shh."

Eventually, I see the end of the lane ahead, where a small figure sits on what looks to be wooden palettes with a thin blanket over the top. The person keeps their head down until we are almost upon them, then the head slowly raises, revealing first the eyes and then the scruffy gray facial hair of Warlock.

The old man looks at Madge, who looks at me and holds her hand out. It takes me a moment to remember the twenty dollars. After I hand her the bill, she nods at Warlock, who reaches into his coat pocket and pulls out a familiar-looking vial.

For a brief moment, the doctor's words enter my mind. He had warned me about taking the cocktail again, that I was one of the lucky ones who lived.

Warlock leans forward, extending his hand to me. I reach out and take the vial, examining the liquid inside the glass as much as I can in the darkness. "Last time this shit put me in the hospital."

"It won't have the same effect on you now," Warlock says. "The first time is always the worst."

I let out a loud sigh and look at Madge. "It's on your conscience if things go sideways."

She grins mischievously. "Drink it."

"Come to me, Little Blue." I pop the small cork top, then close my eyes and empty the contents of the vial down my throat.

The same acrid taste hits my tastebuds, one I couldn't remember tasting until now. I lean against the wall, drop my chin, and wait, homing in on the distant sounds of the city. It takes several minutes before I start to feel strange, light and hollow. I slowly raise my head to look at Madge and then at Warlock. Both are intensely staring at me.

"You should sit," Warlock says. "In case you get dizzy."

With my back against the wall, I unhook my backpack from my shoulder and let it fall to the ground. Then, I brace my guitar on the wall and slowly slide down until I'm sitting on the cold cement. My throat begins to burn and my head feels heavy, too heavy to hold up. Again, I flop my head forward and stare at the ground.

* * *

My eyes focus on the now steel-gray narrow walls as the air grows dense and smells like rotting animals. In a deep haze, I slowly scan the space around me and catch sight of something purple, the same color as Madge's hat. Then, I see a mess of white next to it—must be Warlock's beard. They didn't leave me this time. They're still here.

"Little Blue, are you here, honey?" My voice is distorted and strange. I focus on my breathing as I wait for any sign of my child. "Where are you? I can't see you." I move forward onto my hands, then turn and use the wall to stand.

Maybe she's not coming this time. Maybe she crossed too far over and can't find her way back. Maybe...

I hear a gurgling noise close by, and I turn to see her, my Little Blue, standing next to me.

She looks different this time. Her skin is glowing white, and her eyes are big and shiny black with dark circles underneath. Her once-gleaming hair is frazzled and wild. But I don't care; she's here. My daughter is here. I reach for her. "Come here. Let me touch you."

But she doesn't step closer. Instead, she stares forward as if she's looking right through me.

"Little Blue, it's me, Dad."

Then, as if on a mechanical hinge, her mouth opens wide, very wide, revealing a dark, endless hole. I stare in shock into her gaping mouth. Then I see something moving, her tongue waving back and forth, or...

I gasp loudly when I see the jet-black head and shiny black eyes. Slowly, the creature inches out of my daughter's mouth until it slides past her lips lands with a thud at her feet and slithers away.

Little Blue closes her mouth and tilts her head, finally seeing me, though her eyes are still hollow and black. "Daddy. Is it really you?" She lunges toward me and into my arms. "I've missed you so much. Why did it take you so long to come back?"

"I'm sorry, Little Blue. I had some trouble, but I'm here now."

"I kept thinking that I would never see you again, and it broke my heart. Especially after Claire said she saw you and got to spend time with you. I was so jealous, Dad, it made me crazy."

I move my head back so I can look into her dark eyes. "A little girl named Claire. You saw her?"

Little Blue scowls. "I didn't have a choice. She kept following me, and I couldn't get away from her."

"Where is she now?"

Little Blue looks more annoyed. "Why? Aren't you here to see me?"

"I am, but that little girl's father misses her badly. She died when she was just—"

"Five. I know. She keeps repeating that over and over. It's not that I don't like her. I do. It's just that she's hard to be around sometimes."

"What do you mean?"

"She has temper tantrums when I won't do what she wants, and she is very impatient."

"I know. But she's just a kid. You were headstrong, too, when you were her age."

Little Blue grins for a brief moment. "I guess so, but you wouldn't be so understanding if you were in my shoes. Especially when she starts chanting those annoying words over and over."

"Chanting?'

"Kind of, yeah. She skips along behind me wherever I go, saying "Big Time, Big Time," over and over."

"Just brush it off. She's a kid. Try to remember that she lost her parents, the same as they lost her. I'm not sure why she's attached herself to you, Little Blue. Maybe it's because you have a kind heart, and she feels safe with you."

"I know, Dad. I'm good to her, I promise. But that doesn't take away the fact that she's super annoying."

"Do you see your mom still?"

Little Blue frowns. "Not as much. Like I told you before, she's always on a little hill waving for me to come to her."

"Why don't you go to her?"

"I told you already—if I do, I won't be able to see you anymore. I've seen a lot of people disappear over that hill. People I never see again."

I sigh, feeling selfish. I want her to be happy and with Kim, but I also don't want to lose her again.

"I see Mom crying a lot, but I'm not sure why. Maybe it's because I won't go to her."

"Maybe it's time you do, sweetie." I have to force the words out. "You look different now than you did the last time we met. You look like you're getting sick. I'm sure that if you went with your mom, things would be better, and I bet there wouldn't be any more snakes either."

Little Blue shrugs. "It's a funny thing about them snakes. I never see them until I come to see you. And as far as I can tell, no other person where I am has had problems with them."

"I don't know why they are around you either. I haven't solved much since you've been gone, have I?"

She wraps her arms around my neck and kisses my cheek with her icy cold lips. "It's okay. I know how much you love me. But I do worry about you."

"You don't need to worry about me. I'm fine."

"Do you think you'll have more kids now that I'm gone? If you do, I hope you don't forget me."

I pull her close and gently run my fingers through her now-coarse hair. "I'm not planning on having more children, but if I did, nothing could ever change how I feel about you. Remember, I am always yours, and you are always mine. And since the day you were born, I promised that we are forever connected to each other."

She smiles for a moment while looking into my eyes. Then, a look of sadness comes over her. "I should go now, Dad. If I stay here too long, I start to feel weak."

I reach out and touch her freezing hand. "I wish you didn't have to go."

"Me too, Dad." She turns away.

"Wait, Little Blue. I need to ask you something."

When she turns and faces me, I see tears in her eyes and my heart sinks.

"I need you to try and remember the man who was near you on the night you died. Are you sure about the tattoo of a snake on his arm? Could it have been something else?"

"It was a snake, Dad. Just like I told you."

As I watch her take a few steps away, a light mist begins to seep through the narrow brick walls, slowly filling the alley. I close my eyes, avoiding the pain of watching her leave me.

# Chapter 14

"Hey, mister, are you okay?"

A strong urge to puke rises from my gut as the words pierce through my aching head. Willing my eyes to open a slit, I focus on two elderly women wearing soft-colored outfits standing over me.

"Do you want us to get you some help?" one of the ladies asks.

"No," I groan, fearing another ride in an ambulance and an uncomfortable confrontation at the hospital.

"Are you a street busker?" the other woman asks.

"A what?"

"Your guitar. Are you a street musician?"

Using all my strength, I slowly sit up and see my backpack and guitar beside me. "No, I'm not. Thank you, ladies. I must've fallen asleep here, is all."

"Do you know someone who lives here?" the old woman asks.

I look around and realize I've woken up on the same white stairs in front of the same high-rise apartment after taking Warlock's potion the first time. How the hell do I keep ending up here?

I grab onto the railing and pull myself to a standing position. "Thanks for your concern, ladies. I'm feeling wide awake now."

After giving suspicious looks, the women shuffle up the walkway. I sit back down on the steps and strain to remember how I got here again. But I'm drawing a blank.

Just then, a young guy carrying a parcel walks up the stairs toward the entrance.

"Excuse me," I ask, "but do you know what time it is?"

"Seven," he says, barely looking at me.

Shit! I have to work for Lauren's father at the firm this morning. I feel for my wallet and my phone, which—luckily—I still have in my jacket pocket. I slide my phone out and sigh. Lauren is going to be disappointed that I didn't show up at her place and didn't even call, but right now, I have no idea where I am in conjunction with her place. I need her help, otherwise, I'll never make it to work on time.

I dial the number and do my best to regain my wits.

"Jude. Where have you been? Are you okay?"

I clear my throat so I don't sound as raspy. "I'm fine. It was a strange night and...well, I'll tell you all about it when I see you."

I tell her that I'm kind of lost and need a ride. She asks me to find what street I'm on and the closest building address. I tell her I'll find out and then text her. As soon as I end the call, I see the delivery guy who gave me the time walking down the stairs without the package.

"Hey, I'm sorry to bother you again, but would you possibly know what street we're on?"

The guy looks at me in disbelief. "125 Greenwich Street." He shakes his head as he walks past.

I text Lauren the info, straighten my shirt and do my best to finger-comb my hair. I probably look as bad as I feel. As I wait, I reflect on the last thing I remember, and my heart begins to ache. The snake, like a scene from a horror movie. How it slithered out of my child's black, cavernous mouth. And she looked—awful, ghoulish. Her eyes were empty and dark, and her skin was white as snow and just as cold. But it was her, her essence, her spirit. It was her.

I smile as a tear rolls down my cheek. If I was given the chance, I would've gone with her and left everything behind. All of the pain, the disappointments, the guilt and the sorrow.

I take in a deep breath. If I'm going to see Lauren, I have to get it together. I wipe my cheek, straighten my shoulders and stand up to watch for her car.

Thankfully, my clarity and strength are returning quickly. I'm not sure if I've built up a tolerance to the drug or if Warlock lessened the strength, but whatever the reason, I'm glad I'm not in the same rough shape I was the last time.

As I wait, I look up at the building. The shiny, clean windows on every floor. Why here? Why, when I've seen Little Blue, do I end up on these same steps at the same address?

A white Rolls Royce pulls up, and I step to the side of the stairs. I don't want any more people looking down at me and thinking I'm a busker or, worse, homeless. I hope I have enough time to shower and clean up at Lauren's before I have to be at work. Thankfully, she makes her coffee strong.

The car door opens just as a wave of dizziness hits, and I turn my back to the stairs to hang on to the rail. The car's passengers walk up the stairs, and from what I can hear, one is an older man with a gruff voice, and the other is a younger woman. When I know they've climbed past me on the stairs, I turn and sneak a look. The man is wearing a dark blue tailored suit, modern and pressed, whereas the woman—who, from the back, has a young, athletic body and golden hair tied in a low ponytail—is wearing a form-fitted black dress suitable for a strip club.

The man kisses the young woman when they reach the entrance doors, says, "I'll see you tonight," slaps her on the ass, then turns to walk back down the stairs. It's only a fragment of a second that I see his profile before I turn around, but something about him is strangely familiar.

I listen to the sound of his shiny Italian shoes as he walks past me and gets into the back of the car. After a moment, I watch as the car pulls away from the curb.

Ten minutes later, Lauren pulls up and taps on the horn. I let go of the rail and bend down to grab my pack and guitar, and my head starts to spin. Thankfully, I'm able to right myself and make it to the car. Once my things are in the back, I get into the passenger seat and look at Lauren's concerned face. "You look rundown. Are you okay?"

"I'll be fine. I just had a bit of a crazy night. I'll tell you later—I really need to have a shower, and if you have any of that strong coffee, that would be great."

* * *

No hangover I've ever had compares to how awful I feel as I step into the elevator, clutching my stomach and struggling to keep from throwing up. I would call in sick, but after learning that Lawrence Banks was at the penthouse when my daughter died, my need to uncover more details outweighs how I'm feeling.

Lauren insisted on driving me to work and said she'd come back to pick me up when I'm done. She's a beautiful person, someone whom I want to get to know a lot better. That being said, after the talk we're supposed to have later, she'll probably think I'm nuts and won't want to see me anymore.

When the elevator door opens, I see Mabel, the senior secretary, behind her desk. She looks up from her computer and waves me over. When I reach the counter, she hands me a small piece of paper with a list of tasks—ladies' bathroom sink leaking, fix table leg in boardroom, change vent filters. "Everything you'll need should be in the utility room down the hall." She points with the end of her pen. "Mr. Banks said that you can leave once you're finished."

I begin with the table issue in the boardroom, a spacious room lined with windows. At the front is a long table where the top executives likely sit, and in front of it are several smaller tables arranged in a classroom setup. I'm moving each table to locate the wobbly one when a man with a broom comes into the room. He wears a long blue shirt with the words janitor over one pocket and Brags over the other.

He looks like a character you might find in a book set in the deep South, a lanky hillbilly with a mullet and patchy facial stubble. "Hi. Are you new?" he asks, pushing the broom closer.

I nod. "My name is Jude. And you're Brags, I presume."

"That's me."

Though he doesn't speak with a drawl, he's friendly and laid back like people from the South. Every time he speaks, he stops sweeping and rests his hands on the top of the broom. He says he's worked as a janitor at the firm for the past five years and has learned a lot about how the other half lives. When I ask him what he means, he says, "I've seen all sorts of things go on here that wouldn't go on at, say, a government office."

Here's my chance to lift the rug on this place. I turn the table on its end and unscrew the wobbly leg. "That's interesting." I keep my voice nonchalant. "What kind of things?"

He steps closer and lowers his voice. "Picture the hottest girl you've ever seen, then take a few years off her age, add jewels and fake lips and boobs. That's the kind of women I've seen at boardroom parties."

"Interesting." I shrug. "There are a lot of wild lawyers working here, sounds like. Do you know any of them personally?"

Brags scoffs. "Yeah, right. As if any of them would want anything to do with a bottom feeder like me. They drive pricey cars to work. I drive a moped."

I nod understandably. "So, most of the lawyers are younger, tattoo-loving kind of guys?"

"Yeah, most are younger, except our boss, Mr. Banks. But he gets his share, too."

I nod. "I bet you could write a book about working here."

"I could. But I wouldn't. I'd have to be pretty stupid to tell stories about lawyers who belong to one of the most powerful firms."

"I guess that's true. Nevertheless, you're an interesting guy to talk to." I'm trying to stroke his ego.

Brags resumes sweeping as I assess the table leg. He asks me where I'm from, and what brought me to work here. I answer with just enough information to satisfy him. Then, as subtle as I can, I ask another question.

"I bet you've seen a lot of stars come through the office, considering this law firm caters to celebrities like Chad Michaels."

His face turns excited. "Just last week, I saw Chad Michaels in this very room."

"Wow! That's incredible! I love his music. Anyone else?"

"Too many to remember. A lot of times, the lawyers leave with the stars, too. They go to big parties to hobnob with them. Lucky buggers."

"When they had parties here, did you see if any of these lawyers had tattoos?"

I realize how odd this sounds and think up a story fast. "I know it's a weird question, but I'm an aspiring tattoo artist, and I always wondered what kind of ink rich lawyer types are into. I'd love to work on people who actually want to spend the money on quality—it's my target market once I get my business off the ground." I hope I sound convincing.

Brags stops sweeping and leans on the broom. "I'd have to think on that. Usually, the lawyers wear long sleeves but sometimes I've seen them roll them up, especially if they're partying on a Friday night. What kind of tattoos do you draw?"

"Snakes, mostly. Sometimes, I draw dragons, too. Let me know if you remember any tattoos, especially snakes. Then I'll know if I'm on the right track with my drawings."

"Fair enough. I'll rack my brain. I've got a couple tats myself. Most of them have gone blue from age and because my cousin used cheap ink."

I ask if his cousin is a tattooist, too, and he shakes his head. "Naw, but he did a lot of tats in jail. He's pretty good, actually."

Brags pulls his shirt up and reveals a mess of faded green on his stomach. He tells me the picture was supposed to be of his late dog, a pug, but ended up looking more like an old woman. I turn my face away just in case I laugh.

When I'm finished rethreading the table leg, Brags helps me turn the table upright. "I may not have as much money as these big lawyers, but I saved a few bucks. If you want, you can tattoo a snake on me for practice."

He's a sweet man. Not the brightest bulb, but he's kind and seems genuine. He would never suggest I tattoo him if he only knew how poorly I draw.

* * *

Waiting in the lobby for Lauren's car to pull up, I reflect on my first shift working at the firm. My tasks were easy, and everyone was friendly, but the biggest bonus of the morning was meeting Brags, who hopefully will prove useful in gaining information about the lawyers at the firm.

Lauren pulls up, and I get in.

"How was it?" Lauren asks, looking pleased to see me.

I tell her the short version—how straightforward my duties were and that I met the janitor. Lauren then tells me a surprising story about Brags. "He was a patient at the hospital who'd suffered a major head wound from a motorbike accident. After he finished rehab, he lived at a halfway house and was put in a work program my father sponsors. Anyway, my dad gave him a job, and he's been working at the firm ever since. His real name is Bradley, but when he suffered his head injury, he couldn't say his name. When he tried, it came out as *Brags*. Even though his speech is better now, the name kind of stuck."

"I'm amazed. I mean, he looked a bit different, but I never would've guessed he had brain damage. Does he still live in a halfway house?"

249

"No. A number of years ago, my father rented him an apartment, and continues to pay his rent as long as Brags works at the firm."

"That is very cool of your dad." Lawrence came off as a bit of an egotistical prick on our first meeting, but maybe I was wrong about him.

"Did you see my father this morning? Sometimes, he sleeps at the office on the lounge sofa when he's working on a big case. My mom said he's spending more and more time there. As much as we have our issues, I do have respect for his work ethic."

"I didn't see your dad."

She looks at me perplexed. "That's strange. I spoke with my mom this morning, and apparently he'd said he was staying at the office last night because he had an overseas video call early this morning."

I don't want to concern her, so I try to smooth things over. "I don't think I went into his office at all, so he very well could've been in there,"

Her expression relaxes. "Yeah, it's a big office, that's for sure. It's easy to miss someone."

I nod.

As soon as we open the door to Lauren's apartment, a rich aroma fills the air. My first guess is pot roast or stew. "You cook?" I ask, kicking off my shoes.

Lauren shrugs. "I wouldn't say that I'm a cook, I'm more of a dabbler."

On my way to the sofa, I breathe deeply through my nose. The smell reminds me of growing up at home, where we didn't have much money, but my mom made the best comfort food from what we had.

"It's stew," Lauren says, grabbing a couple of bowls from the cupboard. I get up to help set the table, and when she turns, she bangs into me.

"Sorry. I just thought maybe you needed a hand setting the table and—"

Holding the dishes, she looks up at me, smiles, and softly presses her lips against mine. As we kiss, I gently take the bowls from her hands and set them on the counter. Wrapping my arms around her tiny waist, I pull her close. The kiss and embrace send a wave of electricity through me, not sexually, but in a magical, almost surreal way, like two powerful magnets coming together. She pulls her head away slightly and whispers, "The stew."

* * *

I can smell the sea tonight and feel the Atlantic breeze sweeping through the city. Lauren offered to drive me to work at Skully's, but I don't want to get too used to accepting rides from her; I don't want her to feel like I'm taking advantage.

As I walk toward the bus stop, for the first time in two years, I'm thinking about buying a car—granted, a beat-up one within my budget—so I'm not always stuck on the loser cruiser. If I'm going to be spending a lot of time with Lauren, she deserves a guy who's got his act together.

Once I'm seated at the back of the bus, I text Lauren and thank her for the great meal. She replies with a lips emoji.

I smile and scroll through my messages. There's one from Michaels and one from a number I don't recognize informing me that I have been hacked and that my credit card is being charged. Please click this link ASAP to fix it. I block the number, then read Michael's message: "Hi, it's me, Chad. If you have a moment, I need to speak with you." It was sent an hour ago while I was having dinner with Lauren. I get so wrapped up in the moment with her that I barely notice my phone.

I call Michaels and press the phone tightly to my ear, trying to hear him over the noisy sounds of the bus. "Hi, Chad. How are you doing?"

"It's nothing a few pain pills won't fix," he chuckles. "I think it helps that I don't have to deal with anyone nagging at me while I'm healing."

"What do you mean?"

"My girlfriend, Holly, left me. She said it was because I'm still not over my wife and that if I really cared, I would've called her when I decided to leave the hospital. She's probably right. She was beautiful, but I think

I was more attracted to the idea of having someone to come home to."

Normally, I couldn't relate. I've been a dedicated hermit. But now Lauren is in my life, and even though the relationship is new, I can't imagine how crappy it would feel to be back at my apartment alone.

"So anyway, Jude, I was wondering if you ran into that crazy old lady since I last saw you."

As much as I don't want to lie to the guy, I also don't want to tell him that Madge wasn't interested in helping anyone but me. I'd rather wait until I see Madge again and try and talk her into introducing Michaels to Warlock. "My phone is breaking up, I'm on the bus. Can I call you tomorrow?"

Michaels sighs. "Alright. I'll speak to you then."

After ending the call, I lean back in the seat and exhale in relief. My heart aches for him; I understand his pain. As irrational as it may seem to believe in warlocks, ghosts, and spiritual connections, grief can cloud your rational thinking and make you receptive to all kinds of possibilities. I can't imagine anyone not wanting to see a deceased loved one, especially after losing a child.

As the bus heads toward Hell's Kitchen, I close my eyes and recall my last encounter with Little Blue. I'm positive that she really appeared, and despite Lauren's doubts about the reality of seeing my daughter, I know this time it was real.

* * *

Skully's towel-saving system seems to be working, which is apparent when I walk past his office and look at the clipboard on the door. There are dozens of people who signed the paper after borrowing a gym towel. As quirky as old Skully is, I have to admit, he may have solved the towel issue.

Thanks to the odd text back and forth with Lauren, my shift goes by fast, and before I know it, Skully and I are locking up and heading home.

Outside, Skully asks if I want a lift to the subway, and I'm just about to answer him when I glance across the street and notice Lauren waving at me from her car window. I smile, say good night to the old man, and then walk across the road to Lauren's car. Skully hollers out from behind, "Way to go, kid."

Once we're at the apartment, we bypass the living room and head straight to bed. Usually, at Lauren's, I take off my shirt and sleep uncomfortably in my jeans, but tonight, she tells me that the jeans feel rough against her skin, so I might as well take them off. She crawls in and snuggles up to me, skin to skin. I want her, but I'm exhausted and don't want to make love when I'm not awake enough to appreciate every moment.

# Chapter 15

Awakened by a whistling sound and a chilling breeze, I glance at the digital clock on the bedside table: it's 4 AM. Assuming Lauren might have accidentally left a window open, I quietly get out of bed, careful not to disturb her. I tiptoe to the living room and find the open window. A cold gust hits my bare chest, making me shiver.

After closing the window, I exhale and see my breath puff out. As I turn to head back to bed, I hear footsteps and feel guilty for waking Lauren.

But when I return to the bedroom, I see Lauren sound asleep. An eerie feeling settles over me. I sit on the edge of the bed, scanning the room before accepting that I must have just imagined the noises or heard the tenant next door moving around. I slip into bed, gently resting my head on the pillow as Lauren shifts closer, nestling her head on my chest and draping her arm across my stomach.

I'm just drifting off when I feel the icy chill return. That damn window! But how? I closed it tightly and fastened the latch.

I have to be up for work in a few hours, but Lauren could catch a chill if I don't deal with the window. Slowly and meticulously, I lift Lauren's hand off my stomach, then slide out of bed. With my eyes barely open, I walk into the living room and over to the open window. When I shut it this time, I make sure the latch is closed correctly. Just as I turn to go back to bed, I catch something: a figure moving in the corner chair.

I'm staring, trying to focus when suddenly, the figure stands up and slowly floats toward me. A blast of icy cold wind rushes through the room, and my eyes dart quickly to the window, open again. I look back at the figure, frozen in fear and disbelief as it gets closer.

When it passes through a thin beam of light coming through the window, I see the face, a child's face, pale as the snow and framed by black hair cut into a bob.

"Don't be scared, Jude." The haunting voice echoes through the room.

"Claire?" I whisper.

The ghostly child nods.

"Why are you here?"

"You are Little Blue's daddy."

I nod. "Yes. Did she ask you to tell me something?"

"No, silly. I came here to tell you a secret."

"A secret. Okay. You can tell me."

"I'm not a ghost, you know. I'm just a kid. If I were a ghost, I'd be scared of myself because ghosts scare me."

I feel my fear vanishing. "I understand. Do you want to tell me your secret?"

She nods, then frowns. "I do want to tell you, but it makes me very sad and angry when I think of it."

"Maybe if you tell me, it will help, and you won't have to feel that way anymore."

She looks at me and tilts her head, confused. "You don't make sense."

She's wearing the same red outfit and shiny black shoes she wore that day at the park. She fidgets uncomfortably with the hem of her dress. "It's about my mommy."

"Your mommy? Is she in your world with you?"

"No, silly. My mommy lives in this world but she's very sad all the time. When I'm allowed, I go to see her, and sometimes, when I'm there, she goes to her bed and cries all night. Sometimes, when she cries, she holds my picture. My daddy does that too, but not as much as Mommy does."

"I'm sure your parents miss you very much."

"They miss me because I'm special."

I smile. "Yes, Claire. Of course, you are. Now, what's your secret?"

She sighs and fidgets once again. "It's about a bad man who hurt my mommy when my daddy was singing at the studio."

"A bad man? Do you remember his name?"

She shakes her head in disappointment. "No. But he let me play with the snake drawing on his arm."

"A snake drawing? Where on his arm was it?"

Claire points to my forearm. "There."

"Do you remember what he did to your mommy that hurt her while your daddy was recording?"

"Yes. He took my mommy and me out for ice cream. Then we stopped at his home on the way back to see my daddy."

I'm afraid to learn more, but I need to know if there's something I can do to help her. And I can't help but focus on the snake tattoo. "Okay, go on."

Claire tells me that a man who knew her daddy very well took her mom and her to his place. While they were there, the man took Claire's mom to a back room. "I heard my Mommy saying 'stop' but the man wouldn't. I was crying and banging on the door, but it was locked. I was very scared."

I take a deep breath and exhale. "I'm so sorry that happened."

Claire looks up at me with furrowed brows. "I hate him for what he did."

"Did you ever talk to your daddy about what happened?"

She shakes her head and sniffs, though I can't see any tears. "When the man had my mommy in the room, I heard him say that if she told anyone, the man would hurt my daddy. And after my mom came out of that room, she took me to the bathroom with her and told me to never ever tell daddy. Then she wiped our faces, and the man drove us back to my daddy's studio. After what happened to my Mommy, I got very sick, and I had to stay in the hospital. My mommy and daddy don't live in the same house anymore."

My guts wrench for the child. I wonder if Michaels ever found out what happened.

"Who are you talking to?"

I turn abruptly. Lauren is standing in the doorway, rubbing her eyes.

I look back at Claire. She's gone, and the room feels warm and still. "I just got up to close the window."

"What do you mean?" Lauren sounds confused. "The windows don't open in the living room. They never have. They were painted over years ago, and now they're permanently stuck."

I look, and sure enough, the window is closed tightly.

"I must've dreamt it was open," I say, thinking quickly. "Let's go back to bed."

* * *

My head spins that morning as I try to process my sudden meeting with Claire. Given everything that's happened lately, I

259

don't question what I saw. Little Blue is real, or at least her ghost is, and so is Claire.

The snake can't be a coincidence. The man who hurt Claire's mother must be the same man who caused my child's death. There has to be that connection—why else would Claire be linked to Little Blue in the spirit world and now to me in the real one?

I feel terrible for Claire, hearing her mother being abused. What a horrible burden for a child to bear. I'm not sure what I can do to help her find peace. All I have to go on is a man with a snake tattoo on his forearm.

"Hey man, how goes the battle?" Brags walks into the bathroom, where I'm changing a lightbulb.

"All good. How's your day?"

He looks at his watch and smiles. "Almost over." As he props the door open and grabs a mop and bucket, I notice his physical disability, a sort of limp which I hadn't picked up on before.

Brags rambles on about the weather and how he's saving for a new Vespa. Then, out of nowhere, he whispers, "Do you remember when you asked about the lawyers who work here and if any have a snake tattoo?"

I finish with the light bulb and face him. "Of course. Why? Did you find out something?"

Brags grins proudly. "There's a junior lawyer they call Michael Fedora because he always wears a brimmed hat. He spilled his coffee in the lunchroom this morning. When I went to mop it up, he bent down to wipe off his shoe, and I noticed a squiggly line on his arm that looked like a snake's tail. When I asked to see his tattoo, he refused and went back to his office. I don't think he likes me much."

My heart is hammering. "Interesting. Do you think he goes to a lot of celebrity client parties with Mr. Banks?"

Brags nods. "I've seen him leave the office with celebrities, along with Mr. Banks and a few others. He's a real party type, especially on Fridays in the boardroom. His is always the loudest voice in the room."

"Is Michael Fedora here right now?"

Brags shakes his head, "No. I saw him leave about an hour ago. But he's here a lot, so I'm sure you'll meet him."

"Thanks, Brags. I appreciate your help."

I'm excited about what Brags told me. Any lead is better than none. When I'm finished working, I walk past the front desks on my way to the elevator, but Mabel stops me. "Jude, are you going anywhere near Greenwich Street?" She picks up a small box and places it on the counter. "I was supposed to send this out today, but I plumb forgot."

The street name sounds familiar, and I glance at the box and see the full address. Holly Scott—name doesn't ring a bell—Apt 2011, 125 Greenwich Street. I suddenly realize that it's the same building whose stairs I woke up on twice after seeing Little Blue.

"You'd be saving my butt," Mabel adds.

* * *

I've never approached the white steps from this direction before, so I have to read the address on the buildings to make sure I'm in the right place. But as soon as I see the white steps and the railing, I remember.

I'm not sure why I thought this was a smart idea. It's not like I was just going to show up here, and answers about why I was brought to this place twice will suddenly fall into my lap. I guess I was just hoping for some kind of break-through or sign.

Maybe I will see the same Rolls on the street. Even though I never got a good look at the driver, I'm positive I've seen him somewhere before. But then again, if he was rich enough to afford such a pricey vehicle, I might've seen him on TV or something.

I read the name on the package again: Holly Scott, Apt 2011. As I take the first step, I hear a man and woman arguing in the distance. I climb a few more steps to see over a bush and spot a grey-haired man and a younger woman walking quickly on the sidewalk toward me, engaged in what looks like a heated argument.

Instead of minding my own business and continuing up the stairs, I stay put and watch the duo as they quickly approach.

Both are too engrossed in arguing to see me watching them as they hurry up the walkway. It's only when they get to about fifteen feet from the stairs that I recognise the couple. It's the same people I saw getting out of the white Rolls.

I only saw the side of the man's face then, but now, I see him clearly. It's Lawrence Banks.

Before I know it, they're walking up the steps. I don't want him to see me, but there's no chance I'll get away unnoticed. Panicking, I look down at my shoe, place the parcel on the step and fiddle with my laces, obscuring my face.

"I haven't been with anyone but you, and you know it," I hear the woman say.

"Nobody makes a fool of me. Definitely not some ex-stripper from the Bronx."

The energy between them is intense, and I can feel the negativity as they walk past. I exhale a sigh of relief when I hear them continue moving, and then they suddenly stop. Slowly, I hear one set of footsteps walk back down the steps and then stop beside me. I hear him breathe and can tell he's looking at me, studying me.

"Look, Holly. You've got a package."

Damn it! I forgot about her name written in bold letters and in plain view on the box I'd set down beside me. Knowing I'm busted, I slowly stand and face a very angry-faced Lawrence.

We stare at one another for several of the most uncomfortable moments of my life. Finally, I lean down, pick up the box, and offer it to him. "Hi. I was asked to deliver this to a Holly Scott." I smile sheepishly.

He stares for a few more moments, expressionless, until the woman, Holly, calls out, "Are you coming?"

A broad, slow grin spreads across his face. "Thanks, Jude. I'll make sure she gets it." He then places a finger over his lips, signaling me not to say a word, and carries the package to the doorway. "Look, I bought you something. It was supposed to get here before now."

I quickly head down the stairs and, without glancing back, hurry up the street.

I get on the first bus I see and find a seat by the window. Looking out at the busy traffic, people and streets, I struggle to make sense of everything.

It's obvious that Lawrence is cheating on his wife with a mistress, and knows I've seen them together. This is not good. If I'm honest with Lauren, she'll be devastated and will tell her mother, who will also be devastated. But if I say nothing, then I am betraying the one person who is managing to pull me out of my depression, who showed me I'm still capable of having true feelings. No matter which way I decide to go with this, it doesn't end well.

Why is it that whenever something wonderful happens in your life, an equally powerful but negative force seems to try to destroy it?



A mouth-watering aroma of leftover stew and baked goods fills the apartment.

"How was your shift?" Lauren says softly.

"Great, everything is perfect." Of course, it is, and here's me with this dark, devastating secret gnawing at my guts. I force my best fake smile, then walk up and pull her close.

"I had a great day too. A little weird, but great." She smiles, then hands me a full bowl.

"Why was it weird?" I say, sitting at the table.

She sits across from me and shrugs. "I was on Broadway at a music store, and on my way out, I saw an elderly homeless man crouched against the wall of the building. I asked him if he needed help, and he mumbled something, so I called for an ambulance and sat with him until they got there."

"That's sad. Was he okay?"

She frowns and shakes her head. "Unfortunately not. By the time the paramedics got to him, he was already gone."

I reach over and touch her hand. "I'm sorry you had to see that, but it was very cool of you to try to help him. But, you're right, that was a weird experience."

"Unfortunately, homeless people die every day in New York. It's tragic but a sad reality. That wasn't the weird part."

"Okay. What was?"

"There was a homeless woman who showed up not long after the police arrived, and the paramedics covered him with a sheet. One of the officers noticed the woman standing by the dead man, so he asked her if she knew him. From what I overheard, she said she knew of him and that his name was Warlock."

I barely choke down the food in my mouth. "Warlock?"

"Can you believe it? Didn't you say that there was a street guy you met, the one that gave you a vial of drugs, whose name was Warlock as well?" I slowly nod. Lauren shrugs. "It must be a popular name for con men on the street. Still, it was very sad."

I put my spoon down and fold my arms on the table. "You mentioned a woman who spoke to the cops. Did you happen to catch her name?"

She looks at me quizzically. "No, why?"

"Maybe it was the same duo. You never know."

"I doubt it. There are thousands of homeless. The odds are too great."

"True." I try to act indifferent. "But just as a process of elimination, what did she look like?"

"Well, she was interesting, that's for sure." Lauren giggles. "I don't think she was too worried about dressing to impress. I love colorful people, and believe me, she was colorful. She was wearing an oversized neon mu-mu and red socks that came up to her knees, and to top it off, a bright purple hat with a long feather sticking out the side. She was sweet, though. She told me I was beautiful and that I looked smart."

My eyes widen. She's described Mad Madge perfectly, so it had to be the same 'Warlock' as her. But what were they doing on Broadway? That's a hell of a jaunt from Hell's Kitchen, especially considering how decrepit the old man was.

I look down at my food and pick up my spoon, attempting to hide my shock. As I slowly eat, I can't help but think of what this means for me and future visits with Little Blue. Madge didn't have the ability to connect me to my daughter. Only Warlock did. Now he's gone. Does that mean that any chance of me seeing Little Blue again died with him? But maybe Madge knows someone else who creates the serum that Warlock gave me to help me see my child again. I swallow hard. I hope that Madge didn't disappear now that Warlock is gone. I have no idea how close the two were.

"Wait. I do remember something else about the woman. She mentioned that she was from Florida and had only been in New York for a few months. She was complaining about the difference in weather."

I breathe a slight sigh of relief. Madge told me she was born and raised in New York. "What color was her hair?"

Lauren thinks for a moment. "Blond, like a natural blonde, and very stringy."

Thank God. There's no way that Madge's hair could be mistaken as any other color than flaming red, and her hair was bushy and fuzzy. I grin. "It doesn't sound like the same woman I met. So, tell me, what were you doing at the music store?"

She smiles and motions to the loveseat, where my guitar is resting on a cushion. "I went and bought you some new strings. Yours were looking pretty old."

The rest of the night goes by too quickly, with Lauren sitting across from me on the sofa and me playing her some of my original songs. Surprisingly, I manage to get through each tune relatively smoothly, considering how long it's been since I've put this much time into playing.

In bed, I can feel her pressing against me, clearly wanting more, but the stillness of the room lets my mind wander through the day's chaos. My thoughts churn—Michael Fedora, the lawyer with a snake tattoo; catching Lauren's father with another woman at the same building where I woke up after a drug-induced haze, thanks to Warlock; and the shocking news of Warlock's death, found far from where he was supposed to be, and discovered by Lauren. My mind feels like a mass of tangled strings. No matter how hard I try to process everything, I'm overwhelmed and a world away from making sense of it all.

* * *

Morning breaks, and a bright sunbeam illuminates Lauren's face, making her appear ethereal as she lies motionless beside me. She is everything good and pure, and I am the darkness, dragging weighted baggage and bad news behind me. I don't deserve a woman like her, and if I were a better man, I would walk away before her feelings deepen, only I can't. I am too selfish to let her go.

# Chapter 16

The clock reads 7 AM, and I am scheduled to work at the firm, but how can I show my face there after what I saw? If Lawrence is at work, I'll be setting myself up for confrontation.

But how do I get out of it? Lauren got me the job, and if I bow out without reason, she'll think I'm ungrateful, and she'll lose respect for me. With everything else going on, I'm not sure I could handle that.

As soon as I move my leg, intending to slip out of bed undetected, Lauren wakes and looks at me. "Are you getting up for work?"

I wrap my arm around her and squeeze. "Actually, I was thinking I could stay here with you, then later catch a show or something."

She smiles and tells me she has to meet with Jan at the hospital in a couple of hours. "Besides, you don't want to take a day off work yet, do you?"

Desperately. "No, I was just kidding."

After a few more minutes of cuddling, Lauren heads to the bathroom for a shower while I lie in bed, growing increasingly anxious about the probability of a confrontation with Lawrence.

* * *

After I kiss Lauren and thank her for the ride—the hospital is close by—I wait for her to drive away before turning to face the building that used to captivate me. Its once-beautiful glass now appears dark, reflecting the turbulent gray sky and giving the building the illusion of an ominous, shadowy tower. Swallowing hard, I reluctantly enter the lobby and walk to the gold bank of elevators.

When the metal doors open, Mabel is the first person I see. I smile at her, but she doesn't return the sentiment. She's probably heard that Lawrence intercepted the delivery of the box and was undoubtedly reprimanded for not getting the parcel delivered through commercial channels on time. This means Lawrence is most likely here—not good.

Mabel slides a piece of paper toward me without making eye contact. Fix blinds in the boardroom, check crown molding in lunchroom. It sounds like an easy enough shift, provided I don't run into Lawrence. Though, I wouldn't mind bumping into Michael Fedora to sniff out what I can about the supposed snake tattoo.

I start in the boardroom and re-adjust a few slats on the long blinds. It was that

271

easy—can't these people do anything themselves?

Next, I head to the lunchroom to check the moulding issue. I laugh when I see a tiny nail sticking out of the corner piece. Nothing one whack with a hammer won't fix. I'm just entering the storeroom to get the tool belt when I look across the hall and see Lawrence's door open. I try to hurry past him undetected, but then— "Jude. Can I see you in my office?"

Shit! I can almost taste the impending doom in the air. This can't end well. From the time it takes to walk from his doorway to the chair in front of his desk, I decide to respond to whatever he has to say as if nothing has happened.

"Have a seat." He motions to the chair, then sits behind the desk and leans forward with his hands folded in front of him. "Are you liking working here?"

I nod and try to sound cheerful. "The few people I've met here seem nice, and I haven't had any issues with the work."

He nods. I can tell he's putting on a front, like me.

"Is there something you want to talk to me about?"

He grins. "You said you work at a boxing gym in the evenings, right? Skully's, is it?"

I'm confused by this change of topic. "Yes."

"What's the old guy like?"

"He's great," I say, not understanding the point of this.

"How great? He's like a father to you?"

I shrug. "I suppose. Like a secondary father, I guess." I'm starting to feel a little defensive. Why the hell is he asking about Skully?

"About our little surprise meeting yesterday." He raps his fingertips on the desk. "You haven't mentioned that to anyone, have you?"

I shake my head.

Lawrence leans back in his chair and exhales a sigh of relief. "That's good, Jude. We need to keep it that way. Do you comprehend?"

"Sure."

"These matters can be sensitive, and if my little secret got out, it could hurt a lot of people. Mainly me. It would cost me, and I hate nothing more than parting with my money. I'm sure you understand."

Actually, no. You smug bastard, how the hell could I understand? I'm not a cheat, and I'm not rich. I nod. "No problem."

"Good." He stands, then walks around the desk and pats me on the shoulder hard. "Just remember, I didn't get to where I am by being a sweetheart. You remember that, and we'll get along fine."

I speed through the rest of my tasks, fueled by anger and a little fear. Lawrence was trying to intimidate me. I could feel it. Not only do I feel disgust toward him for being a bully, but he's also put me in a bad position with Lauren. Every moment I'm keeping her father's secret is a moment I'm part of his betrayal.

I am just walking past the front desk when Mabel barks out, "Mr. Banks doesn't need you to come in for a couple of days."

* * *

On my way to the bus stop, I text Michaels and ask if he's up for a quick coffee somewhere. I want to see if he knows Michael Fedora and then break the news about Warlock.

I'm not sure if I should mention seeing Claire. If I do, he'll want to know what she said and, for the life of me, I can't begin to know how to tell him about his wife.

Secrets, all of these damn secrets. I feel heavy keeping the truth hidden from people who have only shown kindness to me.

After missing one bus while waiting for a response from Michaels, I decide to take the next one when no messages come through on my phone.

When I get back to Lauren's, there is no aroma of food cooking in the air, and she's not standing at the doorway greeting me with a smile. Instead, she's sitting on one half of the loveseat with her legs folded to the side and a Kleenex in her hand. Her eyes are red, and it's obvious she's been crying. I kick off my shoes, walk over, and sit beside her.

At first, she brushes off the fact that she's been crying and then tries to ask me about my day to divert the attention from herself. But she's been so supportive and compassionate with me from the very beginning that I want to do the same for her. I place my hand on her back. "You can tell me. I'm here for you."

Wiping her eyes with the Kleenex, she looks at me. "There's nothing wrong with me. It's my mom. I feel awful for her."

"Is she sick?"

She shakes her head. "No. Not physically, but definitely emotionally." Lauren sniffs a few times, then continues. "My father called her from work and tore her apart over a bill he'd gotten for car repairs. He said she got ripped off, then called her a dumb cow and said that if he knew she was this stupid when they met, he never would've married her. Then, he did the unthinkable and told her that she repulsed him because of her ugly body."

"That's terrible."

"He knows how badly she feels about her appearance after having a double mastectomy, and he homed in on that weakness and completely destroyed her. She was crying so hard, Jude. It broke my heart. My father has always had a mean streak, but I never thought he'd stoop this low."

"Is your mother going to be alright?"

Lauren shrugs. I wipe a fresh tear from her eye.

"She thinks that he's trying to get rid of her because he's found someone new, but I told her that he's too old to be out there trying to find someone else."

I accidentally scoff out loud.

Lauren sniffs again and looks into my eyes. "What?"

I shake my head. "Nothing."

"No, really. Why did you make that noise?"

She's too vulnerable. There's no way I can lie to her or avoid the question. I sigh and look down. "You're mother is right. Your father is having an affair."

Lauren tilts her head, and her eyes open wider. She asks me how I know this, and with no other option, I tell her about the package and how I was asked to deliver it to the same address Lauren picked me up at on Greenwich Street. I explain how her father and a woman named Holly were arguing, and I overheard. "They were very familiar with each other, and it was obvious they were having a relationship dispute." Then, I tell her about how Lawrence called me into his office and told me to keep my mouth shut.

Her sadness quickly turns to anger. She clenches her hands and, through gritted teeth, says, "I can't confront that bastard; he'll just lie. That's what makes him such a successful lawyer. He's a king at bullshitting. I want you to write down that Holly woman's address. Do you remember her apartment number? Her last name?" Lauren leans over to the coffee table, opens a small drawer, and pulls out a square pad and a pen. "Please, write it down."

I do as she asks. "Listen, Lauren. I know you're upset, but that's all the more reason to think before you act. It's better to strategize and figure out the benefit of confronting this woman and not just show up with verbal guns blowing."

Lauren looks at me with new tears forming but nods. "I know you're right. It's the same thing we tell our patients. Think before you react." She wraps her arms around me and hugs me tightly.

I can't stand that son of a bitch. I knew he was a scumbag the moment I met him.

"There's no way I'll let him destroy my mom. I don't care how powerful he is. I'll do whatever it takes to make sure that doesn't happen."

* * *

Lauren's restlessness, combined with frequent trips to the front room to pace, make for a sleepless night for us both. It's obvious that the news of her father's infidelity and, more importantly, her mother's frail emotional condition is playing hard on Lauren's mind. Thankfully, I don't have to work at the firm today and can avoid any further awkwardness with Lawrence. I make a mental note to call Skully, confirm my shift, and see how he's doing.

Lauren makes me a couple of eggs on toast and forgoes breakfast herself, citing an upset stomach, no doubt because of the burden she's packing. She kisses me on the cheek, then heads to the bathroom for a shower.

I'm just rinsing my dish when I hear my phone buzz from afar. I walk into the bedroom to retrieve my cell from the bedside table, assuming the message is from Michaels, as I never heard back from him yesterday.

But when I check the notification on the screen, it's not him. It's Lawrence, who tells me to meet him today at 1 PM at a yacht club on 44th Street.

My gut clenches. Why the hell does he want to see me, especially out of a work environment? I sit on the bed and try to figure out his reasons. The only rationale I can come to is that he's still worried I'll talk to Lauren and either wants to intimidate me some more or to play me like a fool and pretend to befriend me. Either way, I want nothing more to do with the guy. No amount of extra money is going to make me stay near the likes of him.

My phone buzzes again, and I look at the screen. Another message from Lawrence. "I'll be at a table with some other lawyers from my firm."

Other lawyers? Maybe Michael Fedora? This news changes things. There's no doubt that I am quitting, which means I won't have access to the law firm or this Fedora guy. Showing up at the yacht club is my only chance to meet him, but I'm not sure how to explain this to Lauren. She already feels betrayed by her father, and I don't want her to see me the same way.

Unfortunately, I don't have much choice. I'll have to tell a small lie about where I'm going. If I manage to find Michael Fedora, make a connection, and spot a snake tattoo on his arm, I'll then have the chance to question him about being at my daughter's recording contract celebration. Once I have all the information, I'll come clean to Lauren.

I manage to type out, "I'll be there," and send it just as Lauren walks out of the bathroom. "Feeling any better?" I ask.

"I'll be fine. It's a lot to process, but I'll get through it."

She tells me that she has business to take care of and will be heading out soon, which relieves me of having to come up with a lie about meeting her father. Once she's ready, she kisses me on the cheek—not with her usual kiss, but a more mechanical, her-mind-is-some-place-else kiss.

Once I'm alone, I hang my only collared shirt in the bathroom and turn on the hot water to steam it. I only have one clean pair of jeans—I hope the yacht club doesn't have a dress code.

* * *

An archway decorated with intricate vine designs frames the entrance to the yacht club. I look beyond the man in a dark uniform and white gloves standing at the front of the foyer to the big doors at the back that open up to the water. It's definitely a more formal atmosphere than I was expecting.

Feeling seriously out of place and increasingly anxious about why Lawrence wants to see me, a part of me—a big part— wants to turn tail and leave, and I would, except for the off-chance that Michael Fedora will be here.

I approach the doorman and ask where the lounge is. He gives me a friendly smile and gestures to an open door inside the entrance.

As I step into the room, the first thing I notice is the wood-paneled walls and the red carpet. The space is furnished with dark wood tables surrounded by red velvet cushioned chairs. At the far end of the room, a bar is staffed by a man with slicked-back hair and a bow tie, busy mixing drinks.

Before moving farther in, I scan the room, looking for Lawrence. I spot him near the back of the room, engrossed in conversation with three others. He catches sight of me and waves me over to the table where he's seated.

"Jude," Lawrence says. "You made it."

Unlike the other times I've seen Lawrence, he's not wearing a suit. Instead, he's dressed casually with a short-sleeved shirt and beige chinos. The other men at the table are much younger than him, probably close to my age, and dressed semi-casual. One guy is wearing jeans, making me feel a bit more relaxed about my attire.

Lawrence introduces me to each guy and mentions they are lawyers at the firm. As soon as their names leave his lips, I forget them except for one. Michael Fedora.

"We call him that because he always wears a hat, even in the shower," Lawrence jokes. But there's nothing on the guy's head, only wispy hair and a bald patch near the back. I guess that explains the hat obsession.

Lawrence waves to the bartender and then points at me, signalling that we need another seat. I wait as a short, older man scurries over with the chair and sets it between Michael Fedora and Lawrence—one of whom I desperately want to talk to and the other I'm dreading to hear a word from.

Like Lawrence, Michael Fedora also wears short sleeves. When he takes a drink, I watch his left forearm as he raises his glass to his mouth. There's no tattoo.

The men talk and laugh about a case they're all familiar with as I sit uncomfortably in the circle. "Do you want a drink?" Fedora asks me, then raises his arm, the one I couldn't see until now, at the bartender. My eyes zone in on the forearm tattoo, but before I can distinguish what the picture is, he lowers his arm. Soon, a waiter walks over and takes my order—a tonic with a slice of lime. By the looks on the men's faces, I can tell my choice of beverage stands out as odd, the same way I do.

When their chatter pauses, I lean closer to Michael. "Interesting place for a tat. Can I see it?"

He shrugs and shows me the artwork. A large tiger is inked into his arm, seemingly crawling from his forearm to his bicep. The tail of the creature is long and winds around the bottom of his arm, making me understand how, if Brags only saw the tail on this man's arm, a quick glance could mistake it for a snake. I exhale with frustration, further than ever from the truth.

"Alright men, I've got to talk to Jude alone, so I'll catch you at the office," Lawrence announces.

Like little soldiers obeying their sergeant, the three young lawyers quickly stand, grab their jackets, and head for the exit. Inside, I'm shaking my head. How powerful is this guy to be revered like he is? I would hate to live my life bowing down to a mere mortal, especially one as big a jerk as him.

Lawrence stares at me and chuckles. "So, have you told anyone about our little secret?" His mouth is only inches from my face, the putrid smell of processed scotch hitting me.

I shake my head. A lie.

"Good. Good." He pats my shoulder.

Just then, a stodgy-looking man in a white captain's hat, white pants and a blue blazer enters the lounge. As he walks toward the bar, he glances over at our table and smiles before making a beeline toward us.

"Oh shit, Big-Mouth Bobby," Lawrence mutters under his breath, then raises it in a fabricated happy tone. "How ya doing, old codger?"

The old man reaches the table and holds his hand out to shake Lawrence's. Lawrence raises his hand, exposing his left forearm, and I let out a low gasp when I see the faded tattoo: a staff with wings that has not one but two snakes wrapped around it.

Hearing my gasp, Lawrence follows my eyes to his arm, then looks back at me. "I got it years ago, in the navy."

I can't speak, not yet. My mind is too busy connecting the dots. Lawrence was at the penthouse the night Little Blue was honored for signing her recording contract. He had access to her and is an intimidating presence that no one at the party would've challenged or betrayed.

He stares at me, and in his eyes, I can see it clearly. As sure as I'm sitting here, I know he's the one who drugged my child—the person she remembers as the cause of her death. His gaze never wavers from mine. The look of guilt on his face is undeniable.

*I gotcha, you sonofabitch!*

"That's some kind of staring contest," the old man interrupts.

Lawrence looks at the man, but I keep my gaze on him as I think about my next move.

My phone buzzes in my pocket as the two men converse. I quickly slide my cell out of my jeans and glance down at the message. It's Lauren. "911. Call me."

I take a deep breath and stand. "Nature calls."

Once I'm in the washroom, I go into a stall and dial Lauren. She answers on the first ring. "Jude. Where are you?"

I tell her I'm at the yacht club, which seems to stun her for a moment before she continues. "I went to see her." Her tone is excited.

"Who?"

"My scumbag father's mistress, Holly. I went to see her, and boy, did I find out some crazy shit."

Not knowing how to respond, I ask her if I can call her back in a while.

"There's something else, Jude. When I was driving away from Holly's, I heard some news about that boxing gym you work at, Skully's."

"What do you mean? What news?"

"Someone tried to burn it down."

My mind slips into a confused daze, and I can't find the words to respond. "Are you sure?"

"That's what they said on the news."

She offers to pick me up. I don't care any more about her finding out that I met her father here. All I care about is that I found the man responsible for Little Blue's death. I tell her to pick me up at the 44th Street Yacht Club, and then I end the call and walk back to the table, where the two men are still talking.

Lawrence glances at me. "You look a little flushed. Everything all right?"

I grin. "Not yet, but it will be."

I nod to the elderly gentleman and walk out of the lounge. Once I'm at the entrance, I quickly call Skully's. The phone rings and rings before, finally, someone answers. "Hello?"

I recognize the voice right away. It's Myles, one of the trainers. Once he knows it's me, he tells me about the fire in his office. "It happened late last night. But the only damage was to the front entrance. Whoever started it was an amateur, that's for sure."

"Where's Skully?"

Myles sighs. "That's the real bad news. He was here late, as he always is, and from what the police gather, the old man caught the arsonist in the act. After a brief scuffle, the criminal took off. Unfortunately, the stress was too much on the old man, and he had a heart attack. I'm sorry, Jude. Everyone knew how close you two were."

There's a sharp pain forming in my chest.

This can't be happening. There must be some mistake. Skully was old and feeble, but strong as an ox. A lot of people tried to mess with him since he started the gym, but no one ever managed to defeat him. I feel an overwhelming urge to vomit.

Lauren's car pulls up. I walk toward it, my knees weak and my hands shaking. I don't look at her when I get into the passenger seat. I stare through the windshield in silence.

"I don't believe it! That bastard is here!"

Lauren slows down as she passes a white Rolls Royce, the name *Big Time* on the licence plate.

# Chapter 17

"Why were you there? Did you go to meet with my father?"

I nod as she unlocks the door, and we walk into the apartment.

The corners of her mouth are downward. "How could you meet with him after you caught him cheating on my mother? You knew how upset I was."

I do my best to push Skully's death out of my mind for now so I can focus on her. I put my hands on either side of her head and look into her eyes. "You have to trust me, Lauren. I didn't go to meet with your father to make friends. I went for a far more important reason."

She looks at me, and gradually, the intensity of her anger fades. "I'm not sure why, given that we barely know each other, but I trust you."

"Why in the hell would you ever go and visit your father's mistress?" I shake my head and smile.

Lauren shrugs. "I guess I needed to see the heartless woman who's tearing my parents apart, face to face. Only, she wasn't heartless at all. In fact, she is just as much a pawn in my father's game as my mother is."

I look at her quizzically.

"Holly was a stripper when she met my dad at a bar where she was working a year ago. She told me he was very depressed because his wife was divorcing him. Apparently, it took Holly quite a few months to figure out that wasn't the case. From what she told me, she knew something was wrong with his story when he avoided introducing her to his friends or meeting hers. He didn't want her to visit his office and would never stay at their apartment for more than a night or two."

"So, why didn't Holly leave?"

"My father threatened her whenever she tried to leave. He pays for the apartment and convinced her to quit her job. He warned her that if she took up dancing in a bar again, he would have the club owner turn over her earnings, making her work for nothing. He also threatened to spread horrible lies about her if she started seeing someone else. She felt trapped like a bird in a gilded cage."

I nod. "Did she say anything else?"

"Lots. She spilled the beans on him. I think she's looking for a way out and saw me as a catalyst to do that. Safety in numbers, I guess."

"Spilled the beans? How so?"

"Well, here's the gist: she told me all my dad's assets are in my mother's name. I never knew that because my mom never mentioned it. He did this to protect his assets in case he faced any legal issues or lawsuits, and of course, he also has his offshore accounts."

"So, that's good news for your mom then, right? I mean, it'll be harder to screw her over if she's holding all of the cards."

Lauren sighs. "It's not that simple. My mother is a genuinely honest woman—one of the things I admire most about her. Her real concern isn't money. It's because she trusted him and has remained loyal for all these years. That said, I don't think she'd want to face him in a legal battle over money; he's ruthless. What devastates Mom is that my father has started being abusive and demeaning. He was her whole life. I'm worried that when she finds out about Holly and how my father has been in a relationship with her, it might push my mom past the breaking point."

"I understand. Is that all Holly told you?"

"She told me that if I promised to help her escape from my father, she would reveal something to me—something my father would never want anyone to know. Once I agreed, she read from a small notebook." Lauren took out her phone. "She let me take pictures of the pages."

Eager to hear something damning and criminal that could implicate him, I listen intently.

"I thought she was going to read me little notes about his crooked legal practices or something, so I was dumbfounded when she read an entry from her book about a bad fight my father and her got into." Lauren looks down at her phone and begins to read from the photographed pages. "'The fight ended with him choking me and saying he could do anything he wanted. He told me that because of his power, he doesn't operate within the confines of the law.'" Lauren looks up at me. "Then he gave Holly an example of a time that he got away with something that would've landed anyone else in jail."

"Does it say what he did?"

Lauren's eyes well up, and she looks down at her phone to read. "'Lawrence bragged about being at a party a couple of years ago for a teen singer who had just signed a recording contract.'"

Suddenly, my breathing stops, and my vision narrows.

Tears fall from Lauren's eyes as she continues. "'He boasted about the girl paying attention to him, not the younger guys in the room. He said he spiked her drink, just to help things along, then followed her into the bathroom, where she was obviously ready for him, but then she got dizzy, and the stupid bitch fell and hit her head on the porcelain sink.'"

I remind myself to breathe as tears drip down my face.

Lauren lowers her phone and puts her hand on my leg. "If this is too hard, I'll stop."

"No. I need to hear this."

"'Lawrence laughed as he remembered the next part, saying all he had to do was claim he was trying to help the girl get to the washroom because she was dizzy, and his word was never questioned. *The funny part is,* he said, *I had drugs in my pocket when the police arrived. So, let that be a warning to you, Holly. I am untouchable.*'" Lauren puts down her phone. "Holly said it was after that conversation that she knew she had no way out."

My first instinct is to jump up and grab a knife from the kitchen, then head out to find Lawrence. My rage must be obvious, as Lauren tells me to calm down and rationalize. "Don't think of doing anything rash. You'll only be hurting yourself." Then, she moves my chin so our eyes meet. "Listen to me, Jude. I know you're churning like a storm inside, but you have to let things take their natural course. What my father did is deplorable and unforgivable, but we have no proof, only Holly's words written in a small notebook. If you want justice for your daughter, you have to wait until we find more concrete evidence. My father was right when he told Holly that he's untouchable; unfortunately he can and has gotten away with a lot of bad things, but I believe that good always eventually takes over evil. We just have to wait. Will you make me a promise not to do anything impulsive and vengeful?"

Her eyes are sincere and caring. I can tell she's got my best interest at heart. She can't comprehend the severity of how I feel, how any parent feels who has lost a child. Still, the logical side of my brain knows she's right. If I could get to Lawrence and somehow overpower him, who's to say I'd succeed at killing him? Even though I have youth on my side, he's a big man, a lot bigger than me, and if I failed, he would make sure I was thrown in jail to rot for the rest of my life. Lauren is right; reacting out of rage is the wrong approach.

I nod reluctantly.

She asks why I went to meet her father at the yacht club. I explain that my goal was to meet the lawyer, Michael Fedora, and verify whether the tattoo on his arm was indeed a snake, as Brags had claimed. When I recount what happened next—how, after the lawyers left Lawrence and me alone, I saw the snake tattooed on his forearm and realized that he was responsible for my child's death—her eyes widen. It's not just the tattoo hunt that surprises her, it's the fact that my source of information is from my daughter, who has been dead for the past two years.

"Little Blue told you about the tattoo?"

With no strength left in me to lie or dismiss my interaction with my daughter as a mere hallucination, as Lauren suggested it was before, I sit in front of her raw and vulnerable, armed with only the truth. "Yes, I was told by Little Blue that the man who drugged her had a tattoo of a snake on his forearm. I know it sounds crazy, but I did see my daughter's spirit, and she did tell me about the man with the tattoo."

She remains silent for a few moments, then shrugs and tells me that as much as her beliefs usually run parallel to what can be scientifically proven, she does not doubt that I am sane and lucid. "As hard as it is for me to wrap my head around paranormal communications if you truly believe what you've told me about Little Blue, I promise to do my best and be open-minded."

I smile and hug her. "Thank you. Your opinion matters to me very much. And just so you know, until recently, I felt much the same as you do regarding ghosts and the afterworld."

My phone buzzes, and I look to see a message from Chad Michaels. As much as I don't want to tell him about seeing Claire and what she told me about what happened to her mother, after finally finding out who was responsible for Little Blue's death, I now know that it's not my secret to keep.

"I'm off tonight," Lauren says. "I need to seriously consider how to approach my mother with everything. But I need to give my brain time to process it first. Is there anything you have to do?"

I nod and tell her I am thinking of going to Skully's gym to learn more about what happened. Lauren hugs me and then offers to come with me to Hell's Kitchen.

* * *

We park off to the side of the building, where a fire truck is just pulling out. A police car and a fire investigator's vehicle are parked side by side, their occupants leaning over to speak to each other through open windows.

The walkway to the entrance is saturated in water, and there is a sign on the door that reads *CLOSED UNTIL FURTHER NOTICE*.

I'm just about to approach the officer to ask if I can go inside when I see Myles exit the side door. I yell his name, and Lauren and I walk toward him. Bald and almost seven feet tall, with a physique like Tarzan, most people would never guess that Myles has the kindest, gentlest demeanor. Skully kept him around the gym in case any out-of-the-ring fights happened, which were diffused quickly once they saw Myles.

"Are you all right?" I ask.

Myles shakes his head in disbelief. "I'm fine. I wasn't even here when it happened. I wish I were because I would've made the guy who tried to torch the place pay dearly."

I think this is the first time I've ever heard him mention violence. I ask him if they have any clues on who would've done this, and he tells me that although Skully could be a real jerk sometimes, everyone respected the guy. "Like I told the cops, I never knew about any enemies the old man had."

Myles reaches out and puts one of his baseball glove-sized hands on my shoulder, "I am sorry about Skully, truly. In all the years I've worked here, I never seen him take to anyone like he did you."

I nod and do my best to keep from crying. "So, what happens to this place now?"

Myles shrugs. "Dunno. But I know one of the cops who was called to the scene. He told me that a distant relative of Skully's is coming from Florida to deal with things. My friend said he'll let me know if anything is new."

Back in the car, my cell rings as we pull out of the lot. It's Chad Michaels. "Hey, man. Why didn't you answer my text?" His voice is anxious.

I apologize and tell him that I've had my hands full.

"Well, I need to talk to you. It's urgent. Can you meet me?"

I tell him I'll call him right back, then ask Lauren if she will be disappointed if I meet with a friend. "It's important."

She tells me she was thinking of calling and checking on Holly anyway, just to keep a friendly alliance. "We might need her testimony down the road."

I get Lauren to drop me off in Tribeca, at a small bistro across from The Woolworth Building on Broadway and tell her I'll take the bus back to her place when I'm done.

"Don't get into any trouble," she says, half jokingly.

* * *

Claire's grim story bubbles to the front of my mind as I sit and wait in a small booth. I have no idea how Michaels will receive any of the awful news I'm about to tell him, first as a father and then as a husband. He's going to go crazy with anger. I know if I was handed the same news, I'd go crazy.

I order a tonic and lime from the waitress just as Michaels walks through the door and spots me. As soon as he slides into the booth across from me, I am aware that he's gone through something pretty traumatizing. His eyes have dark, sleep-deprivation circles, and his face is pale.

I ask him if he's all right, and he says, "Crazy things have been happening at my place, Jude. You wouldn't believe it." The hand not in the sling nervously taps on the table.

The waitress appears, sets my drink in front of me, and then asks Michaels if he'd like anything.

"I'd avoid ordering coffee," I say, looking at his fidgeting hand.

He gives me a sideways look, then lets out a laugh.

After foregoing a drink and once the waitress leaves, he continues his story. "She's been at my place. Running the halls, knocking stuff over."

"She?" I know the answer, but I want him to say it.

"My daughter, Claire."

I may be the only person he knows that believes him.

He continues with widened eyes and a fast-paced ramble. "There was this thing in the mirror after I got out of the shower this morning. It looked like words written in the steam."

I smile inside, remembering the fog on my apartment bathroom mirror, only it was a snake, not words. "Could you make out what the words said?"

"Yeah, I think so. From what I could see, they spelt *Big Time*. Which makes no sense at all." Michaels rubs his face with his hand. "I don't know, Jude. Maybe I'm losing my mind. Maybe I'm just reacting to the pain medication I've been taking or something."

"I don't think that's the case at all, Chad. I think there's a huge possibility Claire did visit you." I want to tell him what I know, but I don't. Instead, I wait for the opportune moment and continue to listen.

Michaels goes on about how he's been speaking to her, even reading stories and singing songs. "I'm not sure if she can hear me, and she never shows herself. But I know it's her. I feel her essence. I don't know what to do. Why is she visiting me now? It's been two years since she died."

I take a deep breath. I already feel bad for him, and I can't imagine how he will react to what I feel obligated to tell him. "Maybe Claire is visiting you because she needs to tell you something?"

He thinks for a moment, then says, "What could that be?"

"Your daughter visited me too. I saw her only for a brief time, but she was there."

"What do you mean? When? Why did she go to you?"

I shake my head slowly. "I'm not sure. She must know that there's a connection between you and me. My daughter also mentioned her and spoke about how she is in the spirit world. Claire was with her. Little Blue told me that Claire often chanted the words *Big Time*."

"Are you serious? You're not messing with me, are you?"

"Not me. And as weird as I know it sounds—believe me, I can barely believe it myself— it's all true." I divert my eyes from his and look down at my hands folded on the table.

"There's something else, isn't there?"

I nod. "Yes, and you may want to brace yourself for this one."

I can feel his eyes on me as I tell him what his child, or the spirit of his child, said to me. As best I can, I reiterate what Claire said about the night Michaels was recording. How a man was in the studio and offered to take Claire and her mother for ice cream, then took them to his place, and how he'd pulled Claire's mom into another room and locked the door. My heart sinks when I tell Michaels about the screams, the pleas from his little girl's mother, and the man's threats to stay silent.

By the time I gather enough nerve to look into his face, Michaels' expression has changed from sadness to pure rage. His lips are pursed, and his eyes are severe and squinted. "Who did this?" he hollers, causing the other patrons to turn.

"Think back to when you were recording that day."

"I can't remember. I was distracted because we had problems with the nerve console, which the in-house servers holding the hard drives didn't recognize. Emily and my daughter were in and out of the studio; Claire was never blessed with the ability to sit still for long. I do remember that the session went on for a lot longer than anticipated, and I remember Emily was in a strange mood when we finished for the day, and I think Claire was, too. I should've figured out something was wrong, but I thought they were both tired from waiting all day." He glares into my eyes. "If you know who hurt my wife and daughter, tell me now."

"The name *Big Time* doesn't mean anything to you?"

"I don't know, should it?"

"Think hard, Chad." I want him to connect the dots and figure it out on his own.

"Other than big time, as in someone achieves a high level of success, or my lawyer's licence plate, that's all I can think of."

"Bingo."

"What? Bingo, what? The success thing? The guy who did this to my ex-wife was successful. I don't get it. Quit playing games with me."

I lean in. "The licence plate."

"What are you saying? My lawyer assaulted Emily? Is that what you're telling me?"

"First of all, I didn't say it. Claire did. And secondly, I have no problem believing that Lawrence is capable of doing such an awful thing."

Michaels grows quiet for a long time before he stands up and nods goodbye.

"What are you going to do?"

"I don't know yet. But right now, I need to go to Maine."

"Why Maine?"

"That's where Emily is."

# Chapter 18

It's midnight when the buzzing from my phone wakes me. I quickly get out of Lauren's bed, slide on my jeans, grab my cell, and move to the sofa so I don't wake her.

"Hi, Jude. It's Myles. I know it's late, but my cop friend just called with some news that I thought you might find interesting."

"All right. What did you hear?"

Myles tells me that they have the arsonist in custody. "Apparently, the guy walked into a local precinct with burns on his hands and a gash on his head from where Skully hit him with a bat. From what my friend said, the arsonist is simple and was very sorry about what he did."

"Wow. He actually turned himself in. That's crazy. Did they tell you his name?"

"It's Brags or Begs or something like that."

Brags. I can't believe it. Lawrence must have sent Brags to set the gym on fire, probably as an intimidation tactic to keep me too scared to reveal his secret. And poor Skully died as a result. Myles adds that Brags gave a statement saying his boss ordered him to do it. Apparently, he's willing to testify. It won't bring Skully back, but at least they know who's responsible.

Not wanting to attach myself to the person who did the crime, I don't tell Myles I know Brags. Instead, I thank him for the info and end the call. Leaning back on the loveseat, I close my eyes and shake my head. It's incredible how so much crap can happen in such a short period of time.

I get up and am about to go back to bed when there's a sudden rap on the door.

Who would be knocking at this hour? Considering I haven't heard the intercom buzz, it's likely one of Lauren's neighbors. I consider quietly going back to bed, but I know if they knock again, it'll wake Lauren.

I slide my phone into my pocket and walk to the door, hoping that whoever is there is easily dissuaded from bothering us and I can go back to sleep.

As soon as I turn the knob, a burst of power thrusts open the door and sends me to the floor. I scramble backwards and do my best to focus on the intruder in the dark.

"There you are, you little bastard."

When he passes through the light from the streetlamp outside, I see Lawrence's crazed face and pinhole-sized pupils; he's high on something. He looms over me, gripping a gun in his hand. With massive force, he kicks me in the ribs, sending a searing pain into my lungs. "What are you doing?" I groan.

Lawrence leans down and, through clenched teeth, growls, "I'm trying to decide if I should blow your head off or beat you to death."

"Why?"

He snorts in disgust. "My so-called do-gooder daughter went and paid Holly a visit." Lawrence kicks me in the ribs again; I hear something crack. "I heard all about their little chat. After Holly unloaded everything on Lauren, she had the nerve to call my wife. And let me tell you, now that my wife's armed with Holly's pathetic sob story, it'll be a cold day in hell before I get back what's mine!"

I pull my knees up to help let air into my lungs. "I don't give a shit about you or your damn money. It was you who drugged my daughter, wasn't it, Big Time?"

He tilts his head and, through his drug-infused brain, says, "Bravo, Jude. And now you'll have a reason to quit snivelling when I pull the trigger and unite the two of you."

I feel the cold barrel push into the side of my skull. Teetering on consciousness from the pain in my ribs, I close my eyes and ready myself for what's to come. I hear the gun cock and try to picture Little Blue.

There's a loud *crack*. Immediately after, the dead weight of Lawrence's body slumps to the floor beside me.

I look up to see Lauren with a cast iron frying pan gripped tightly in her hands.

She drops the pan and crouches over me. "Are you okay?"

I nod. "It's my ribs. Help me get up."

If I could take a deep breath right now, I would holler out in pain as Lauren does her best to help me off the floor. Once standing, the agony in my ribs dissipates enough to allow me to take in air.

"He looked stoned out of his mind on something," I gasp. "He was acting like a crazed animal. What should we do?"

Lauren bends over and feels her father's neck. "He's got a strong pulse. He'll be fine, but we should probably get out of here in case he—" Suddenly she screams; Lawrence has grabbed onto her ankle.

I spring into action and pry his fingers, which have the strength of vise grips, off her. "He's coming to, Lauren."

"We need to get out of here."

"Okay, grab what you need."

We head to the bedroom, where Lauren slides her feet into sandals, and I grab my trainers.

We freeze in place and stare at each other. Then, I motion for her to stay back as I slowly walk to the doorway and peek around the corner. Lawrence is on all fours, scrambling to get up, gun in hand. "We have to go. Now!"

Lauren sprints across the room. I wince in pain as I grab her hand and run through the living room and out the front door.

We reach the bottom of the stairwell when the sound of the door closing above echoes down. With Lauren safely behind me at the exit door, I look up the gap in the stairwell and see Lawrence looking down.

I push open the door that leads to the alleyway in the back of the building and run with Lauren. "He's obviously gained his energy back," I huff.

"It's the drugs. But he's also in really good shape, a fitness buff."

"Great!" I exclaim sarcastically. "Where are you parked?"

"Jude, I didn't have time to grab my purse, my phone, or my car keys."

I reach for my wallet in my jeans pocket and realize I left it on the bedside table. Thankfully, I find a small amount of cash in my front pocket. "I have enough for the subway. We can go to my apartment." I don't have my keys, but with Lauren's help, I can try to get into my bathroom window via the fire escape.

At the front of the building, we see Lawrence's car parked near the entrance. Together we jog toward the subway station, looking behind us every few minutes. Thankfully, the adrenaline pumping through me is helping numb the pain in my ribs.

* * *

The subway is crowded, more so than usual for this time of night. "I'm scared, Jude," Lauren says, clutching my hand.

"Don't be. I won't let him hurt you, I promise."

The pain in my ribs comes in waves of sharp stabs, but thankfully, we only have to wait a few minutes before seats open up at the back. Lauren plunks down between a portly woman reading a newspaper and me. At least, I think it's a woman because of the bright pink Lycra socks; the newspaper hides her upper body.

Lauren leans into me to avoid rubbing up against the stranger. "It's a blend of interesting odors in here," she says, waving her hand in front of her face.

I nod. "I usually try to breathe through my mouth on these rides. "

I can feel Lauren's grip loosen slightly as the woman beside her engages in conversation. I'm not listening to what they're saying, too focused on the other passengers and the doorways, praying that Lawrence doesn't find us.

When I'm sure we're in the clear, I let out a long breath. "As soon as we get off the subway, I'll call the cops to meet us at my apartment."

Now that my anxiety is dissipating, I home in on Lauren's conversation with the woman. "You're a pretty little thing. I was, too, once. But after a stint in the crazy house, I never looked the same." The woman cackles.

I know that voice. It can only be one person. I lean forward to see past Lauren to the woman, who's wearing a purple hat on top of her unmistakable red fuzzy hair. Madge looks at me, then winks. "Is the gentleman your husband?" she asks Lauren.

"No. I guess he's my boyfriend." Lauren looks at me and smiles.

"You'd better treat this girl right," Madge says. "Or I'll find you." She snorts.

The next stop is just around the bend, and Madge struggles to her feet and walks up the aisle. Lauren looks perplexed. "What an odd woman. She was friendly enough but obviously deeply disturbed. She said something very strange to me."

"What was that?" I say, not wanting to tell her just yet. We've got bigger things to worry about right now.

"She introduced herself as Marjorie Gamble."

"Why was that strange?"

"Do you remember when I showed you my family album, and the picture of my distant grandmother, Marjorie Gamble?"

I nod.

"Talk about a coincidence," Lauren says.

Madge shuffles behind the exiting crowd and right before getting off, she turns and looks back at me, then nods.

* * *

I'm feeling relieved as Lauren and I walk up 6th Ave toward my apartment. Even though it's a bit of a walk, I feel a lot safer now that I'm back in the familiar surroundings of Hell's Kitchen.

We don't talk much during the walk. I can tell by her concentration that she's trying to process everything that just happened.

"My father is a beast, a monster," she says in a low voice. "And because of his wealth and status, he's pretty much unbeatable."

"It may seem that way, but one way or another, good will trump evil."

She scoffs. "I wish I could believe that."

"You're the one who told me that, Lauren. It stuck with me."

Finally, I can see Wong's restaurant sign ahead.

Lauren looks around as we walk. "It's funny. I always thought Hell's Kitchen would be much more active than this at night."

I smile. "Like what? Did you think the Irish mob was still ruling the streets?"

"No. I didn't mean busier as in a criminal way. I just thought there'd be more, you know, action. Colorful people and vendors and such."

"Most people, even the night lovers, go indoors after 1 AM, especially this time of year."

308

I can tell our chatter is relaxing her a little. Even though my apartment is a far cry from her posh digs, at least it's a safe place to sit and come up with a viable plan.

We're approaching the Plexiglas-covered bus stop when the roar of a speeding engine suddenly erupts from a nearby alley.

A white car barrels onto 8th Avenue and skids to a stop beside us. There's no mistaking a Rolls Royce, with the high grille and the Spirit of Ecstasy statue on the hood.

"What do we do?" Lauren's voice trembles.

But before we can even pick a direction to run, the driver's door flies open and out steps Lawrence, dried blood caked on his forehead, gun in hand. Lauren and I step backwards until our backs are against the Plexi-glass shelter of the bus stop.

"Looky here. And you almost made it," Lawrence sneers. His eyes have the same wildness as before.

We are so fixated on Lawrence that we don't notice the figure at the entrance of the dark alley until her voice cuts the night air.

"You've been a bad boy, just like your distant grandfather."

Madge steps into the light.

"You're the descendant of an evil that has corrupted this family for many decades." Her voice booms as she steps in front of us, facing Lawrence.

"I don't understand," Lauren says, terrified. "What's going on? How did she get here?"

"Shh," I whisper.

"What this family needs is a reckoning. A purification from the disease that has plagued its men for generations." Madge grins like the Cheshire cat, sending chills down my spine. "It ends with you, Lawrence, and it ends now."

"What the hell are you rambling about, you crazy old bag? Back away. I've got no qualms about taking you out as soon as I finish with these two." His eyes are wild and as blazing red as Madge's hair.

I step in front of Lauren. "Don't do this. You'll only be making things worse for yourself."

"Ha! How the hell can things get any worse for me? I'm ruined. You two shit disturbers saw to that." Headlights from an approaching truck reflect off the steel barrel of the gun. "See you in hell." He squeezes the trigger. In the same instant, in a flurry of fast-moving color, Lawrence is hurled off the sidewalk and directly into the grill of the 5-ton truck. I turn to see the fresh bullet hole in the bus stop plexiglass behind us.

Lauren cries out as the truck screeches to a halt. I wrap my arms around her tightly.

Everything seems to move in slow motion as I watch the truck driver get out to check what he hit. The streetlight flickers over the scene, and a light fog blankets the road. As Lauren sobs against my chest, Madge turns to face me. "Take care of her," she says, gesturing toward Lauren, who doesn't seem to notice.

I nod and mouth, "Thank you."

Madge steps into the street and crosses to the other side, where two other figures have gathered—a child and what appears to be a young woman. Madge reaches them just as distant sirens begin to wail.

Madge looks back and smiles, and as the young woman steps off the curb, I instantly recognize Little Blue.

She walks a few feet into the mist on the street. My heart races as I gently release my hold on Lauren and step toward my child, while Madge and Claire watch from a distance.

"Jude, where are you going?" Lauren sniffles, apparently unable to see what I see.

A small crowd forms around the truck, their voices melting into the background as I reach the center line. I'm afraid to close my eyes, fearing that my child might vanish if I do.

"Hi, Dad." Little Blue smiles. Unlike the last time I saw her, she looks beautiful now—radiant, healthy, and forever young.

Overwhelming love rises in me.

"I'm glad it's finally over." She glances at the accident. "Now you can live in peace."

"That was the bad man from your party that night, wasn't it."

She nods slowly. "I like Lauren, Dad. I think she'll be very good for you. She's strong and kind."

"Remind you of anyone?" I wink.

She giggles. "Nah. I am way cooler."

Tears form in my eyes. "I'm not going to see you again, am I?"

The corners of her mouth drop. "You will, but not for a long time."

"Can I touch you?"

A slow tear runs down her cheek, "Yes." Then, she leans weightless into my arms. "I will always love you, Dad."

"I will always love you too, my Little Blue."

"Jude. What the hell are you doing? Get off the road." Lauren grabs my arm as I turn to see emergency lights speeding toward us.

I look back for Little Blue, but she's gone.

Lauren pulls me backwards, and as I glance across the road, I see my daughter stepping up to the curb. She smiles, and a wave of warmth floods over me once more.

Little Blue takes Claire's hand, and with Madge in the lead, they walk a few feet before disappearing into the night.

# Epilogue

With no one challenging Lawrence's finances and holdings, Mrs. Banks will be set for life. Lauren mentioned that her mother offered to buy her a house, but Lauren turned it down. Even though she thinks her mother earned every penny by putting up with her awful husband, Lauren won't take a dime. But we make ends meet just fine without her father's riches.

As for Holly, she was finally freed from Lawrence's control. Although she couldn't keep the apartment—that property went to the estate—she was allowed to keep her jewelry, designer clothes, and the small dog Lawrence had bought for her. Holly called Lauren a few months ago, saying she was moving out of the city and planning on finding a small town where she can start over.

Brags is in a facility for people with disabilities, kind of like a camp rather than a real prison. His psychiatric evaluation showed he's not likely to reoffend. Because of his reduced mental capacity and the fact that he didn't fight back during Skully's attack, the courts were lenient and gave him a light sentence.

And as for me, it turns out old Skully didn't have a fondness for his extended family. Only a month before he died, he wrote his will and left me the boxing gym. I have no idea how to run such a business, but I'll learn, and Skully's legacy will live on. And, of course, I'll remember to count the damn towels at the close of every day.

* * *

The cool Atlantic breeze rushes up the shore and dances around the picnic table, causing the edges of the white linen tablecloth to flail over the open food. Emily and Chad are quick to place the salt and pepper shakers on the corners of the fabric before continuing our lunch. I smile across the table at Lauren, who looks ethereal under the midday sun.

"Will you keep this place or sell it and move to the city?" I ask our hosts.

Emily and Chad look at each other and shrug. "It doesn't really matter where we end up, as long as we're both there," Chad says.

Lauren flashes a grin my way, her leg brushing against mine with a soft nudge. I return her smile, reflecting on everything we've endured since that first encounter. While Lauren can't replace the void left by Little Blue, she surrounds it with warmth and fills my life with renewed hope. She makes me feel alive again.

314

After lunch, Lauren and Emily clear the table while Chad and I walk across the freshly cut grass to the beach.

"She doesn't visit any more."

"Who?"

"Claire. Since Em and I got back together, I don't feel her with me."

"Maybe it's because you were ready to let her go."

Chad nods. "And what about your daughter? Do you wish you could see her again?"

"No. I like to think she crossed over the barriers that kept her tied to this world—to me—and now her spirit is free."

Chad stops walking and looks at me. "But you must miss her."

I glance at my left forearm, grinning at my latest tattoo: a snake pierced by a sword through its eyes. "I do, but I carry her essence with me. From the moment she was born, I knew I would always be her dad, and she would forever be my Little Blue."

## The End

Jay Lang grew up on the ocean, splitting her time between Read Island and Vancouver Island before moving to Vancouver to work as a TV, film and commercial actress. Eventually she left the industry for a quieter life on a live-a-board boat, where she worked as a clothing designer for rock bands. Five years later, she moved to Abbotsford to attend university. There, she fell in love with creative writing and wrote five novel manuscripts in a year. She spends her days hiking and drawing inspiration for her writing from nature.